We are perfectly concealed. Men will continue to notice us only for their sexual and nesting needs—which is what we want them to do. By the time they observe that there has been an astonishing number of births of baby girls, it will be much too late.

I am Minerva the historian, and this is the first chapter of our saga . . .

*   *   *   *

Review Excerpts, DAUGHTERS OF A CORAL DAWN

"Throughout . . . are passages of musical beauty, droll perception, and the sort of lyrical sexuality for which Katherine Forrest is celebrated . . . DAUGHTERS OF A CORAL DAWN is . . . a love song to the beauty, strength, and ingenuity of women."

Ann Bannon, Gay Community News

"The novel is beautifully erotic in a setting of almost theatrical splendor . . ."

Bay Windows, Boston

"Women have waited for years for good lesbian science fiction. With DAUGHTERS OF A CORAL DAWN, the waiting is magnificently fulfilled."

Lesbian Connection

". . . A definite must for fun and laughter, for the sheer pleasure of having a book completely suspend you in time."

Angles, Vancouver, BC

"Forrest spins her story with a sureness and a sagacity that are charming and seductive, and in the process proffers that rarity — a story one wishes did not end."

Update, San Diego

". . . surely destined to be a classic . . ."

Mom . . . Guess What! Sacramento

Daughters of a Coral Dawn

BY
KATHERINE V.
FORREST

THE NAIAD PRESS, INC.
1994

Printed in the United States of America on acid-free paper
First Edition

First Printing May, 1984
Second Printing January, 1986
Third Printing July, 1989
Fourth Printing April, 1993
Tenth Anniversary Edition
First Printing September, 1994

Cover design by Bonnie Liss (Phoenix Graphics)

Typesetting by Sandi Stancil

Library of Congress Cataloging-in-Publication Data

Forrest, Katherine V., 1939–
    Daughters of a coral dawn.

    I. Title.
PS3556.0737D3   1984   813'.54   83-21964
ISBN 1-56280-104-X

ACKNOWLEDGMENT

To the Third Street Writers Group — Lorraine Ackerman, Montserrat Fontes, Janet Gregory, Jeffrey N. McMahan — fine writers and good friends.

Over our three years we have learned from each other and grown together.

I thank you all with love.

BOOKS BY KATHERINE V. FORREST

CURIOUS WINE

DAUGHTERS OF A CORAL DAWN

AMATEUR CITY
A Kate Delafield Mystery

AN EMERGENCE OF GREEN

MURDER AT THE NIGHTWOOD BAR
A Kate Delafield Mystery

DREAMS AND SWORDS

THE BEVERLY MALIBU
A Kate Delafield Mystery

MURDER BY TRADITION
A Kate Delafield Mystery

THE EROTIC NAIAD
Edited by Katherine V. Forrest
and Barbara Grier

THE ROMANTIC NAIAD
Edited by Katherine V. Forrest
and Barbara Grier

FLASHPOINT

To Sheila
For all the beautiful years

Daughters of a Coral Dawn

PART ONE

MOTHER

I

The idea to smuggle Mother off Verna III came to Father when Jed Peterman fell down a hill of keteraw and proceeded to smother in a pile of mutherac, managing to do this in spite of all his training and thorough briefings on the planet's topography. Father, his crew chief, found him, and in disgust kicked him further down the hill, starting an avalanche which buried poor Peterman forever.

Why would Father risk years of severe punishment to bring an alien to Earth? Mother looked like one of the Sirens of Earth legend. Glossy dark silken hair reached to her voluptuous hips and covered cantaloupe-sized breasts. As if that wasn't enough to capture a young Earthman there were her extraordinarily beautiful eyes—the color of pure emerald. And Mother, an inexperienced Vernan child of only forty-five, was enthralled with Father's virility and willing to go with him anywhere.

Father cut Mother's hair to collar length and concealed her remarkable eyes in gray infra-protect lenses. Judicial application of plastisculpt coarsened her nose and chin and ears. The barest touch of a surgiscope knife added temporary lines around her eyes and mouth. Still, his plan would never have worked except for the flappy tents the space crews wear which hid Mother's cantaloupes.

Exercising his authority as crew chief, Father accused "Peterman" of violating Earthcode MCLVIII—sexually harassing a female alien, a misdemeanor—and imposed a sentence of solitary confinement for the duration of the

3

return trip to Earth. Of course, only Mother's days were solitary.

Upon arrival on Earth, poor "Peterman" vanished, AWOL from the Service. And Father took Mother to the pleasure capital of Vega where he married her. So long as she did not have to be fingerprinted or have her blood tested she could easily pass as an Earth female, albeit spectacularly endowed; and given her extreme youth it was unlikely that she would face exposure through medical discovery for many years. Perhaps by then, Father reasoned, the laws would have changed. And so Mother and Father set up house-keeping in Calivada.

Mother did have her idiosyncracies. She made noises at night—sometimes like the klaxxon warning of a fluoro-carbon alert, sometimes reminiscent of nineteenth century war-whooping Indians. She was by now pregnant and since Vernan babies become conscious in the womb after the first month, the first words I heard were from Father, grumbling during one of her spectacular effusions: "Great Calvin Coolidge, can't you hold that down a little? Everyone in the neighborhood knows what we're doing."

"A Payrungasmad curse on the neighbors. Can you do that again, dear?"

Father was furious when he learned of her pregnancy. "Great James Garfield, how could you let that happen!" he bellowed. "We've been married only six weeks! You said you'd take ovavoid!"

"No I didn't, you just gave me the pills," Mother informed him coolly. "I did what all Vernan females do when their males leave it up to them. Each time before we made love I concentrated hard and thought negative thoughts." She shrugged. "Sometimes it works, sometimes it doesn't."

For a while Father screamed incoherently, then asked in a hoarse voice, "Why didn't you take the pills? Why why why?"

"Those things have never been perfected in three hundred years! Imagine what they'd do to a Vernan. At least we don't have to worry about birth control for a while, dear," she said seductively. "Isn't that good?"

Father, who was accustomed to adjusting swiftly to emergencies in space, had calmed down somewhat. But he said plaintively, "What do we do now? How can I take you to a med station to have our baby? I'll have to find someone, pay a huge bribe. Then worry about blackmail. Maybe I can think of a way to smuggle you back to Verna-Three."

"Don't worry," Mother said. "I'll manage."

Meanwhile, reports of Mother's foibles had spread throughout the district, especially after she daily emptied tea leaves from the vacuum tubes and explained to a curious neighbor that she always sprinkled tea leaves on her floors, tannic acid being wonderful for the disposition. And when another astonished neighbor watched Mother pluck choice leafy tidbits from the front hedge and eat them for her lunch, Father realized that even in Calivada Mother was a bit too outre. So he hustled her off to an isolated but fully mechanized farmhouse near the border. She did not mind in the least; pregnant Vernan women crave solitude. She spent much of her time telescanning Earth's history and culture and learning agronomy and hydroponics, which she realized we would soon need.

Vernans do not require an interminable nine months for gestation; mother and baby work together to make things much more efficient. And so five months later, Mother gave birth. It took about an hour for us to be born, one by one.

"Great Ulysses Grant!" Father screamed, tearing at his hair. "It's a goddamn litter!"

"It's all your doing," Mother retorted, more than a little miffed. "The male determines the number. That's how it is on Verna. The more sperm, the more chance for more eggs to be fertilized. And Geezerak knows you're a regular sperm factory."

"Great Woodrow Wilson, how could I know that," Father

said shakily as Vesta and I were born, the last two, bringing the grand total to nine, all of us girls.

"One Y chromosome," Mother grumbled at him. "You couldn't spare even one Y chromosome."

"Never again!" hollered Father. "No ovavoid pills, no more you know what!"

"Suit yourself. You could take them yourself, you know. I'll be sore for a day or two, anyway. And lower your voice," Mother said as we all began to wail, "you're disturbing the girls."

In a voice shaking with horror Father said, "Clothes! Great Herbert Hoover, clothes for nine girls!"

"I'll manage," Mother said.

"How will you ever take care of them?"

"I'll manage," Mother said.

"Even choosing names for nine girls!"

Mother said distractedly, fastening liquiblots to each of us, "The girls and I settled all that before they were born."

"What!" Father shrieked.

Frightened by him, I began to cry. "There there, Minerva," Mother cooed, picking me up. "Dear," she said to Father, "it's a . . . strong communication. It's gone, now that they're born. I can't really explain. Anyway, males never understand how it is between mothers and babies."

"What have I wrought," Father whispered, tiptoeing away.

Little did he know.

Isis was the first of us to indicate special gifts. When she was eight, Mother discovered that she had full comprehension of a teleclass in spatial calculus. I had already chosen my specialty—history—and was able to explain to my family that mathematical genius usually manifests itself quite early. It was then that Mother warned us all to be careful, that our family could not afford the bright light of publicity. Isis, soon bored with calculus, entertained herself by plotting stock market curves.

Thanks to Mother's agronomy and hydroponics expertise, the farm had become virtually self-sufficient, and Father and Mother managed to conceal our existence for quite a while. After that, although the nine of us drew attention, we had grown at very different rates and were physically dissimilar. To our chagrin, we had inherited more of Father's build than Mother's; but fortunately, we had also acquired finger-prints.

Father spent more and more time away, volunteering for missions of six months and longer duration, coming home for a few weeks of loving attention from Mother, then blasting off again. It was hard to blame him. During his time home nine squealing little girls climbed all over him, but he was frustrated in his attempts to enjoy us; he was unable to win so much as a game of gin rummy or any other game of skill by the time we were six. Hera knew more about the space ships he flew than he did by the time she was eleven. He was less and less able to participate even in dinner table discussions of any kind.

As we turned sixteen, Father had been gone for more than a year. A beribboned representative from the Service visited, gazed at us in astonishment, then broke the news that Father had been last seen pursuing a fellow crewman in a shuttle craft and had vanished near a black hole.

"He was a hero," said the representative.

Hera, by now an expert in astrophysics, said through her tears, "If he'd just known to set the coordinates for—"

Mother sobbed loudly and stamped on Hera's foot.

The representative went on to explain Mother's survivor benefits. "Rough going, supporting such a big family," he said sympathetically. "Even with generous benefits."

Mother dried her tears. "I'll manage."

The stock prognostications of Isis were now invaluable. Mother's investments financed travel and advanced educations for us all.

Once we completed our home-based education and

ventured out into the world we thought it would be more difficult to hide our gifts, especially when we all performed spectacularly well scholastically, and later, professionally. But we had one overwhelming advantage: We were women. Scant significance was attached to any of our accomplishments.

It was Diana, now a geneticist, and Demeter, a meditech, who made the first great contribution to our future. They discovered through experimentation that most Vernan genes are dominant and consequently mutation-resistant.

"It's why you had girls," Diana explained to Mother. "You couldn't have had a male no matter what."

Venus, our biologist, joined in further research. Additional experiments showed that our life expectancy was thirty years longer than an Earth male's; that unlike Mother who was pure Vernan, we were more likely to bear only two or three babies at most at one time, all girls; and that they would inherit the intellectual capacity of their mothers.

Selene the poet and Olympia the philosopher made the final valuable contributions, documenting and forecasting the continuing irrationality of Earth beliefs, customs, and mores, and clearly demonstrating the need for concern—and change.

We have just completed a week-long meeting of extraordinary scope, and have made our plans.

We will all marry. We will all have as many births as our individual situations allow. And pass the word on to our daughters.

Isis has shown that if we have multiple births, and succeeding generations continue at that rate, exponentially there will soon be a female population explosion.

And we are perfectly concealed. Men will continue to notice us only for their sexual and nesting needs—which is what we want them to do. And by the time they observe that there has been an astonishing number of births of baby girls, it will be much too late.

I am Minerva the historian, and this is the first chapter of our saga . . .

II

2199.2.21

Our Unity has assembled where we could not possibly be noticed—in an inland area of Southeast Calivada bearing the glorious history of having been a gunnery range, a nuclear testing site, a missile base, then a late twentieth century disposal for nerve gas and nuclear waste, which despite government denials did indeed, according to Hera, achieve critical mass in the year 2160, disintegrating even the sagebrush within a seventeen hundred mile radius. The site is perfect. But to further guarantee our secrecy and privacy we have posted bright graphics around the perimeter: WARNING—PARALYTIC FOAM TESTS IN PROGRESS.

We are six thousand now—precisely six thousand two hundred and forty-one, according to Isis—a three point seven average birth rate adjusted for a miniscule death rate . . . to which I have contributed far more than my fair share . . .

Some have chosen to camp out amid the scouring desert winds, but most of us are sensibly comfortable in the dome which was dropped into place and inflated by the resourceful Kendra and her transport crew, and then air spray painted to resemble ancient and blackened bomb craters.

It has been a time of exhilaration: The five generations of our Unity are together. We are but eight original children now; Selene died many years ago deep-sea diving off Antarctica. And I am consoled by my hundreds of descendants—of myself, and my four daughters, who to my great and abiding grief perished along with their father in the great transport collision that took the lives of so many in '72.

This meeting of the Unity is, of course, Mother's idea.

"No later than one month from now," she had informed us, smiling from the lumiscreen and adding, "No kidding, this is urgent." She had just moved from the carnival city of Rio to the monument city of Omaha, and had been amusing herself scanning twentieth century television tapes.

"Mother, do you have any idea of the logistics?" Hera demanded. Even when we were children she had been the only one of us to dare challenge Mother. "Bringing our six thousand together in a safe and private—"

"I know you girls can manage," Mother said serenely, and switched off.

I know you girls can manage. We had heard that phrase all the days of our childhood. And still we were girls to Mother.

But as always she was right. We managed.

We came from everywhere, many of us extricating ourselves from personal and professional entanglements. Some came from the orbital space stations, dozens more from the planetary development settlements. None were in deep space now—the Federated Governments had again conditioned acceptance of women into the Service based upon waiver of privacy rights.

On this first day there was continuous blending and co-mingling of us in colorful pulsing currents, a babel of excited conversation and joyous laughter as we exulted in being together. We were women with the shared experience of stretching toward excellence, and we celebrated ourselves. Some blending and co-mingling extended well into the night; our sleeping modules were of styroplast, makeshift and far from soundproof.

Accompanied by Mother who was also wakeful, I strolled through the darkened compound late this night. The soft moans and choked sounds of ecstasy from all around us evoked memory in me. After my devastating personal tragedy I had found the dearest woman on Earth, who had healed much of my pain and left me herself only in death; and after that there had been other variously rewarding liaisons, the most recent with a veritable child of twenty-five, who had gone on to another; but the unexpected joy of five years with her had left only gratitude in me, not grief. My sisters had followed a path similar to mine, all of them finding later-life relationships with loving women.

"Six thousand I've spawned," Mother grumbled, "and I'm the only heterosexual left." She took my arm. "I'll go back to my quarters now, dear. Tomorrow is a day of great decision."

Mother and the eight of us had met in a quaint and uncomfortable replica of a twentieth century hotel in Omaha, under the shadows of depressing gray buildings low against an endless empty sky, in view of abandoned nuclear silos and fields filled with museum pieces—bulbous-bodied aircraft and tiny warplanes looking like deadly insects. "An appropriate atmosphere," Mother had said grimly.

My Inner Circle, she had always called us. The first born, her elders. And we truly needed all the wisdom and knowledge we had accumulated among us. During hours of grueling debate, extending our minds to fullest capacity, we carefully analyzed the decision facing us.

On the final day, all areas of discussion exhausted, Mother announced, "What now remains is the choice of a leader."

"Leader?" Hera demanded, astonished as were we all. "You, Mother. As it has always been. Or a consortium like this if you choose not to lead."

"There are many reasons why you're wrong, Hera dear. But," Mother added generously, "I'll mention only a few. We need a leader who acts from primary logic, not preconceived ideas and the experience of a lifetime. Who makes decisions instantly. There will be circumstances—perils— none of us can foresee, and no time for decision by committee. We need a leader with immense intellectual reflexes and self-confidence and enormous energy. Someone young."

"Kendra," I said. "Hera's daughter has always possessed great inner strength and impressive personal magnetism."

"Thank you Minerva," Hera said to me, "but Kendra has focused her talents in my field, which is insufficient in scope. And she is not young."

Vesta said dubiously, "A young woman? To command respect and obedience?"

"To command respect," Mother corrected. "Obedience will follow respect." Her face was somber. "There may be no individual all of us would follow. And that will diminish our odds for success considerably." She brightened. "But in a garden of roses sometimes it's difficult to see at first the one rose that stands out above all others. Let's try data extraction."

"Wait," Hera said. "There is another descendant of mine, Regina's daughter . . ." She trailed off, her face thoughtful. "A master engineer at age twenty, and she—"

"I know of her," Isis interrupted. "Her accomplishments have been noted in all the Journals. Graduate school in Gdansk, the highest scores in their history—"

"Yes," Hera said proudly.

Isis shook her head. "She's amazing. She's still doing advanced study in Houston, yet some of her basic designs have already been incorporated into Jupiter Station. And she's one of the few women they've ever allowed into that all-male sanctuary."

Olympia said, "Mother, all of us have intellectual qualifications—"

"For what we need—"

"Mother," Olympia said in some exasperation, "*personal* qualities are necessary, perhaps more so than—"

"She has remarkable personal qualities," Hera said. "She has . . . presence."

"Enough," Mother said. "Let's look at her."

Diana fed in coordinates, and we all read in silence as data blipped down the screen, line after line cataloguing academic excellence and professional achievement.

Vesta murmured, "But she's only twenty-three. How has there been time?"

Demeter said in awe, "Her days must be twenty-five hours long."

"Incredible engineering skill, incomparable dedication," Mother mused. "Diana, show her to us."

Diana tapped a key. A tall, blade-slender figure with tousled dark hair, simply clad in a white shirt and dark pants, looked up from a computer board, long slim fingers holding a laser design stylus, rectangular green eyes irritated as if in resentment of having to relinquish these moments to have her likeness recorded.

"She has your eyes, Mother," I said. "That exact remarkable color. I know of no other in our Unity to inherit that color."

Venus murmured, staring at the screen, "I'll follow her anywhere."

"Of all my girls," Mother said to Venus, "you are the most aptly named." She asked Hera, "Is she . . . attached?"

"Not to my knowledge."

"For lack of time, not opportunity," Mother mused, appraising the arresting figure on the screen. "Historically it hasn't been necessary, but it's advantageous for a leader to have . . . physical appeal. Especially if she remains unattached."

Venus said with a shudder, "The only major leaders in history to remain celibate were the rulers of that religious sect—" She knitted her lovely brow.

"Catholicism," I supplied.

"And numbers of them were none too faithful to the ideal," Olympia said tartly.

"Never has a leader faced this situation," Mother said thoughtfully, "except for the leader in that Biblical legend of the Promised Land . . ."

For some hours we debated leadership attributes, fed coordinates into our data banks, examined and discussed other possible candidates—but all of us had been stirred by the imperious young woman who had stared at us with such impatience.

"The first one," Mother said. "Let me see her again."

Again the young woman stared resentfully at us with her arresting emerald eyes.

"A leader should always dress consistently," Mother said thoughtfully. "She may very well do . . ." She smiled. "Diana dear, what is the etymology of her name? Not that I believe in portents, of course."

All of us hid smiles. Her selection of our names had placed even greater expectations upon all of us. Diana's slim fingers fed the question to the data banks.

"Well well," Mother said as we all read the answer on the screen. "The strong and the able. Many aspects appear to favor her, this . . . Megan."

III

2199.2.22

Our Unity is a dramatic sight: six thousand on two darkened semi-circle tiers in enclaves of sixty or so, gathered around pack-powered lumiscreens. On a raised platform, gazing out at her remarkable progeny, Mother sits resplendent on a huge chaise, her green lustervel cape in majestic folds around her. She seems smaller with the passing of the years—her cantaloupes more like grapefruit now—but still, somewhat past her prime and years of greatest vigor, she possesses an aura of indomitable self-confidence and undiminished magnetism.

In a phalanx behind Mother we sit—the Inner Circle. My sisters and I are grouped as usual, Isis, Hera, Venus and Diana together in their brilliantly hued garments; and Vesta, Olympia, Demeter and I—the quiet ones—in our simple robes. Selene, while she lived, had also belonged with us, the quiet ones. We have all aged well; we have maintained good health; we look much as we did at half our age. Diana has told us that we may reasonably expect thirty more optimum years, and more beyond that if breakthroughs in delaying of the aging process occur as anticipated.

Thirty more years of physical vigor will be especially prized by Venus, who at this historical time gazes not at Mother nor the impressive audience of thousands, but at the slender young woman with tousled dark hair framing her face, her elegant height emphasized by close-fitting lustervel pants of burnished black and a puff-sleeved, high-collared white silk shirt. She stands beside a data bank, motionless, statuesque, gazing at Mother with eyes of pure emerald.

Mother has honored several young women with invitations to share our platform—ostensibly to monitor visual and data banks—but we all know her purpose: "This Megan," she had said. "I wish to observe her."

Venus, Diana, and Demeter begin their presentation, Venus taking her eyes from Megan only as she moves to join her sisters at the projection module.

So many years ago we sisters had held a similar council with Mother. Now we have far less time to impart far greater information—and never will the stakes be higher.

My sisters' four-hour presentation is splendid, opulent, a fully comprehensive oral-visual tribute to the contributions of women to the civilized growth of every country on Earth— from the comparative handful who shone their lonely light through dark centuries of abysmal ignorance, to the brilliant achievements of our own group. The micro-recording made of this presentation will always be the one truly accurate review of women's history in existence; and no description of mine could ever convey its acuity and luminosity.

Olympia and I are next. We have condensed the work and knowledge of our lifetimes into a historical and philosophical perspective of women throughout recorded history, and we give our projections, Juno's mathematical constructs and Olympia's theorems based upon the principles of Aristotelian logic. Our projections are dismal enough without necessity for additional conclusion.

And now it is time for Mother to speak.

As the gigantic lumiscreen behind Mother dims with the ending of our presentation, she slowly revolves her chaise to face the two-tiered semi-circle.

In a pool of gold light in our darkened enclosure she

sits for some moments amid absolute silence. Then she smiles. "Hello, dears. You're all simply beautiful."

She is forced to raise a hand before the tumult will subside. "Dear ones, the lines of history are intersecting again as the girls have just shown you. On this dreary planet it's all so depressingly predictable. Males become spastic with terror everytime women break through to new choices and freedom. And this most recent freedom—no longer needing the poor things at all to make babies for us—well, have laws ever been passed more quickly? Really, my dears, the *death* penalty for the sale of Estrova? *Sperm certificates* for approval of pregnancies and births? One retreats from contemplating what they may think of next."

Outside our quiet enclosure the harsh desert winds, whining and howling, hurtle at us. Mother says mournfully, "Raising such wonderful ones as you I suppose it was inevitable you'd find each other more interesting than anyone else. But how could I ever have known you'd end up falling in love with each other?"

Mother leans forward. "It has never been the female nature to seek or want power. And so in this primitive culture we have been at the whim of its inferior leadership. But when those in power learn that certain of us will never surrender control of our bodies or our lives—"

Again Mother has to raise a hand for quiet. "We will soon be the most visible women on Earth." She sighs. "You know, girls, they will never tolerate us."

She sighs again. "My dear ones, let's just get the hell out of here."

For some minutes cheers and applause reverberate through our enclosure. Mother beams. And finally raises a hand. "Hera will now explain the options open to us."

Crimson cape flowing out behind her, Hera stalks to the projection module and confronts her audience, standing with booted feet planted apart, cape swirling about her black mesh trouser-suit. The tallest of us sisters, she has always been the most flamboyant; and her descendant, the graceful young woman attired in black and white who assists her at the console, has inherited Hera's dramatic presence—without necessity for any flamboyance.

"There is this possibility," Hera intones. "On-planet relocation. We have the means, the technology to remain undetected—with certain precautions, within certain parameters."

The huge lumiscreen behind Hera contains the globe of Earth. Megan's slender fingers dance over the touch-plates of the console, bringing into closeup one section of Earth after another as Hera speaks.

"Except for mineral exploitation, these areas of the Arctic and Antarcticas are untouched." With a laser pointer Hera dextrously circles areas within the geographic regions. "Other northern possibilities include the Yukon and Siberia. Another virtually deserted area is in South America, the southern half of what was recently Brazil. However, as you know, territorial claims are still in dispute," she says distastefully.

"The northeast section of Australia—" The continent appears; Hera forms a circle with her laser light. "Algeria and Libya," she continues, "and a section of southern Russia." Circling a section in southwest America, she says contemptuously, "Here, where we presently are. Where the craters of the moon are lovely by comparison."

"None is an Earthly paradise." Mother's voice is mild. "Unpopulated areas are unpopulated for good reason."

"If we wish to remain on Earth," Hera proclaims, "we shall have to choose one of these areas, and Isis and Venus inform me that rigid population control will be required. Greater than ten thousand of us would result in certain exposure."

There are murmurs—of dismay, disapproval.

Mother says quietly, "We are women of sensibility, we all need beauty in our lives. I believe we need—"

A shout from the second tier: "Our needs are for us individually to decide!"

In the shock that follows this outburst, amid a rising tide of murmurs, a slender figure steps into the pool of light illuminating Mother and stands in a still, angry tension, silk shirt fluttering in the air currents. "No one shall interrupt Mother when she speaks." Megan's voice is bell-like, a command, reaching to the farthest tier without audio-enhance.

"Come here."

Mother's voice matches Megan's in command, and her eyes are fixed on eyes of identical emerald which look into hers with sudden uncertainty.

Mother reaches to her. Megan hesitantly, reverently takes Mother's hand. Mother pats Megan's hand, releases it. "Stand here next to me," she orders, "until Hera needs you again."

Megan is not accustomed, as we sisters are, to Mother's disconcerting blend of steeliness and affection; and she stands beside Mother's chair gazing at her in bemusement, ivory skin heightening in color.

"Charming," sighs Venus from beside me.

Mother says, "To whomever spoke, your point is well-taken. If impudently made. However, I had thought it unnecessary to state that each of us must choose her own course. Continue, Hera."

Hera casts a stony glance toward the second tier. Her arms crossed, she says loftily, "That imbecilic remark was uttered, I trust, by no descendant of mine. I will continue. Another possibility is our own solar system. With varying degrees of difficulty all the planets are habitable. And although it would appear that we could exist there in open freedom, feasibility is marginal. It is Vesta's opinion—concurred in by all of us since there is ample historical precedent—that we would not be allowed to peacefully exist, that we would be regarded as alien, threatening, unacceptable. Reasons such as territorial claims would be found for the destruction of any world we attempted to openly build. And there is another critical factor. Our leaving Earth would result in a sudden and drastic siphoning off of Earth's intellectual resources—what was termed centuries ago as 'brain drain.' It is doubtful we would be allowed to leave."

The tiers of women stir; there is a murmuring, a disturbed undertone.

"Mother's home world has low population density and a sophisticated civilization," Hera says. "Certainly they would welcome Mother. But we, her offspring, are basically Earthwomen, and it would be expecting the improbable to think that any civilization, however advanced, would react without xenophobia."

She turns and stalks to her projection module, cape swirling, motioning imperiously for Megan to remain at Mother's side.

The curving screen behind Hera suddenly glows with glittering pinpoints, the outer pinpoints fleeing as focus narrows to the sphere rotating above the North celestial pole. The focus narrows further, until a circle of constellations hovers on the screen: the fiery belt of Orion; the scattered stars of Gemini with Castor and Pollux blazing; the farflung stars of Perseus; the modest triangle of Aries; the sprawl of Taurus.

The focus narrows further, moves slowly across Orion and the brilliant Rigel and Betelgeuse; across the great flaring Aldebaran, one eye of Taurus—and stops over the other eye, a cluster of five radiant stars.

"The Hyades," Hera states.

The focus moves very slowly across, stops again. The screen is filled with blazing globes in a field of diamonds, clothed by reflection nebulae—illuminated fluorescent clouds like silken transparent hair.

"The Pleiades." Hera's hushed voice pervades our enclosure. "Minerva," she says with a touch of sharpness.

I start; along with everyone else I have become immersed in the overwhelming splendor on the screen, have forgotten my part of Hera's presentation.

"Minerva will relate to us the legend of these stars from antiquity," Hera says, speaking more gently. "It seems somehow . . . symbolic."

"The Pleiades and the Hyades are in Taurus." I arrange

my thoughts with effort, my eyes still hypnotized by the radiance on the huge screen. "Taurus is the second sign in the Zodiac. In legend, Taurus the Bull carried Europa across the seas to Crete, and then Jupiter placed him in the heavens. The Hyades are five sisters who nursed Dionysius as a baby, and they were raised to the heavens as their reward. They are sisters to the Pleiades—what we look at now—the seven daughters of Atlas and Pleione. The daughters grieved so over the suffering of their father that they were changed into stars. The sisters all produced divine or heroic off-spring."

"Excellent," Mother says, beaming. "Simply excellent. Not that I believe in portents," she adds.

"Thank you, Minerva." Hera continues, "Taurus also includes the great Crab nebula which went nova in the eleventh century, and the great red giant Aldebaran, twenty-one parsecs distant from us. The Pleiades are an open star cluster in the galactic arm of Perseus, ninety-two parsecs distant. They are an unusually compact group for an open cluster, and surrounded as you see by wisps of illuminated gas. This brightest star—" Hera taps with her laser light. "—is Alcyone. She is a third magnitude star. Of the hundreds of stars within this cluster and around it, these are the ones of interest."

Hera circles a jewel-like sprinkling. "An unusual concentration of G-two stars—which as we all know is the classification of our own sun." Hera pauses to allow the significance of this statement to penetrate.

"Limited information dictates limited choice," she states. "Two hundred or so years of galactic probes, a hundred years of manned star probes—comparatively small wedges of the galaxy are mapped or explored. And have thus far been analyzed only for chemical content and evidence of intelligent life—and then exploited only to the extent of trade agreements, as with Verna-Three, Mother's planet. Earth continues to subdue and colonize its own hostile planetary system, has analyzed no other star system for colonization."

Hera crosses her arms and says with considerable satisfaction, "It was not difficult to feed in basic data of life support on Earth and compare it to what has been received from all the star probes, and to further narrow that into definitive form. I caution you, what I will show you now does not nearly represent the wealth of knowledge we have amassed."

She turns to the projection module. A blurred globe appears on the screen—a reverse negative of Earth, misty coral in place of blue seas, with streaks and swirls of pale ivory and coral continents.

Again Hera stands with her arms crossed. "This is a ninety times magnification from a galactic probe as well as a composite," she says calmly. "And because of the atmospheric shroud, it is the best penetrative representation we have."

Murmurs of disappointment—and dismay—can be heard. Hera says brusquely, "Yes, there is much we do not know about this planet, but a great deal that we do know. In very general terms, chemical and gas composition from spectrographic study. The atmosphere contains the four vital components necessary to sustain life as we know it. The vital constituents of living cells—nucleotides—are present. There are massive ocean areas. Radiation readings provide atom absorption rates and gas densities. Obviously we have approximations of the mass, radius, and density of this planet, its orbital path, and we know that three small moons surround it. And we have studied its star."

On the screen appears a sun and planetary system which at a glance could be mistaken for our own solar system.

"This sun is a white-to-yellow G-type star." Hera's voice is flat, as if she is explaining the commonplace; she has always been supercilious in the sharing of her knowledge. "Our spectroheliograms have given its luminosity, color index, spectral sequence and class, to mention the most basic factors." She says impatiently. "The coordinates for all technical data are on your individual screens. Sequence them, scan the data. Then I will entertain questions.

Intelligent questions," she adds forbiddingly.

A musical rise and fall of women's voices begins, soft-toned discussions. Megan bends to Mother, murmurs. Again Mother pats her hand. Megan illuminates the huge platform screen and moves to a data board and for herself runs the coordinates Hera has given, sequencing them with great rapidity. Then a flow of equations races across the screen. Since I possess only cursory familiarity with Isis' field, these are of a complexity beyond me. But Isis looks on with rapt interest, as does Hera, who ceases her impatient pacing to stare at the stream of symbols, head cocked to one side in her habitual manner when her mind is fully absorbed.

The flow of symbols ceases; a final equation stares from the screen. Megan turns and gazes at Isis with an expression of deference.

"You are correct," Isis tells her. She adds in a low tone to us, "Hera and I arrived at that answer only after much combined effort. The technique is rough but her leaps in logic are astonishing."

"About what is she correct?" I inquire; but as Megan extinguishes her data, the first question for Hera has appeared.

The lumiscreen reads, "SINCE THIS PLANET IS LIKE EARTH, WILL IT NOT ALSO HAVE INTELLIGENT LIFE, AND MANY LIFE FORMS?"

"The planet promises to have life forms more intelligent than some in this room," Hera snaps. Her dark eyes are indignant. "This planet is *not* like Earth. It is Earth-*like*—a billion degree difference as any cretin knows. In a universe with untold star systems, countless numbers have planets favorably endowed for maintaining life. But the permutations of life forms are also incalculable. Of the few hundred thousand star systems which have been mapped, this planet is a close approximation of Earth-type conditions. But there will be differences that cannot be imagined, much less foretold.

"As for the lucid part of the question, even a stage-two intelligence has discovered fire and attempts rudimentary forms of communication with its own kind, and there are no surface irregularities, no atmospheric disturbances, no patterned pulses indicating purposeful use of energy. The most primitive technology would produce uneven readings, variance in the radiation readings, and based on every standard of judgment there is no evidence of civilization—which does not mean that intelligent life does not exist. The star system appears relatively young—in the four billion year range—and probably is still advancing along a typical median evolutionary scale. There are readings we cannot take unless actually there. The organic molecular structure of the ocean . . . DNA readings. But the basic molecular keys for the evolution of life forms are present, and we may assume varied life forms exist. Next question."

"WHY NOT A DOMED SETTLEMENT IN A CLOSER STAR SYSTEM SUCH AS ALPHA CENTAURI?"

Hera nods acceptance of the question. "Vesta? Perhaps you would answer."

Smiling sweetly, Vesta stands. The gentlest among us, she is perhaps most loved. She is a social scientist—the gentlest of the sciences—and an incredibly wonderful cook. She has lived for the past twenty years with Carina, a descendant of Selene, a big shy woman so reticent and tender with Vesta that it seems miraculous they managed to come together.

Her huge gray eyes fixed on the audience, Vesta says in her soft voice, "If we wish to live in the combination dome-subterranean type settlements Earth has established on its other planets, we could of course go to any planet not totally inimical. But the domed planetary settlements have this in common: they were built for mining purposes, secondarily as colonies. They possess an underlying impermanence. Anyone there has the choice and option of returning to Earth, a scant few days' journey. Many studies support claims of harmful long-term effects of enclosed living. But in the Pleiades we may have an optimum chance to live in the open. If we find conditions that preclude this, then one would hope we would make this planet a temporary refuge until we find another which will not condemn us to living as artificially supported expatriates. One where we can live freely, as a naturally coexisting part of the ecology. A planet to be our home."

A planet to be our home. These words echo eloquently for some moments before the next question appears.

"WHAT ARE THE ODDS FOR SUCCESSFUL COLONIZATION?"

Hera nods in satisfaction at the question. "Venus, perhaps you would assist."

Venus moves gracefully to join Hera. By far the most beautiful of us now as always, she wears a soft blue flowing robe which suggests rather than conceals the womanly curving of her body. She gazes at her audience with azure eyes, and speaks in a voice of sensual tones which nevertheless contains authority.

"The risk is enormous. Initial tests may dictate a restricted existence to us immediately, as Vesta has suggested. We can do only so many laboratory tests, we can duplicate only conditions we are aware of, that we can forecast. The long term effects of this planet are the key. Will there be bacteriological conditions beyond our knowledge? Ultraviolet differences, to change the properties of our genes? Or will we adapt with a minimum of side-effect? We do not know."

Hera flings out her arms. "But we will not be like Christopher Columbus on an uncharted sea. Nor Robinson Crusoe with limited resources on a desert island. We will be the best prepared exodus in all history."

"HOW FAR A JOURNEY TO THIS PLANET?"

"A descendant of mine has just determined that answer," Hera says proudly, "and Megan will speak."

Megan looks only momentarily startled. "Thank you, esteemed Hera."

She moves to the projection module. An equation appears on the screen. "Eighteen days to the Einsteinian Curve, as we all know." Another, far more complex equation appears. "With optimum current starship technology, ninety-seven days beyond that to orbit and planetfall."

"Excellent, my dear," Mother says, beaming.

"HOW CAN WE BUILD A STARSHIP AND REMAIN UNDETECTED?"

"We cannot," Hera declares in her most imperious tone. "Megan, call up coordinates point niner-four-five and six."

Against the backdrop of the ghostly gray-white craters of the moon floats an immense brown brindled carrier ship, with faintly discernible Cryllic lettering repeated at intervals along its massive hull.

There are murmurs of surprised recognition.

"The *Brezhnev*," Hera confirms, and falls silent, allowing us to contemplate it.

Brezhnev's one venture beyond the Einsteinian Curve has given it justifiable fame: it carried back to Earth the oxyplants that had cleansed the pollutants from the atmosphere. Afterward, it had made numerous solar system circumnavigations, but the continuous reshielding required for spaceworthiness had eventually reached the point of diminishing returns for the Eastern Bloc; and more than a decade ago they had built the *Tolstoi*. *Brezhnev* has been in parabolic lunar obit ever since.

"Through my daughter Kendra's company we inquired about salvage rights to this abandoned and mothballed ship." Hera smiles with immense satisfaction. "Our generous initial bid has been greeted with great eagerness by the Eastern Bloc."

"Of course if they hadn't been eager, we'd have taken it off their hands anyway," Mother adds, to laughter. "But it's so much nicer this way."

"Yes," Hera says, "especially when we have no use for credits where we're going. Megan, please key in coordinates niner-four-seven and eight."

A research station turns in stately slowness against the blue and white swirls of Earth. Hera does not bother to identify this historic station which was abandoned when the solar laboratories were built.

"Kendra's company has a two-year maintenance

contract with WACASA," Hera says.

She strides to Mother's side and stands illuminated in the pool of gold light. "Our plan is simple. We will buy *Brezhnev* and all necessary supplies to outfit it. And use *Skylab* as warehouse and waystation for ourselves and our equipment. We will expend a great many useless credits purchasing what we need, and in return we can never be accused of theft—which will confuse the issue of pursuit, perhaps. All reshielding and testing will be accomplished while *Brezhnev*—which we will rename, of course—is on orbital pass on the moon's dark side. Preparations will require total cooperation from all of us who choose to leave, and a coordination of effort on the most massive scale imaginable." Hera stalks back to our group, and sits down.

"CAN OUR SHIP LEAVE UNDETECTED? WHAT IF WE ARE PURSUED?"

Isis stands. "We cannot leave undetected. We can assume pursuit, for many reasons—mainly irrational. At best we can evade pursuit. We have the advantage of *Brezhnev's* orbital configuration, and leaving from the moon's dark side. There will also be Earth's decision-making time— minutes to perhaps hours. Our computations have determined that except under the worst possible circumstance we will reach the Einsteinian Curve first. Our odds then of being found in hyperspace drop to fifty percent or less, given the ingenuity of the navigation plan we will devise."

"I have an idea how we may reduce those odds even further," Mother says musingly, "but it needs more thought."

"HOW WILL WE AS INDIVIDUALS BE ABLE TO LEAVE EARTH SAFELY AND UNDETECTED?"

As Olympia stands to answer, erect and dignified in her gray robe, Mother snorts, "Details, mere details to be worked out. Next question." Olympia sits down.

"DOES OUR NEW PLANET HAVE A NAME?"

Smiling, Demeter stands. She is the most reflective of us, sweet-natured and humorous, totally immersed in her work which, as she has grown older, has tended more to the research aspects of the medical arts. She has lived with Aleda, a lovely descendant of Vesta's, for many contented years.

"The planet is currently designated on WACASA maps as M233.143-3," Demeter says. "As Mother's elders we have taken the liberty—certain that we would have your approval—to name our world after Mother."

First Mother glares at us, then scowls at her audience until the tumultuous applause dies and everyone sits down. "Forget it," she says. "I refuse to set foot on a planet called Mother."

Demeter's rejoinder is soft. "We have named our world . . . Maternas."

"Maternas," Mother muses.

Applause builds, swells, thunders. "All right, all right," Mother grumbles, holding up a hand. "Who is your poor Mother to argue?"

We know she is pleased.

"WHEN DO WE LEAVE FOR MATERNAS?"

"The best question so far." Mother thumps her chaise in emphasis.

I rise to answer. "Nine months to a year. With proper coordination of our efforts, we can reduce the time. The crucial element in our preparations is coordination."

"And I have some ideas about that," Mother says, her eyes drifting over to Megan. She gets to her feet. "I'm tired, dear ones. And you know how details bore me. Hash everything else out among yourselves. I know you girls can manage."

To continuous cheers and applause, Mother makes her way to the corridor leading to her quarters; then she turns and beckons, for Megan.

IV

Personal Journal of Megan
2199.2.26

It is not that I am reticent—although others may judge me so. In a brief life where time has been insufficient to my needs, verbal expression—either recorded or spoken—is an expenditure I make as carefully as any other. Minerva has told me that a journal containing the personal thoughts and observations of a leader will one day be a vital part of the history of a new world. That will never be. I will never permit access to my personal thought. But at this moment, the reflection required to record this is soothing to me, and will perhaps make concrete the dreamlike events of the past days.

Before our Unity met, I had extrapolated that one day we would no longer retain meaningful productivity and motivation in our lives, that a growing sense of futility would eventually bring a period of withdrawal, of isolation, perhaps even exile. But my mind had not made the conceptual leap to exodus . . .

The instant I saw on lumiscreen our new world—its indistinct coral and ivory hues defeating my staring efforts to discern a revealing feature—I knew I would offer every skill I had, every talent, all my training, to help build this world . . .

But never did I dream that I would play a part such as I have been given . . .

When we reached Mother's quarters, she arranged herself

30

on her chaise, and I began to pace. It is impossible for me to sit quietly; I am too conscious of unused time slipping past. Mother, who contemplated me as I paced, no longer disconcerted me; I now knew that her ways are not meant to disconcert—they are simply her ways. And so her eyes followed me, the eyes which somehow have come down all the generations of her descendants to me. My mother has grey eyes; my natal sisters Lilia and Tara have inherited her eyes and diminutive stature. As I recall, my male parent's eyes are a nondescript variant of hazel. I seldom cast a thought to him; he displayed interest in me only when my achievements rewarded me with a small degree of renown, and his is an interest I see no reason to return.

"Sit down, dear," Mother suddenly directed.

Smiling, I sat where she indicated, at the foot of her chaise.

"Of course you're coming with us," she said.

"Nothing could prevent me."

She said tartly, "Then tell me how you will contribute."

I replied with caution and deference. "In the area Minerva referred to as coordination of effort. I have completed advanced study in colony design, several of my concepts have been applied on Jupiter—"

Mother said impatiently, "I know all about your accomplishments."

I said in surprise, "I am honored. I suggest that three essential plans must be devised. The first priority is outfitting a ship previously an ore carrier to make it habitable over many months for more than four thousand of us, and—"

"Four thousand? Why do you say four thousand?"

"A mere guess," I said swiftly, apologetically. "It seems . . . a correct number. Some of us will have powerful ties here. Others will be psychologically unable to leave—"

"Four thousand or so was the number Isis arrived at," Mother said, "except that she used one of her curve charts—" She waved a hand. "Details bore me. Continue."

"The configuration of our ship's interior must be planned

in minute detail, supplies and equipment precisely computed. The talent among us must be correlated, allocated, applied. At planetfall, while preliminary tests are undertaken and Maternas is surveyed and charted, while decisions are taken about where we shall locate, the transition period from the ship to Maternas must be planned and organized, a well-conceived and flexible structure for our living arrangements must be designed in advance—"

"Enough," Mother said.

She reached to me, took my hand, patted it; and said the words—casually—that have reverberated in my mind all these days since: "Megan, my dear, you are my choice to lead our exodus and settlement on Maternas."

I could only stare at her. Then stammer, "There are others . . . I'm young—"

"If you ever get to be my age which Geezerak knows nobody is—well, most of you young people are quite boring, I must admit. But aside from that, age is irrelevant to almost everything." She looked at me, eyes distant and containing an expression I could not identify. "You have skills uncannily matched to our needs . . . as if a seed has come to fruition at the precise moment its fruit is most badly needed . . ."

"Mother," I said as she trailed off, "only you should lead us."

She looked at me acutely then, her eyes aware, compelling. "Leadership is simple. It requires only the ability and willingness—the courage—to make decisions. I believe that you have that courage. I will help, dear one. But this is a time for youth. Your time."

I did not answer. I could not. My mind was filled with visions.

"There is a price," Mother said. "There always is."

I looked at her.

"Loneliness."

I smiled. "I have been most of my life alone."

"A very short life. Dear, choice is so very different from necessity. Do you know anything of leadership dynamics?"

"Some," I admitted. "As part of my studies. As a facet of colony reorganization. And enough to know I will not be readily accepted by women as talented as I, women of vastly more maturity than I."

Mother sighed. "I know I'm old as dust but wisdom is such an effort . . . Listen, my dear. It's really very simple. Beginning tomorrow you'll be seen always in my company. Decisions I and my Inner Circle are required to make will be referred to you. Until the idea of your status is firmly implanted. Then it will be up to you to build your own authority and power base."

My mind was already grappling eagerly with the immensity of such responsibility. "I dedicate myself to—"

Mother waved a hand. "Skip the homilies, dear. And try to keep one thing in mind at all times. Even in a group such as this, all aspects of leadership psychology apply. Leadership imagery, for instance. Black and white are power colors—so dress all the time just as you are now. Power attracts, Megan. Irresistibly. My gifted children are no more immune to the charisma of the leader than anyone else . . . especially such a leader as you. Many women will soon want to occupy your bed, however briefly. I'm sure they do anyway," she added, coolly surveying me.

I laughed, warmed by so offhand a compliment. "If I haven't had much time before, I certainly won't now, Mother."

"No, you won't." Her face was more somber than I had yet seen. And tired. "Lovers—a family—distract. Dilute attention and energy. And create jealousies, factions. Our circumstances will be unforseeable, with the survival of thousands at stake. The stakes are much too high for—"

"There will be no one," I said firmly. "I assure you it is a loneliness I can accept."

"It is a most difficult loneliness. One that grows more difficult. I know all about the difficulties," she murmured, and lay back, her eyes shuttered from me. "And that aspect of your life has been open to you for so short a time . . ."

"I accept it without reservation," I said, knowing it

would be easier for me than most. Perhaps I should have revealed the extent of my innocence to Mother—this missing element in my life—but I decided that I would not; it was an innocence in which I took no pride. "I give you my word," I said. "My solemn word."

She murmured, eyes closed, "It begins tomorrow, Megan. My Inner Circle contributed heavily in the choice of you . . . they are eager to support you . . . to have you join us . . ."

"I sleep little," I replied, "and rise early. I will—"

But Mother's breathing had become the slow rhythms of sleep. Carefully, gently, I covered her with a soft fleece thermolet, and walked soundlessly from her quarters, thinking that she had looked tiny and vulnerable . . . and knowing that I would protect her at any cost, this woman to whom I had willingly, unhesitatingly, pledged my life.

V

2199.4.6

Mother has told me, "If you insist on pursuing this eye-witness history of our journey, then focus it on Megan. The leader always provides the history, the legends."

But how shall I record Megan?

In these days of chaos, amid the maelstrom of our preparations, she has been peremptory, dogmatic, abrupt, impatient, even rude. Yet she has been our rationality, our strength.

No, she has said to the fabricators that we argued were essential to our new settlement. "Synthesizers only. If we cannot build our own fabricators after planetfall, then the planet's resources are insufficient to our needs."

No, she has said to equipment for full oxygenation. Her tersely given reason: "Oxygen only on the living levels, and we will draw that partly from photosynthesis in the green-house areas. The rest of the ship will be sealed except to repair crews."

No, she has said, her finality implacable, to all pleas, no matter how rending, for personal possessions of any kind. "Supplies for transit and planetfall are the only priority. If anyone cannot leave behind her possessions and mementos, she may stay behind with them."

No, she has said to modification requests for the tiny and starkly bare cubicles that will be our living quarters. "If anyone cannot accommodate to four rigorous and tightly disciplined months in space, then she does not belong with us."

She has assigned responsibility with a maximum and flattering degree of trust. "You and Olympia choose, assemble your own team," she has told us. "The decisions about what knowledge we store to take with us are yours alone."

She speaks seldom, and then with simplicity; but she has full appreciation for a task well thought out and completed with excellence, and a brief word of praise from her seems eulogy. A task completed below her expectation will bring silence—and redoubled effort to transform that silence.

Hera has established the team which is redesigning the ship we purchased—and have renamed *Amelia Earhart.* Megan's design contributions based on rotational principles are brilliant, Hera says, and have enabled Hera to release part of her team to begin the critical work on *Amelia's* power drive.

Isis, in charge of supply distribution, says that Megan's instant computation of the most complex weight to stress ratios is astonishing . . .

She is everywhere. And her presence is exhilarating.

I have tried to analyze that presence. She is constructed of tension: the slender body always erect, blade-straight—never conceding fatigue, although she seems never to sleep. The ivory skin luminous and tight, as if polishing the sculptured planes of her face. The mouth finely shaped, but often drawn taut with concentration, the lower lip caught in even white teeth. She seems fully energized, like an entity in perfect exercise of its powers—like a cat stretched out in certain pursuit of its prey.

When she pauses to observe or listen, her long legs move in unobtrusive rhythm; she cannot remain motionless. But her hands are calm; she holds schematic printouts in an acute still tension; and she taps in emphasis when she speaks, with purposeful fingers long and slender and translucent.

She seems to tower a head above us, yet is no more tall than the tall among us. Her garb is utilitarian—the white shirt and black pants starkly simple—yet on her they acquire elegance. Her habitual gesture is to brush a hand through her hair, hair which is always in disarray, yet pleasingly so, separating into dark curling tendrils over the collar of her shirt. And those emerald eyes. Always those extraordinary eyes.

Her authority is now unquestioned—which is not to say that her decisions have gone unchallenged. We listened carefully to the protests which came to each of us—and pronounced unsympathetic judgment. Mother—the ultimate source of appeal—of course was her usual ungracious self: "Phosh. Do as Megan commands or I will be seriously annoyed."

Fabrienne—a descendant of mine I must admit—had the temerity to complain to Mother, "This is a dictatorship!"

"Of course it is, my dear," Mother answered cheerfully. "Who has time for democracy? We'll get into all that business on Maternas."

But Mother has had daily meetings with Megan, private meetings in Mother's quarters. And often after these meetings Megan's decisions have been changed or modified. And so Megan learns flexibility ... But with each passing day she grows in competence and authority; fewer and fewer of her decisions are challenged; the meetings with Mother become less and less frequent.

So it has become known throughout our Unity that Megan has full support from Mother. And that she has won loyalty and staunch support from Mother's Inner Circle. It has become apparent to us all who observe her daily that she possesses an integrative faculty of stunning dimension, seeing the whole and its parts with equal acuity whatever the complexity of the whole. Many are born with great gifts for an hour which never comes. But she is perfectly designed to lead us, and we support her with our hearts as well as our intellect ... Increasingly, with our hearts ...

Venus somehow manages to find moments from her

work to disturb Megan. And she does disturb her . . . If noticeable to very few, the signs are unmistakable. Brief breaks in her concentration when Venus is nearby. A sudden stillness in her body when Venus comes into the room; the subtle heightening of the ivory coloring.

It is easy to forget how very young Megan is; her appearance is so imposing, her presence so electric, her decisions made with such quiet assurance . . . But I see her sexual awareness of Venus, and her confusion . . . As does Venus. As does Mother.

Several days ago Mother and I came into the command room to consult Megan. She stood with eyes fixed on her drafting board, face flushed. Venus leaned casually toward her, a finger tracing slow circles in deliberate teasing distraction over the design Megan was revising.

"—anti-grav unit in my quarters," Venus was saying. "Let me show you. Sensation beyond imagining. You—"

"Venus," Mother said curtly, "get lost."

Startled, Venus looked at Mother, brow prettily knit.

Also annoyed with her, I explained with satisfaction, "Get lost is a twentieth century phrase. Closely related to the word scram."

As Venus continued to look bewildered, Mother said, "We have business with Megan, Venus dear. Go talk to your plants."

As Venus strolled gracefully away, Mother asked Megan in a voice that contained a gentleness I had heard as a child, "Is Venus a problem to you, dear one?"

"No, Mother," Megan answered immediately. "No, she is not."

"I can help—"

"Do not. There is no problem."

Mother nodded. I had never heard anyone address Mother in a tone so closely resembling a command, nor her accede so willingly. Megan had inherited Hera's pride, I thought— with a most considerable addition of her own. But I had seen her involuntary glance as Venus had left; and I looked at her in concern, knowing too well how vulnerable she was.

I have read or heard somewhere a definition of sexual appeal in a woman: it is merely the reflection of that woman's own sexual interest.

The two major and equal interests in Venus's life have always been her work, and the exploration of the sensations possible to her body. She has a sexual confidence I have never remotely possessed, not even during the years when my body was at peak attractiveness. The sexual shimmer that surrounds Venus has not diminished with the years. She seems the most youthful of us, and her effect on women remains, to this day, mesmerizing. Her body is fully fleshed, her breasts exquisitely shaped; and her movements are languorous, sensual. I have seen women stare at her lips, which possess not only perfection of shape but a slightly swollen, ripe aspect. Many times I have seen Venus's azure eyes meet the eyes of another woman with a candid eroticism that intensifies until the hot blue seems the very edge of orgasm.

It has been years since Venus abandoned men. "Boring. Too easy," she had told me with an expressive shrug. "Women are challenging. And physically much more . . . interesting."

Megan had forbidden Mother to help her—but not me.

But I said to Venus without much hope, "I think you should leave Megan alone."

"Don't be disagreeable, Minerva." Venus was brushing her silver hair. "And silly," she added.

She lay on her chaise in a filmy one-piece trouser suit of palest blue. I sighed; such firm breasts surely had to be a matter of sheer will power. "She's too busy," I argued. "She doesn't have time to dally with you."

"Of course she does. There's always time. If necessary it can take a very short time. Short but frequent can be oh so very sweet." She looked off away from me, smiling.

"She's young."

A shrug. "So? I've had younger."

"She could be hurt. And that would certainly distract her from her work."

"Love never destroyed anyone." This was a maxim of Venus's, repeated frequently. "And I love her. I do love her, Minerva."

I had heard this from Venus so many times over the years that I made the appropriate rude snorting noise.

Venus took my hands. "Dear sister, why this interest? It would be good for her. She hasn't anyone, all she does is work work work."

I fired my last salvo. "Venus, Mother doesn't approve."

"Mother has never approved. She thinks," she said with a delicate shudder, "that I should be like Demeter, settled down all these years."

I said tartly, thinking of the lovely years with my own beloved Serena, "If you've never tried—"

"Have any of you ever lived as I do? But perhaps this is the time for me, Minerva. I believe, I truly do, that I will be with Megan forever. But why worry about her? I'll be good for her. She never sleeps, never relaxes. She needs distraction. Just let me get my hands on her. Inside that white shirt of hers. And after that, most of all . . ." Venus smiled. "Those black pants. Ah, those black pants . . . she won't relax for a certain most exquisite time, but afterward she'll be very relaxed. And sleeping a very sweet sleep."

"You're incorrigible," I muttered, and left without further protest. I myself could not see that Venus would be particularly harmful to Megan; my only concern was that Megan seemed disturbed by her . . .

VI

Personal Journal of Megan
2199.5.25

Exhausted, I'm exhausted . . . Yet sleep is not what I need, no more than would a computer . . . And I am adjunct to our computers, synthesizer of their data . . . judgment maker . . .

Continuously I analyze, fit each piece into the whole, yet I maintain mental fluidity as the data accumulates and constantly changes. I walk on a wire suspended over a precipice, confident and fearful both. But amid the fearful tension of negotiating the peril is an exultation I have never known . . .

We are three months ahead of schedule. An incredible achievement by us all. Tomorrow we leave, those of us who have worked out of our desert compound, for *Skylab* and the final weeks of preparation before we board *Amelia Earhart.*

Four thousand and forty-five have chosen to go at latest count, and cutoff date looms but five weeks from now when we finalize all designs and weight tolerances. We have emphasized that afterward under no circumstances will anyone be allowed to change her mind and join us; reconstruction of *Amelia* and all preparations will be complete.

Two thousand and eleven state that they have made their irrevocable decision to remain. They are here with us, most of them working on plans to occupy this compound and create beauty in this desolation where they will be un-detected and safe.

This time of exhilaration, of eagerness for the adventure that lies ahead, is greatly tempered by the grief of partings. No one of our Unity is untouched, immune from the wrench-ing emotion of this time, least of all me.

Even the Inner Circle has been shocked by not one but two defections: in these past few days Olympia and Isis have suddenly chosen to stay. Mother exhibits a placid demeanor to us all, but she spends considerable time secluded in her quarters—as do I now, having learned only today my own grievous news. My mother has chosen to stay, and my two sisters. On this greatest adventure of my life I will be cut off from those I most love, especially Tara, the sister dearest to me . . .

One hundred and ninety-seven remain presently un-decided. Some are claustrophobics who wrestle with the knowledge they must live in the honeycomb which will be our home for three long months. Agorophobics fear the knowledge that they will drift through an unimaginable void. Sedation is possible of course, but it is Vesta's decision whether these women should accompany us, whether they can successfully adapt after planetfall. Other cases are also difficult—women who struggle with powerful emotional ties that bind them here. Still others—the most tragic—are women who love each other, but one wishes to go, the other to stay. These women Vesta also counsels.

I am recipient of admiration for my responsibilities, but never could I perform Vesta's work. Never could I carry such burdens. She has taken the anguish of these women into her. And if I am exhausted, she is wrung dry.

Last week I found her in her chamber, head bowed to her console. Her limbs trembled and twitched as she slept, whether from tension draining from her or from tormenting dreams I knew not. But I decided then that I must recall Carina from *Skylab*. However important her duties there, they could be no more urgent than to be nearby and give comfort to this most precious and deeply valued woman as she performs her vital work.

I saw them together the day Carina arrived. I had come into the chamber at the late end of the evening to obtain projected figures. Vesta stood with her head on Carina's shoulder, shaking with sobs. Carina, tall and powerfully built, held Vesta, stroking her hair, murmuring to her, her voice musical, soothing. I stared, compelled by her tenderness. Then Carina picked up tiny Vesta as if she were constructed of feathers and carried her to a chaise, and knelt beside her and opened Vesta's robe. She took a breast into her hand as if she were holding a frightened bird. I left then, soundlessly, sealing the chamber.

If only I could retain control and command when Venus is near.

Her desire for me is palpable, I can almost sense the pulsing of her blood. And she draws me to her. While I have controlled everything else in my life, I cannot prevent my response to her. Around her my balance slides off its axis and threatens to topple . . . The balance I manage with such effort . . .

I fear what I cannot fathom, the depth in me I do not understand.

I must look the fool to her. She thinks—surely—that I have the experience of most young women my age. No one knows, not even Tara . . . no one can guess my innocence. And Venus is puzzled that I will not acknowledge what is so clearly between us. It would be difficult to acknowledge even if I were free to do so; I do not know how. Never have I felt so awkward, so inadequate. Even Mother has noticed, has offered to help . . . as if I were a seven-year old . . . I will not permit her interference.

I have managed to have others about, to not be alone with her. But this night she found me in the data room.

I would not look at her; I knew her eyes would weaken

me again; her lips, her breasts would stir me again.

"Megan."

Her voice vibrated within me, my body was electric with her presence. She came close to me without touching me. She seems to sense that she should not risk her touch.

"Megan, do you think I'm attractive?"

Not looking at her, I answered with a quick nod.

"Do you find me . . . old?"

I looked at her then, amazed. Among our Unity like ages are the most often together, I suppose because of simultaneous awakening or common sensibilities; but wide disparity frequently exists. These relationships between the generations have always moved me with their beauty—the enjoyment and appreciation of each woman for the other, the tenderness and nurturing such as I had seen between Vesta and Carina. Youth seems to me no advantage; it is merely . . . a gift. And it seems that age would also be a gift, of another, richer, kind.

"You are not—" I said the word with distaste for the way she had used it, "—old." Then I realized what it must have cost to ask such a question and I said, "I cannot imagine you more beautiful than you are."

She smiled then, a radiant, entrancing smile that forced me to again look away. "You find me beautiful?"

Feeling as if I had been cut adrift in an unfamiliar sea in which there was no mooring anywhere, I whispered, "Yes."

"I offer it to you. I can make you very happy. I can give you pleasures you have not experienced in your young life."

"I . . ." I lost my voice. ". . . cannot," I finally managed.

"Megan—"

I continued, because her voice was further weakening me, "It's . . . best if I remain as I . . . am. You make it difficult . . . as it is. All my concentration is required . . . for what I do."

Her voice was soft. "I disturb your concentration?"

I would not look at her. I nodded.

"You're so very shy." Her voice was amused. And pleased.

I muttered, "You must think me . . . ridiculous."

"No. Only very strong. And most . . . desirable. Think about that, Megan. Because I'll be here. Always, for you."

She left me then. Drawing deep breaths, I watched her walk from me, the silken blue garment she wore flowing over the curves of her body, and I thought of how very easy it had been so many months ago to make my solemn vow to Mother.

VII

2199.9.21

We have accomplished the greatest clandestine movement of people and materiel in history. In seven months we have come to this day.

It is difficult to say what has been the more intricate, the movement of the people or the materiel. As we learned when Megan did not return to Houston after the meeting of our Unity, our disappearance has had to be judicious. She is celebrated enough a personage and her talent so significant a loss to the government of the Americas that her sudden disappearance caused an investigation, international accusations, and comment on Worldscape newscasts. And so the notable others of us have vanished one by one, only as our talents became indispensible to our goal.

Many purposefully remained in society up to the last, to perform vital responsibilities. The conversion of our property and other assets into credits for purchase of supplies was critical to our success and had to be carried out inconspicuously. Even more inconspicuous and cautious were our actual purchases. The synthesizers were the major problem. These machines, which will extract our new planet's ore in usable form, are perhaps the most essential components we must have for successful settlement, and cannot be bought without notice and comment. But we managed. We obtained one from a warring faction in Brazil; they were in dire need of credits and asked no questions. Then, instead of attempting to locate the additional one needed, we simply bought from the international underground at a vast expenditure of credits the parts sufficient to construct a synthesizer and effect any vital repairs until both synthesizers can be placed into full and self-replenishing operation.

Another object has been bought—an object of great secrecy—which I learned of by mere chance. One night a week ago I could not sleep, and went out to *Skylab's* observation deck. I watched the silent and trustworthy Carina, under cover of darkness, assist Megan and Hera in swinging a magnetic hoist. An oblong object was placed into a chamber which Carina then sealed with permaweld.

I realized that knowledge of this had been kept from me and the others deliberately, and when the three, along with Mother, came onto the observation deck, I drifted into the shadows and listened with both resentment and curiosity.

Mother said to Megan, "Dear, will everyone be in restraint during the nuclear fusion that propels us into hyperspace?"

"Yes, Mother. We've made the monitor assignments, and the monitors will then be—"

Mother waved a hand. "You know how I dislike details. How long will it take for the leap into hyperspace?"

Hera replied, "At the instant of fusion, a millisecond."

"So how much margin for error do we have?"

"Less than a millisecond."

"Great Geezerak, will you speak a language I can understand? If I were on Verna playing kottlebash and this were a throw of the dice, what would the odds be?"

"This *is* a throw of the dice, Mother," Hera said darkly, "which I fervently hope will not be necessary. The computer will be programmed to nanoseconds. Our little surprise package will be released on the same computer sequence that performs the time sequence. At least ninety percent or better. But it's never been done before—and the risk is immense. For what we risk."

"Phosh," Mother said. "It is not, for what we could

lose, and for what we gain. But we can always abandon the idea. Megan dear, you've had months to deliberate. Do you still agree?"

"I agree with Hera in hoping it will not be necessary," Megan said quietly. "But if the circumstances warrant, we go with it."

They left then. I knew better than to inquire; if I had not been told before, I would not be told now. And so I kept my own counsel, and remained watchful.

Only today was the oblong object moved again, loaded onto *Amelia* and into another sealed chamber. I observed; and recognized the insignia on its leaded impervisteel wrapping. It has come from Algeria, that notorious renegade member of the Arab bloc.

VIII

2199.9.23

Final transport is now complete. We four thousand one hundred and forty-four are on board our *Amelia Earhart*, transferred in wave after wave on Kendra's service ships. Many of us who worked on *Skylab* had but a short hop to *Amelia*, the rest have been transported directly from three separate locations on Earth.

Discipline begins as each of us sets foot on *Amelia*. We are issued feather-light one-piece trouser suits of synsilk, and boots of plastifilm. Every item of the clothing we wear is surrendered, to be placed in *Amelia's* decomposition tubes. We are assigned living space, the sleeping time when we will be allowed to occupy it, and our daily schedule of duties and activities.

Thirteen women are aboard under sedation—our phobics. Vesta has passed them; they will journey with us in chemically-induced tranquility.

Everyone is in her assigned place. We, the Inner Circle—but six of us now—are in the command center with Kendra, our ship's commander, and her four co-captains.

There is searing pain in these final moments. We have, all of us, grieved these past days for those who will part from us. But this is the pain of irrevocable parting, now. To leave some of our Unity behind is amputation. Worse. Those we leave are like deaths to us. As we must be to them. My dear sister Isis. Beloved Olympia . . .

As we wait in unspoken communion, I look at us. We are all dressed alike, but our synsilk clothing is multi-hued, vari-patterned, flows as we move and walk and is uniquely attractive on us all. Megan also wears synsilk, but hers—only hers—is white. Mother's orders, I am certain. Perhaps it is because I have come to know Megan over these past months—have grown to love her lonely strength—or perhaps I am more aware of women physically, having been so long a time without loving—but as the flashing lights and colors of the command room reflect on Megan's luminous skin and clothing, she seems incredibly beautiful. And I see that I am not the only woman she affects; the gazes of others of us are drawn to her also. And Venus does not gaze, but stares—with an expression I have never seen on her, but have often seen on other women who look at Venus: help-lessness.

As I record this historic moment, I watch the huge red numerals count down on the computer sequencing screen. Final systems check continues, the diminishing red numerals in synchrony with *Amelia's* orbital path. On the viewscreen, and at our curved crystal windows where others of us are gathered, the bright pocked surface of the moon passes beneath us as we sweep ever closer to the sharply etched dark shadow that will be our cloak. It is a heart-stopping sight—but my own heart pounds, I am swept by chills as the moment of our new beginning comes ever nearer, as we drift ever closer to that great shadow.

"T minus one minute," Kendra says calmly, for the benefit of those who listen all over our vessel, who wait as tensely as we. "Systems check sequencing is complete."

Megan and Mother stand at Kendra's side where she sits in her commander's chair, burly and imposing, her bearing imperious as her mother Hera's, her white hair queenly, her gray eyes cool as slate.

"Mother will speak at the moment of departure," Megan says.

"Of course," Kendra replies.

The great shadow nears. The red numerals descend in blinking inexorable rhythm. They reach zero. We are engulfed in shadow.

Mother says softly, "My dears, we're on our way."

Acoustically it is impossible, but still I hear the cheers that reverberate through *Amelia*.

There is no perceptible difference in *Amelia's* motion. True, her power has been fired, and waits in readiness; but the thrusters edge her smoothly out of her familiar weary path around the moon's dead face. Kendra has told me there will be no discernible difference as *Amelia* gathers speed, as she begins to hurtle us on solar winds toward our galactic arm and the Einsteinian Curve... We will feel, realize *Amelia's* enormous strength and power when nuclear fusion is sequenced into the power drive and impels us like a watermelon seed into hyperspace—a sensation Kendra says cannot be described.

Except for Demeter and Vesta who have been called to care for some psychological and physical problems a number of women have developed (I feel slightly queasy myself, and avoid the crystal windows), none of us leave the command room. We watch the instrumentation hypnotically, not knowing how to look for what we look for, but expectant and uneasy.

It is five hours later. We have crossed the orbit of Mars, and the huge bands of Jupiter are filling the viewscreen and the windows. And Kendra has said—only to us in the command room—"We are pursued."

Megan walks to her. "How many?"

"Four. Three from Earth." Kendra smiles thinly. "I assume representing the Eastern Bloc, the Sinobloc, the Americas. The other has just taken off from Mars."

Megan frowns and Kendra shrugs her broad shoulders.

"By the time it achieves escape velocity and matches our speed it will be no closer than the ships from Earth."

Hera says, "I'll calculate response time."

"I'll set up coordinates." Megan touches dials that project a grid onto the lumiscreen.

A few minutes later Hera says tersely, "Nine minutes."

"They have never made up their collective minds on anything so fast," Mother grumbles. "What's our situation?"

"Close," Megan says. "They will intersect with us at the Einsteinian Curve."

"I know you girls can manage," Mother says serenely. "I'm tired. I'm going to bed, such as it is. Demeter dear, did you remember to make sure my quarters are nowhere near the children's compound?"

"Certainly, Mother."

"I know I should try to act more decently," Mother says, "but frankly, after raising nine of my own I'm sick to death of children. And I'm sure by now they're all asking how soon we'll be there."

IX

2199.10.11

We have concealed from the Unity that we are pursued, there being no reason for the entire ship to be in a state of agitation for the eighteen days to the Einsteinian Curve.

We, the Inner Circle, and Mother, spend quantities of time in the command room watching as our instruments track our pursuers. Their lighter faster ships, which do not carry so precious a cargo as ours, close inexorably on us.

Even in my limited knowledge of such matters, I see no advantage in the leap to hyperspace. Our pursuers should be close enough then—a matter of hours, according to Kendra —so that they can track and catch us no matter how evasive our escape pattern among the star systems. But I keep my own counsel.

Several days ago hostilities began on the Interplanetary Frequency Channel, the threats streaming across the top of our viewscreen.

IDENTIFY YOURSELVES IMMEDIATELY STATE DESTINATION was repeated at two minute intervals for four hours.

REFUSAL OF IDENTIFICATION WILL RESULT IN CLASSIFICATION AS OUTLAW SHIP was repeated for another four hours.

Then: OUTLAW SHIP IDENTIFY YOURSELVES OR DECLARATION OF HOSTILITIES WILL BE ISSUED. This message blinked ominously for a day.

Then: HOSTILITIES DECLARED. VIOLATION, UN-AUTHORIZED USE OF EARTH RESOURCES.

"Phosh," Mother said. "It must have taken all day to think up that one."

We have not acknowledged any of their transmissions; we remain on steady course for the Einsteinian Curve. But the distance between us and our pursuers closes . . .

We are but four hours from the Einsteinian Curve. And *Amelia* has just shuddered.

"Laser electron gun," Kendra announces laconically. "Nowhere close."

SURRENDER OR HOSTILITIES COMMENCE, reads the screen.

"Answer them now," Megan says softly. She stands beside Kendra, arms crossed, watching the viewscreen and the four tiny blips picked up by our rear probes, four lethal insects pursuing us.

STAND BY FOR MESSAGE, reads our response.

They have waited an hour . . . And now *Amelia* shudders again.

"Begin sedation of the children," Megan says quietly to Vesta, who sits with Carina, gazing raptly at the viewscreen. "And the adults as well. It's a little early, and everything's under control, but we might as well do it now. Tell anyone who asks that *Amelia's* just going through a meteoroid shower."

She turns to Kendra. "Status?"

"I've laid in the evasive course to begin in one hour. Those electron bursts are nowhere close now but they will be by then."

One hour later everyone on the ship is unconscious and in restraint except for the hardy few who have refused sedation. This includes myself—surely not hardy but certainly determined.

"It is my duty to remain conscious," I inform Megan firmly. "I am Minerva the historian."

"You may soon decide to change your profession," Kendra tells me with amused and knowing eyes.

Mother has also chosen to remain unsedated. She sits dwarfed by her restraining pod, and grinning. "We Vernans are tough," she says. "And I want to watch . . . what happens."

"I know all about your little surprise package," I tell Mother. "I've seen it. You might as well tell me what it is." I have already begun to feel queasy; while there is no discernible change in the motion of the ship, our evasive maneuvers have begun, and the stars roll sickeningly on the viewscreen and outside the windows.

Mother says proudly, "It's a fifty megaton hydrogen bomb."

"What!" I sputter, "where—there aren't—"

"None is supposed to be in existence since the Johannesburg disaster," Mother says, "but anyone who believes that is an idiot. All it takes to get one is plenty of credits."

"But what—you surely can't—"

"You'll see," Mother says. "Sit back and relax, dear. Carina's already loaded it into the ejection tube."

Carina and Vesta lie in a restraint pod, Vesta in Carina's arms; their bodies move in the slow breathing of deep sedation.

Amelia shudders and continues to shudder from continuous electron bursts all around her.

"Next message," Megan says.

We transmit, WE ARE IN VIOLATION OF NO RECORDED TENET OF INTERNATIONAL, INTERPLANETARY, OR GALACTIC LAW.

Five minutes later the response comes: YOUR DEPARTURE UNAUTHORIZED. SURRENDER IMMEDIATELY.

"Megan," Kendra says easily, "the bursts are closer but still no danger. The computers confirm we will be fully exposed for two minutes before we reach the EC."

Megan nods. "As we calculated."

Amelia's shudders continue. At seven minutes to the

Einsteinian Curve, Megan says, "Send our next message."

STAND BY FOR MESSAGE, we transmit.

REFUSED, is the immediate answer. HOSTILITIES CONTINUE.

"Even the fools that they are," Mother says, "they're on to that one."

"Next message," Megan orders.

To my amazement, our message reads, CEASE FIRING. GIVE SURRENDER TERMS.

Amelia's shudders cease. The screen reads, FULL COURSE REVERSAL, FOOLISH WOMEN.

"So they know who we are," Kendra says, smiling. "How gratifying. And they seem to be gloating, don't they?"

"I don't think it took them eighteen days to figure it out," Mother says, "although it may have, the poor things."

TERMS ACCEPTED, we transmit. ADVISE DESIRED COORDINATES.

As the series of mathematical equations stream across our screen, we are three minutes from the Einsteinian Curve.

COORDINATES RECEIVED AND BEING PROGRAM-MED, we transmit.

Under two minutes, now.

"Next message," Megan says tensely.

REPEAT COORDINATES, we send. APPEARS ERROR.

Again the equations appear. And an additional message: ONE MINUTE ALLOWED FOR COURSE CORRECTION. DO NOT ENTER EC. YOU ARE NOW IN POINTBLANK DESTRUCTION RANGE.

Our countdown numerals have dropped to fifty seconds to the Einsteinian Curve.

"Excellent," beams Mother. "Simply excellent, girls."

"We've won," Megan breathes. Her slender body relaxes; she inflates her restraint pod.

"Yes." Kendra's face glows. "Detonation sequence has begun." She also inflates her restraint pod.

"My message," Mother says.

"Coming up on sequence right now, Mother," Megan says. "At five seconds to hyperspace."

We watch the huge red numerals count down, reach five.

WE'RE CHANGING OUR MINDS, BOYS, reads Mother's message. THIS IS AMELIA EARHART, OVER AND OUT.

Zero, I remember reading.

Then my eyeballs were driven into my head. My body turned inside out. My mind expanded, contracted, exploded into vivid color. I floated in sickening disorientation . . .

There was the sharp scent of stimulant, a discomfort in my shoulder that I recognized as an injection. As awareness returned I opened my eyes to the color of emerald. I groped. Warm synsilk was under my hands, slender shoulders that were clothed in white.

Megan took my hands. "Minerva, are you all right?"

"Yes, thank you dear," I whispered, smiling idiotically and thinking foolishly that I was half in love with her, and that I was perfectly normal because everyone else was too. Then well-being returned to my body, and rationality. I released her hands. "What—"

"Everything goes well," Megan answered. "We're safe, and on course."

I sit up now, and look around. The pod has been taken from around Vesta and Carina, but still they sleep in their close embrace. Kendra sits as usual in her command chair, smiling at Mother, who gestures to the viewscreen, cackling delightedly.

"Look, Minerva dear. Look!"

On the viewscreen four minute black objects tumble and spin in haphazard grace.

"Our bad-tempered, violent friends," Mother chortles. "Tell her, Kendra. Explain."

"The bomb was detonated the instant after our leap into hyperspace." Kendra's deep voice is rich with satisfaction. "We escaped its effects totally but our four pursuers weren't so lucky. They aren't damaged, and they had time to brace, but they couldn't escape. What you see now are the effects of shock waves which still strike them."

Mother gloats, "Describe what it's like, Kendra."

"They should have turned their ships into the blast," Kendra says, "at least that's what I'd have done. The first shock wave would hit like a tidal wave. And for hours, even though they're in restraint, they'll feel like an angry fist is pummeling their ships."

I whisper, "But can they still track us?"

"By the time they right themselves and synchronize their data," Megan says quietly, "we will be a speck of cosmic dust."

"Mother," I say, "how did such an idea ever occur to you?"

"From a quaint twentieth century film I viewed in Omaha," she answers. "In one of their silly wars, a captain of a submarine vessel faked destruction by ejecting debris to the ocean surface."

"And I expect that's what the fools will claim about us," Kendra says with her deep laugh. "That our ship detonated from nuclear fusion as we leaped to hyperspace."

"You've heard the ancient joke," Mother says, "about women drivers?"

We all look at her, puzzled. Sighing with disgust, she stalks off to her quarters.

X

2199.12.6

I need no pronouncements from Venus nor psychological explanations from Vesta to know that it is not healthy to live in close proximity for long periods of time.

I will not dwell on our discomforts. Mother has exemplified the major one by disappearing into her quarters a week ago and thus far refusing to emerge. "Forgive me dears," she has called through her sealed door, "I love you all but I'm just sick to death of everyone."

Only Megan, Kendra, her co-captains, and of course, Mother, have their own quarters. The rest of us sleep in our catacombs and take care of our bodily needs as our ship section is assigned. For women who have lived their lives with a high degree of individuality, the adjustments have been difficult indeed. At best we are waspish with each other. At worst, quarrelsome and hostile.

My greatest longing is for water sluicing over my body. We are all clean, of course; when scheduled, we line up and file through the chemical mist that cleanses our clothing, our bodies, our hair. But how I long for the simple pleasures of a bath . . .

There seems to be grayness to everything, as if we were in a cave. Megan assures me it is my imagination, that our air is purified thoroughly before recirculation, but it smells musty and thick to me even in the greenhouses, among all the plants and flowers. And even with Vesta as consultant-chef, and meals which are varied and creatively prepared, the food still seems uniform and tasteless. I dream of eating a sun-ripened tomato freshly plucked from its vine . . .

Our days are scheduled, we all have duties and assignments. But we are bored. Our initial delight in our clothes has paled; they have become tiresome. Sexual interest among us has diminished precipitously, even between the most recently together. Privacy to explore sensuality or romantic sensibility is severely insufficient, and this also has not helped the general mood. Venus especially has been in vicious humor for weeks.

All the beauty in our lives lies outside our crystal windows, in the awesome grandeur of blazing star systems, incredibly hued coronas, great illuminated gas nebulae, delicate veils of stardust shimmering with irridescence. The constellations are unrecognizable; the configurations so well known from the days of our childhood were distorted to unfamiliarity as *Amelia* carried us from the solar system. We drift through incomprehensible vastness, our lives entrusted to the rigorous truth of our computations, the faithful silent computers, the subtle skills of our wondrous Kendra.

Our leader, her work to begin anew after the respite of these few months, often walks among us, striking in the pristine synsilk that clings to her slender body. Her serenity soothes tempers and reassures us; her presence reunites us in our purpose. The homeland that awaits us is worth many times the discomfort of our days.

As do most of us, Megan spends time with the children; their capacity for joy and enchantment renews us all. Today I was in one of the compounds when she came in. A tiny towhead with great dark eyes hurtled herself toward Megan, and Megan scooped her into her arms, the little girl shrieking with ecstasy as she was lifted for a ride on Megan's shoulders.

Megan looks relaxed, and for the first time in months like the very young woman she is. And more beautiful than ever, if that is possible.

XI

Personal Journal of Megan
2199.12.12

It is best that my mind be fully occupied, that no time be available for thoughts which torment and are in all ways futile.

But synsilk so reveals Venus's body to me that she might well be unclothed; and her ill-humor these months of our journey, far from unattractive, has added a smoldering quality to her beauty. Her walk—all her movements—suggest images that emerge as longings in the unprotected time of sleep: vivid and heated dreams that drive me from my quarters to pace the corridors of *Amelia*, to uselessly verify course computations in the command room, to unnecessarily review my sketches for colony design in the data work room.

She looks at me. And her trouser-suit, hues of dark blue, enhances the compelling blue of her eyes. Because she is in my sector we often meet in corridors, and she slows her walk—that walk—and looks at me, her eyes leisurely and ever more bold. Her eyes focus upon my lips, drift to my breasts, linger on my thighs . . . She never speaks. Her gaze caresses me; her gaze promises what I more and more long to discover . . .

XII

2200.1.6

We are a matter of weeks away from planetfall. Critically important meetings have begun.

The time away from her responsibilities may have been needed for renewal of Megan's energies, but she seems grateful that her mentalities are once more engaged. All of us on board *Amelia* are eager for new challenges.

The talents and skills necessary to take us successfully from Earth pale in comparison with those that will now be required. Before we left, Megan and we of the Inner Circle had made preparations, carefully selecting four major teams from among the most specifically trained of our Unity.

Erika, the geoscientist, was our first choice. She and her team will map our new world, determine form and gravity values, rock and mineral and chemical composition.

Jolan, our hydrologist, will lead the oceanographic team, analyzing all of the planet's water systems.

Astra, our meteorologist, will lead the atmospheric and climatology team.

Augusta, the zoologist, will spearhead the vitally important group which determines our planet's origin and current formative stage, its present ecology, its plant and animal life.

2200.1.29

We, the Inner Circle, and Mother and Megan, have been

gathered around the viewscreen for hours, since the first faint image of Maternas appeared. We have made our first surprising discovery about her. The blurred montage Hera showed our Unity so many months ago was not a distorted spectral reflectance; our new world is, indeed, coral. Pale coral and white clouds cover coral seas, with land masses somewhat darker, indistinguishable at this distance through the cloud cover.

"Why should we be surprised? Of course it's possible, the solar system planets, all planets vary in color," muses Hera as we all stare at the globe enlarging upon our screen. "Color is only molecular scattering of light . . . a matter of wave length, and white light . . ."

But we are nonplussed; the blue-green seas of Earth are ingrained upon our conscious and subconscious.

Except for Mother. "Verna has high ferrous content," she has told us, beaming, "and lands of many rich colors. Frankly, my dears, Earth was very boring."

2200.1.30

We are in orbit around Maternas, an elongated elliptical orbit because of *Amelia's* size.

How many surprises will this new world have for us? Our sun is not one, but two stars.

"An optical binary," Hera exclaims. "Double star systems are common, far more common than single star systems—Jupiter almost flamed into a star when the solar system was formed. But binaries . . . two stars together . . . and these stars aren't even true binaries, they're light years apart, not gravitationally associated. An optical binary is relatively rare."

The second shock is our planet's nightside, the perigee of our orbit. Maternas has three moons orbiting closely together—two quite small, but all of them brilliant—and a night sky that blazes with star clusters and reflection nebulae. With so glowing a sky, there will be a darkening of the day as our double sun sets, but no night as we have known it.

How will the older children react when they first perceive our new world, a world drastically different from the one they have known? Hera has expressed concern. And has declared that she will prepare the children for Maternas with scientific explanation.

In her gentle way, Vesta tried to disagree, reminding Hera of our own self-sufficient childhood and that many generations have passed since Hera or any of our Inner Circle have raised our own children, and suggesting that our children will more readily adapt than we adults. But Hera is Hera. And so Vesta and I wait in the children's compound for her arrival.

Forced to abandon her cape when she boarded *Amelia*, Hera wears only our standard synsilk garment; but as she sweeps in and whirls to confront her young audience, somehow the cape is in place. The children sit silent, in crowded rows, gazing at her with wide-eyed reverence.

Standing with arms crossed, lips pursed, she finally asks condescendingly, "Would any of you like to guess where every color in the universe can be found?"

A deafening chorus of girlish voices: "In white light!"

Looking somewhat disconcerted, Hera orders, "Please raise your hand if you wish to answer my questions. Do any of you know how pigments acquire their color?"

Every child raises her hand. Looking very startled indeed, Hera points. Rhea stands, Ariadne's ten-year old, a lithe dark-skinned nymph. She says easily, "They absorb parts of the spectrum and reflect whatever remains."

From beside me Vesta chuckles; Hera casts a dark glance toward us, then returns her attention to Rhea. "You understand, then, why plants and grass don't have to be green?"

"Pigment molecules can assume a wide range of structural forms," Rhea answers in a sweet soprano. "The pigment molecules in chlorophyll account for the greenness of plants, they absorb purples and blues, most of the red end of the spectrum, and reflect back green. But if the molecular structure—"

"Yes. Indeed," Hera says darkly. "Would any of you—"

A hand has been raised. Sibyl, Diantha's ten-year old. Hera has stiffened in outrage that anyone would dare interrupt her; but she says gently, "You have a question, child?"

We all know we're in orbit, we know we've arrived where we're going to live. Are the rumors true? Does our world really have coral lands and seas?"

The glance Hera casts at Vesta is chastened. I smother my own amusement; I know better than to incur Hera's wrath.

"Yes, child," Hera answers, "it's true."

Sibyl inquires shyly, "Esteemed Hera, can we see it? Can we see our new home?"

"*May* you see it," Hera corrects triumphantly. "Yes, you may see it." And she marches to a console module amid squeals of anticipation from all the girls in the room.

Vistas of Maternas, seen through our exterior cameras, are greeted with oohs, giggles, ecstatic shrieks. Hera looks on with a wide smile, the joy of our children infectious.

"Tell me, dear ones," Hera says, "can any of you offer a theory why our land and seas happen to be the color of coral?" She points to Calypso, a daughter of Althea, who is enthusiastically waving her upraised hand.

Calypso rises, tidying her royal blue synsilk suit with eleven-year old dignity. "The rumors—well, we hear it's young, our world. We've discussed it and we think it's partly mineral content in the land, partly volcanic activity affecting the atmosphere, along with vapor-filled air close to the surface."

"Excellent, very good indeed." Arms extended dramatically, Hera is beaming. "That's a plausible theory, essentially correct as far as it goes. But—"

Vesta and I tiptoe out.

We have sent our first probes. One to the land surface,

one to the ocean. Meterology balloons were released as the probes landed, and now drift through the atmosphere.

Erika, Augusta, Astra, Jolan, and members of their teams sit with us, all of us in a still tension of expectancy as the first data floods the telemetry screens.

A most critically important conclusion first from the taciturn Astra: "Slightly oxygen-enriched, twenty-one point six percent. But the troposphere is well within every tolerance."

"Feldspars," Erika says, nodding, "sedimentary and igneous rock, also high silica. Soil analysis . . . appears rich in potassium carbonade. Megan," she says, impatiently shifting her slim body in her chair and pushing a shock of unruly auburn hair from her forehead, "this is all very well, but let's send the recorder drones."

"Our coral ocean is good old seawater," Jolan tells us with a grin. Tall and lanky, her body seems folded into her chair; she sits back and casually crosses an ankle over a knee as she continues, "Salinity readings are slightly low but well within norm, and very probably regional. Surface temperature is eighty-one Fahrenheit. Chemically, the major constituents are normal, nothing strange at all. I agree with Erika, I want to see it, too."

Megan nods to Kendra, who releases with a flourish the drones which will fly in rigidly patterned grids above the surface. Augusta and Hera have already made circumference and orbital calculations: Maternas is slightly smaller than Earth, more circular, her daily orbit twenty-four hours and thirty-two minutes long.

As each drone comes to life and opens its electronic eye, we gaze in silence. The first images are from the drones that float over expanses of ocean, but only Jolan follows these, and even her attention is divided; our eyes are riveted upon the screens which will give the first glimpses of our new land. Then jagged mountains soar toward us. Vast flat lands appear, and steeply canted hills. Ivory vegetation vividly tinged with shades of blue . . . We murmur, marvelling . . . but do not speak or move until the drones have completed their first pass and shift to begin the criss-cross pattern.

Then Erika: "The mountains . . . young mountains, all of them young . . ."

No one speaks again until the second pass is complete and the third begins. "Twenty-three percent land mass," Erika says. "Seven great land masses, all separated by great bands of ocean . . . none connected like the continents of Earth—"

"Number nine, Kendra." It is Augusta, the zoologist. "Decelerate it please, and narrow scope."

"Also number four." Ariel speaks, the paleontologist who sits with Augusta.

Kendra protests, "Our readings will go out of synchrony."

But Megan has been observing the growing tension in the chocolate brown face of Augusta, the stillness of Ariel's slight body. "Please slow them, Kendra. We'll recalibrate later."

"I thought so," Ariel murmurs to Augusta.

"And I," Augusta agrees in her calm, resonant voice.

Maddeningly, they stare mutely at the slow-shifting images of pale dense foliage.

"Great Geezerak." Mother has been sitting quietly in her big chair watching the screens and us. "Will you two speak to the rest of us?"

"Angiosperms," Ariel says. "Predominant conifers."

"Much better," Mother growls. "Perfectly clear."

"Flowering foliage and many cone-bearing trees, some sequoia-type," Augusta says, smiling. "Our new world is quite young."

"Younger than suspected?" Megan asks.

"Patrice must determine that, Megan. The land varies so in development, the ocean here is an unusually great barrier to migration and evolutionary forces, as are the mountain ranges. But this extensive, almost unbroken seed-bearing foliage in the equatorial and its adjacent area is very like the Eocene period on Earth."

"The tides, Megan," Jolan says softly. "Smoothly patterned but erratic in height."

"Wind-driven," Dorcas responds, nodding. "It follows. There is much evidence of wind erosion. Some plains areas have a scoured appearance, the mountains are faceted, deeply sculpted. Wind may well be a problem to us, Megan."

"Mean density appears to be slightly less than five point five," Erika says. "Further calculations are necessary but it appears gravity will be insignificantly less than Earth's."

"Kendra, please recall the drones," Megan says quietly. "Those who wish may stay and further analyze data. But in eight hours full teams are to be assembled in the EV area. To prepare for landing on Maternas."

In the silence that greets these dramatic words, Mother climbs out of her big chair. "I'm so glad we're landing. Orbiting makes me dizzy. Good night, my dear ones."

XIII

2200.1.31

Our four extravehicular craft have departed from *Amelia*. The path of Jolan and her hydrology team will be over the coastline and inland lakes of the temperate zone continent we have named Femina. It seems our best settlement possibility. We three others fly in spread formation, several thousand feet apart, our craft in continuous voice and instrument communication. Megan, Mother, and I are with Augusta's team in EV-one, the command craft piloted by Kendra. Others of our Inner Circle travel in the other EVs. Venus is also with us; she sits with Miri, a botanist—a curvaceous young woman with a great quantity of tawny hair, who draws Venus's gaze when Venus's attention is not fixed upon the world below us.

We drift over vast flatlands covered without break by wavy grass-like vegetation and low shrubbery blending gradually into scrub forest, blending further into thick forest intense with ivory-blue color. Miri and Ariel watch this land closely, murmuring into their recorders.

A small grazing herd arrests our attention; the first animal life we have seen. Studying the magnification on her facsimile screen, Augusta states, "Much like Eohippus, the small primitive horse common in the North American West during the Eocene."

Soon we dip low over other herds of animals, some grazing, some dozing in golden sunlight. None seem startled or fearful of our low-flying presence.

"Herbivores," murmurs Augusta, "genus related to cattle, swine, tapirs . . . all ungulates. See how they lack fear? Carnivores seem the exception on this continent, not the rule."

"No dinosaurs?" Mother sounds disappointed.

"That's far from certain yet, Mother." Augusta's chuckle, soft and rich, matches the light chocolate of her skin. "There will be many different life forms on this and all the continents. But dinosaurs and their like were extinct by the late Cretaceous, the period before the Paleocene. Some birds may well be carnivorous—but they aren't a dominant life form, we've seen none of any great size. We've seen no dominant life form as yet," Augusta muses. "There may be predatory land-venturing sea life, possibly Crocodylia."

Erika's voice comes from EV-two. "Megan, an earthquake fault lies directly below, the displacement is evident."

"I don't care much for earthquakes," Mother grumbles as we all stare at the distinct ridges in the land.

"Nor I," Venus says, gazing at Miri. "I prefer the earth to move in other ways."

"Faultlines will be considered along with all other data." The flatness of Megan's voice draws my attention; her eyes are just leaving Venus. They seem cloudy, unreadable.

"Megan, sea level is stable, no unusual coastal erosion patterns." Jolan's voice comes from EV-four. "We've seen no sandy areas at all along the ocean shorelines, vegetation grows down to the tide lines." Jolan's voice has quickened in excitement. "Megan, marine life teems. Even from here we see great schools of fish, sea-going turtles—"

"Also in accord with the Eocene period," Ariel says.

"We're heading inland." Janel speaks, pilot of Jolan's craft. "We'll intersect with you at sector seven."

Kendra acknowledges, with a glance at her topographic map. Sector seven is nearby, an inland lake of considerable dimension cut off from the ocean by a narrow wedge of land.

We pass over a vast windswept area of dark, deeply etched rock. Erika says, "Magma—"

"And deeply wind-eroded," Astra says quietly from EV-three.

"The plants," Miri says in a pretty, girlish voice, "are the best indicators of—"

"Megan!" It is Janel in EV-four. "Megan it's a—We see a . . . a . . . a . . ."

"Janel!" Kendra shouts. "Janel! Janel!"

But there is no response.

"Sector seven," Megan orders tersely, "all EVs full speed."

Hera's voice crackles from EV-two, "Kendra, they're not down. We have readings—"

"As do we." Kendra's voice is low and calm. Janel is her daughter, Hera's granddaughter.

At full power we arrive in only seconds at sector seven, a vast expanse of translucent coral water.

"Great Geezerak," Mother breathes.

The apparition we approach stirs the hair on the back of the neck as it calls forth memory of a primordial past. The creature of nightmare rises at least fifty feet above the surface of the lake in full serpentine horror, its undulating body layered in slimy armor, the immensely high column of neck topped by a scaly head composed almost entirely of bulbous viridian eyes and row upon row of huge serrated teeth.

We approach from the side of the creature, and we see on the horizon Janel's craft. Drifting toward those waiting teeth.

"Janel pull up!" Kendra screams, "pull up!"

There is no answer.

The creature glimpses us, swivels its monstrous head for an instant, the viridian eyes arctic cold.

"*Kendra* . . ." A desperate whisper.

"Pull up! Janel pull up!"

"I . . ." The craft wavers, then resumes its fatal course. And the monster ignores us; it has returned its attention to the victim drifting ever nearer, scant seconds away from those waiting teeth.

Kendra presses the firing stud; a laser flash dissipates harmlessly over the vast lake.

"Kendra!" Megan shouts, "fly at it! Right at it!"

Kendra pulls EV-one around in a sickening swerve and flings us full power at the monster, wild laser bursts flashing as she stabs the firing stud. Other laser flashes expend themselves over the lake; they come from EV-two and -three.

"All EVs," Megan orders, "full speed at its eyes! Full speed!"

We are flying toward those gaping jaws, into annihilation. In my terror I seize Mother—to protect her or myself, I know not which.

The creature's waving head suddenly swivels from side to side as we fly into its field of vision; and tiny bubbles of blue blood appear as several of our laser bursts penetrate the armored body.

An expulsion of breath from Kendra: seemingly inches from those teeth, Janel's craft veers sharply away, flies up and over the creature's head. The creature lunges at the craft, its teeth crashing together like a crocodile snapping at escaping prey.

"Kill it! Kill it!" Kendra shouts. "All EVs fire! Kill it!"

"No," Megan says in a voice of forbidding command. "All EVs to sector six, full speed. And do not, absolutely do not look at that creature."

"*Whatever you do don't look at it.*" Janel speaks from EV-four, in a whisper of compelling conviction.

I am Minerva the historian, and as we speed past the creature, of course I look at it.

I am overwhelmed by the desire—no, the need—to come to those viridian eyes; my body is anaesthetized with tranquility and joyful willingness to be absorbed into those viridian eyes . . .

I am shaken out of my trance by Mother, who is saying in irritation to Megan, "Minerva was always the least obedient of all my girls."

I exclaim to Megan, "It's telepathic!"

"Yes," she answers, "I know."

"Let's kill it." Kendra's voice is low growling fury. "Megan, we'll cover the lake with laser fire from high altitude—"

"No, Kendra." Mother is patting my cheek. "Are you all right, dear one?"

"Yes Mother," I murmur, still somewhat dizzy and confused.

"Mother," Kendra grates, "that horror almost killed my daughter."

"And mine. Demeter is on board EV-four. But all of you are my daughters. And we did not come to this new world to kill. Minerva dear," she says gently, "would you mind getting off me?"

Feeling supremely foolish, I release my grip on Mother and sit up and ask Megan, "How did you know it was telepathic?"

"I realized when I heard Janel call Kendra's name. We had distracted it—it had glanced at our craft—enough so that its telepathic grip on EV-four was broken for that moment. Then I knew our only chance was to cause distraction again in some way so that Janel could escape. Well-armored as it was, there wouldn't have been enough time to mortally wound it before—"

"Yes," Mother says. "You know how I dislike detail, especially gruesome detail. Megan dear, if you had not vindicated our choice of you before—"

"Ariel," Jolan interrupts in a shaking voice from EV-four, "what *was* that thing?"

"It's like nothing I'm familiar with, Jolan. It somewhat resembles tylosaurus—a bizarre variation." Ariel speaks calmly. "With its own highly effective method of food gathering—the rudimentary hypnotic powers of the reptilian species developed to a much more elevated state. First it attracts its prey with the vivid green of its eyes, then draws it with hypnotic trance—"

"Green eyes will do that to you," Venus murmurs. She is gazing at Megan, but strokes Miri's tawny hair. At the height of our peril, Miri had flung herself into Venus's arms; now that the danger is over, she shows no indication of extricating herself; she sits with her head on Venus's shoulder.

"Mother," Augusta asks with a chuckle, "will this satisfy your wish for dinosaurs?"

"Most definitely," Mother says.

Megan's eyes rest briefly on Venus and Miri. Then she runs a hand through her dark hair and says, "A vital question. How prevalent is this lethal creature on this planet?"

"I can make an educated guess about this continent," Ariel ventures. "I would say very likely it is the only creature of its kind. From its size, it requires vast territory from which to draw food, such as that great lake in sector seven. We know there are no other lakes nearly that size on Femina. Another major clue is the ridge of land that separates it from the ocean. It appears to have been upthrust by sudden geological force—"

"Correct," Erika interjects.

"Eons ago," Ariel says, "our creature's ancestors were probably separated from the sea by that ridge of land—"

"We've named the creature GEM," Astra says from EV-three. "Acronym for Green-Eyed Monster."

We all laugh. Ariel continues, still smiling, "From the appearance of its keratin scales, GEM appears to be of great age. If we're correct in our theory that Maternas is following in its own unique fashion the general evolutionary path of Earth, then the equivalent age of dinosaurs has ended, and GEM is the last of its line."

Augusta speaks. "I agree completely with Ariel's hypothesis."

"Very well, my dears," Mother says. "But I want you both to know if we run into any more of these creatures, I'll be seriously annoyed."

Grinning, Megan consults the topographical map. But she has swiveled her chair, I notice, so that its back is squarely to Venus and Miri.

"I believe it would be good to feel land under our feet,"

she says. "And to take a good look at our ocean at the same time. All EVs," she orders, "set course for sector one. We land on Maternas."

XIV

1.1.1

MATERNAS DATE

All our craft have landed, softly, amid waving fields of ivory-blue grass.

"Mother," Megan says, "you will of course be first to set foot upon your namesake planet."

"Don't be silly, dear," Mother responds, reaching up to pat Megan's cheek. "Someone young and agile should assist the aged. Besides, something may very well be waiting to bite."

And so it is that Megan, laughing, first sets foot upon Maternas.

We have visual recordings, of course—in addition to our preserved transmissions sent to those waiting on *Amelia*—of Megan leaping lightly from EV-one, and then standing proudly against the coral sky, her dark hair blowing in the wind, to survey our new world. Then holding out both hands to Mother. And Mother in her green cape, shoulders thrown back, grapefruit breasts thrust forward, stepping with indomitable dignity into the high grass of her namesake planet.

I am next. After all, I am Minerva the historian.

I step onto the wonderful firm land, into the sunlight, and walk weeping into rows of thigh-high bent grass, stroking the lovely blades of it, each blade a distinct pattern of ivory-blue, hearing behind me cries of joy as the others of our landing party also set foot upon our new world.

The soil is a warm red, thickly covered between its strangely regular rows of grass by leafy growth and tiny buttercup-like blossoms. There is the hum of insects, the chittering of small animals, the distant thunder of surf. The air is caressingly soft, and smells richly—intoxicatingly— of grass and flowers and rain and ocean. My step is springy, and I must remind myself sternly of the dignity of my years to resist joining those who like children leap and cavort in the grass. Such considerations, however, do not inhibit Vesta or Diana or Demeter . . .

I come upon Megan already at work, kneeling with Erika and Venus and Miri; they examine a shaft of grass they have pulled from the soil—and evidently with some effort.

"Rainfall is plentiful, conditions ideal," Miri is saying, "the root structure utter simplicity. Why then is it implanted in the soil with so very high a degree of security?"

"Wind," Erika answers.

Megan asks with a smile and a playful tug at the auburn locks that flutter around Erika's face, "Like this breeze, Erika?"

Erika answers somberly, "All evidence points to wind, Megan, including surface configuration. It's less severe here, more erratic, because this continent lies close to the equator. But the winds do blow here—in patterns we must study for our own safety."

Megan nods and takes the shaft of grass from Miri, whips it in a snapping motion to test the tensile strength, then lifts it to her mouth.

Venus seizes Megan's wrists in a grip of such strength that her fingers turn white. "Did you not listen to my instructions before we left *Amelia*?" Her voice is flat with anger.

"I was only testing its properties, Venus. I didn't intend to ingest it."

"That doesn't matter. You must not touch anything to your mouth. You're our leader, you have a duty to us not to be foolish. The immunization shots protect only against bacteria, not—"

"I apologize." Megan is looking down at the hands that slowly release her wrists. "Thank you, Venus."

"The grass is strong enough for many uses," Miri says in the silence. "To create fabric, for one thing—"

Miri has placed the grass in her analysis unit, and we turn our attention to insect life. "Coleoptera," Miri says. "Many of these species are strange to me, but there are many beetles in just this area. If there is any kind of life so perfectly constructed and adaptable, that permeates the universe and will probably inherit it someday—"

"Mother!" someone shrieks. "Something's attacked Mother!"

We run pell mell through the grass . . .

A tiny furry creature is sitting on Mother's arm, feet curled around it, looking up into her face. "Phosh, control yourself Astra," Mother says.

"Mother, stand perfectly still." Kendra walks carefully toward her. Megan approaches cautiously from the side.

But Mother shoos them off with an impatient wave. "This dear creature won't hurt anyone, I can tell by looking at him. If it is a him." She grasps the creature, which makes a sound of whoof, and turns it over. "And assuming," she says, looking down, "that the same rules apply here, then yes indeed, it is a him."

As Mother turns it right side up the creature whoofs again as if in total agreement.

"Mother, it could bite." Megan is smiling in spite of obvious effort to appear stern and concerned.

Augusta is laughing. "Mother's right. A tiny thing like that would never attack anything larger, and he leaped right into her arms. He's just curious, that's all."

"He's much too cute to bite," Mother states.

Perhaps a foot in height, the creature has soft dark fur, four long clumsy-looking limbs, and huge dark eyes that gaze limpidly at me as it cocks its head and whoofs again. It is, indeed, adorable.

Kendra walks to Mother and stands towering over her,

hands on hips, grinning down at the tiny creature. "What is it, Augusta?"

"A primate type, probably with a great many brothers and sisters of similar genus, none very large. His chest-beating descendants will come along eons from now, I would guess. And his sabre-rattling descendants eons after that."

Whoofing, the creature plucks at Mother's sleeve as if puzzled; gently Mother touches, then strokes its soft fur. It utters more whoofs, gazing at Mother with its huge dark eyes, and curls up against her.

"This Eocene period that all of you continually refer to, that this planet supposedly is in now," Mother says, stroking the creature, "how long did it last?"

Erika answers, "About twenty million years."

"Excellent," Mother says, beaming. "Simply excellent."

Venus shrieks, "Vesta! No!"

I no sooner see that Vesta has lifted to her mouth a berry she has found on a low fruit-covered bush than Carina has launched herself in a flying tackle and brings Vesta to the ground, then picks her up by the feet. In spite of my fear for Vesta, it is a hilarious sight, Carina shaking the upside down and thoroughly outraged Vesta until the berry pops from her mouth.

"Down, down, put me down," sputters Vesta.

Venus is already kneeling beside the bush, she has opened her kit and is dropping berry samples into tubes of testing fluid. Carina stands with an arm trembling around Vesta's shoulders, watching intently.

"They're harmless," Vesta protests, "I *know*. I can tell by the smell—"

"It appears so." Venus sighs with relief as none of the fluids change color.

"I've been cooking for half a century," Vesta says indignantly, "and my nose is better than any of your test tubes."

"You won't do that again." Carina now trembles visibly. "Promise me, Vesta."

"I promise." Vesta looks at her with adoration and holds out a hand. "Dearest love," she says.

Vesta and Carina walk a short distance to deeper grass, and embrace.

Mother grumbles, "Here we are on a new world. Sometimes I wonder about my girls and their priorities—"

"It's been a long hard trip, Mother," Venus says, gazing at Miri.

"Shall we go to the ocean now?" Jolan asks. "I long to see it."

"As do we all, Jolan," Megan replies quietly.

We walk toward the distant sound of surf, Mother's little friend curled up in the bend of her arm. Soon we come upon low dunes spread with moss-like cover, so soft that we reach down to stroke it. Miri pauses, gently tugs, pulls harder, finally wrenches a piece of the moss loose; she frowns at the multi-branched root system, then replaces the moss, tamping it carefully into place. We go on. The moss is softer than velvafleece, so soft that I long to remove my boots and further savor it, but dare not risk Venus's wrath.

Then we all halt as one, as if rooted into the moss. The sky is a swiftly darkening coral as our great double sun falls to the horizon. Billowing cumulous clouds are shot through with swirls and threads of gold and red; and under this magnificent sky huge coral waves crash onto ivory-colored moss . . . huge waves in variegated hues of coral . . .

Without a word, we sit to watch evening come to Maternas.

The rich coral of sky and water deepens and darkens. The air grows sharply cooler, so quickly that our clothing is slow to adjust. Erika enfolds the unprotesting Mother to warm her; Kendra holds Hera, her mother; Miri curls into Venus; Carina cradles Vesta; and dear Jolan, next to me, holds me, warms me. Diana, Demeter—others huddle together in clusters nearby. Megan sits alone, apart from us all, gazing off to the horizon, hands clasped around her knees, her white clothing vivid against the gathering night.

And still we remain silent, as unimaginable beauty envelops us. The sky transmutes to deepening shades of blue and begins to shimmer with the silver of brilliant star clusters, the eerie radiance of red and blue fluorescence. One huge moon, glowing gold, is soon joined by two others, much smaller, which slowly rise above the horizon, each jagged in shape as if carelessly formed. Night falls suddenly and completely, and we sit together in a glorious royal blue world illuminated with silver.

It is Mother who speaks, softly: "So lovely a world . . . is surely meant for women."

No response is necessary. Or possible. We continue to sit in contemplation of our awesome ocean and sky—and in the realization that the remainder of our lives will be filled with nights such as these.

We are stunned by a sudden drenching of sea spray—yet the translucent silver waves crash some distance from us, several hundred feet. Then a rising scream of wind strikes with such force that the very breath is driven from me.

The creature that clings to Mother leaps from her arms and with a series of whoofs runs nimbly, in no apparent hurry, over the mossy dunes.

"Take cover!" Erika shouts. "The ships!"

Megan's voice cuts through the screaming wind. "No! Follow Mother's animal! Run!"

"Kendra!" shouts Hera, "see to Mother!"

Kendra sweeps Mother into her arms and we run, run after the tiny furry creature that scampers toward the grass, its feet twice lifted from under it by shrieking gusts. I fall, flung to my knees; I choke for breath. Megan drags me to my feet, pulls me along; I run, stumbling, hand gripped in hers, my eyes burned shut, gouged by the demon wind.

The bent grass has come fully erect; grass is a shoulder-high waving wall before us. We burst through it; it seals imperviously behind us, and we collapse in darkness, crouching together in a sudden and incredible world of tranquility.

Erika brings us light as she tosses from her kit several illumination bars; and I see that we have all reached this safe harbor. Kendra, kneeling, gently lowers the most precious one of us all, who frightens us as she lies motionless. Then she opens her remarkable green eyes and says querulously to Kendra, "You run more roughly than the trogapods on Verna. But thank you, dear one," she adds, patting Kendra's cheek.

We sit, resting, composing ourselves, recovering our wits. Venus tidies her silver hair and that of Diana and Miri; Hera leans against Kendra, but soon sits erect, her dignity returning; Carina fusses with Vesta, brushing invisible particles from her shoulders.

Megan says to Erika, "You tried to warn me of this."

"I had no idea about this, Megan. I had thought perhaps there was a severe monsoon period or its like. This presents formidable difficulties to us." Erika's dark eyes are grave. "Perhaps insurmountable. How can we build structures to—"

"Perhaps not insurmountable," Astra interrupts in a soft voice. "This wind is not part of the meteorological pattern mapped thus far. I suspect—and we'll soon know if my theory is plausible—that this is nocturnal wind caused by the drastic drop in air temperature we all felt when our suns set. Sudden cold air combined with still-warm temperatures can produce a convection-like reaction, a violent squall, a bora-type wind like those found on the Euro-continent of Earth. If I'm correct, then this wind should reduce as surface and air temperatures stabilize. But I share Erika's concern about permanent structures withstanding such a battering, even if for a brief period each day."

"I have an idea about that," Megan says. "But first we must see about your theory, Astra."

Miri reaches up, touches the grass that forms an undulant cocoon over our heads and muffles the howl of the wind. "Megan, it is simple now to understand the toughness and deep root system of this grass, the moss that covers the land down to the shoreline. It protects the land from what would be disastrous soil erosion, it protects insect and animal life. The ecological adaptation here is truly a marvel."

"Great care must be taken about removal of any of this grass for any purpose," Venus murmurs.

"Great care will be taken about the use of all our world's resources," Megan states.

Diana asks anxiously, "Our EVs, will they withstand this wind?"

"They're fastened with retractor rods," Kendra answers with satisfaction. "A cyclone would not dislodge our craft."

"Whoof." Five or six of Mother's little creatures are gathered a short distance from us, apparently attracted by the illumination bars. One approaches Mother.

"Here, come here," Mother coaxes, and it leaps into her arms. "The same one," she says, examining him. "I can tell by the blond markings on his chest. Augusta dear, what kind of animal did you say he was?"

"Primate. Closely resembling Cebus Capucinus."

"Phosh. Much too complicated," Mother pronounces. "I'll just call him a whoofie."

We all laugh, and Mother says to Augusta, "Speaking as the only heterosexual on board *Amelia*, it would be nice to have a male around. Is there a problem about taking him back with us?"

"I'll consult with Demeter," Augusta replies, smiling. "I see no reason why he shouldn't be able to go safely through decontamination. If Megan agrees."

"As an extra precaution," Megan says with a grin, "we'll quarantine him in your quarters, Mother. For his own safety. I think everyone will love him so much they'll stroke his fur off."

"For his food we'll take berries from that bush he was eating from when he found me," Mother says in a pleased voice.

Around us, the grass has begun to collapse into its previous bent shape, and we are in our softly lighted, glorious royal blue world. Erika extinguishes the illumination bars. The wind whips in gusts, flinging our hair about our faces, but it has lost its violence.

"Your theory seems correct, Astra," Megan says, touching the homing signal on her bracelet, the order for us to reassemble for the return to *Amelia.*

Astra says, "Megan, may I remain here and establish site testing?"

Megan nods. "You and your team. But you must remain together at all times and in direct monitoring contact with *Amelia.* Make EV-four your quarters, we won't establish base camp until we select our permanent site."

I see Miri and Venus draw Megan aside. Miri murmurs to Megan; Megan replies—reluctantly and apologetically, it appears. Venus makes a brief rejoinder; her face, turned toward me, is frozen in fury. I cannot imagine what has transpired.

XV

Personal Journal of Megan
1.1.2

I had known, expected that Venus would turn her attentions elsewhere, but not that she would impart such anguish . . .

And I had not expected such a woman as Miri.

I suppose I had hoped that she would be attracted to another woman of my body type. So that I might have favorably compared—even felt some small degree of superiority . . .

Miri is smaller than I by a head. Her tawny hair is thick and rich with curl and reaches below her shoulders—compared with my own brief simple dark crown. Her face is heart-shaped, without the angular planes of my own, her lips fuller than my own. And her breasts . . . here I compare most grievously. Mine are firm and well-shaped, but compared to the swelling glory of hers . . . And she is delicate . . . And with a petite grace . . .

I had first noticed her weeks ago when we assembled the exploratory teams. A woman staring at Venus is not an infrequent occurrence; few women are so arresting as Venus. But Venus met and held Miri's gaze until Miri looked away, her color high. And as our conference progressed, I saw their eyes meet again . . . and again . . .

I saw from *Amelia's* manifest that they had been assigned living areas far separate, and differing sleep and activity times. But they were assigned together on EV-one. Their specialties are related, and I could not prevent it . . .

I saw Venus's eyes go immediately to her as we assembled to board EV-one. And then she sat with Miri. And after that it was as if tinder had gathered flame from a spark.

Amid the unfolding wonder of our new planet, they were on the far outer periphery of my awareness. But still I ached with dull unfocused pain.

Then, after our near-deadly encounter with the creature we have named GEM, I turned to see Miri in her arms, and turned my back again, discovering that my tolerance for pain did not extend even partially this far. And because it was my duty, my sacred obligation, I excised them ruthlessly from my consciousness. With unforseeable danger lying all about us, I could not spare the least part of my concentration.

They did not intrude painfully upon my consciousness again even after we had landed. I worked with them in the examination of the grass-like growth on the planet's surface, working as if I were anaesthetized. Then, as I lifted grass to my mouth to further test its properties, Venus grasped my wrists for my own safety.

It was the first time I had known her touch and the effect upon me was truly extraordinary. Her touch—the touch I had longed for without control—had happened. And the occurrence was simply over with. Dispensed with. Similar, perhaps, to the agency of a lightning rod. A feeling of peace spread through me, and a burgeoning sense of freedom. As I watched her hands release me I felt my yearning for her also release its grip. Memory returned to me of her holding Miri, stroking her hair—memory without pain.

And also the cold knowledge was in me that I could no longer desire a woman who would so casually touch another for pleasure within my sight.

I do not know if her intention was to release me, but as her hands left me I thanked her, not only for my physical safety, but for giving me as well my full freedom. Mother had been totally correct; I needed to concentrate every fibre of my being on guiding us safely through the settlement of our new world.

Lighthearted, I led our group to the ocean, then sat to watch our spectacular evening descend. Even penetrating, deepening cold could not disturb my euphoria; I continued to delight in the changing colors of sea and sky. Venus again held Miri; I glanced once without pain—without actual interest.

My reactions sometimes seem contrary to what they should be, as in my urge to cry when I am truly happy or moved, an urge I ruthlessly control. Since there are things I do not understand in myself, it is no great wisdom to say that I sometimes do not understand the emotion of other women.

As we were preparing to leave Maternas, Miri and Venus came to me, Miri asking permission to remain on the surface.

Venus surely knew that I could not permit this. But if puzzled, I answered truthfully, "We are close to selecting a permanent site and I need to consult with you, Miri. I can permit only Venus to stay."

"I have no wish to stay," Venus said, smiling at Miri.

Realizing that they wished to remain together because there would be no opportunity on *Amelia*, I said, "I can arrange to make my quarters on *Amelia* available to you both for any period of time you wish."

Miri smiled. But Venus's face froze. "You are," she said in a glacial voice, "too kind."

And she took Miri's arm and walked from me.

We have been back on board *Amelia* for some hours now, and I have questions for Miri. But Venus and Miri are together; they use not my quarters but Janel's, who is on orbital duty watch. They have been behind that sealed door for hours and I will not disturb them, but I muttered to

Minerva, the kind woman so dearly beloved and respected by us all, "It seems the time Venus and Miri spend together could be used to greater advantage."

Minerva looked at me with such sympathy that I resolved never again to speak of matters of which I have so little knowledge.

XVI

1.1.3

Knowing that the decision about our colony site was imminent, I walked impatiently into the command room to wait for the rest of us to assemble. Mother was resting in her quarters, and Venus reclined in Mother's chair, gazing at Megan who slept.

We have learned how it is that Megan works so many hours without rest: she sleeps briefly, perhaps half an hour at a time, so deeply that even loud noise does not penetrate the shell of sleep, her breathing so slow to be scarcely perceptible. She awakens as suddenly as she sleeps, refreshed and revitalized.

She had been examining an element of surface data; the same figures continued to repeat across her screen. But her chair was adjusted to its level position and she lay with an arm under her head, dark hair spilling over the vivid white of her sleeve, her body turned so that its slim taut curving was emphasized, the long graceful lines of her legs.

"Where is Miri?" I inquired of Venus.

"Asleep," she answered absently, returning her attention to Megan after the briefest of glances at me.

I asked quietly, "Was it your plan to create jealousy?"
She sighed. "Yes."

"It was a grievous error." I gestured to Megan. "Whatever hold you once had on her is gone."

Venus's eyes did not leave Megan. "Minerva," she said

in the dangerous voice I remembered from our childhood, "how would you like to be stuffed into a decomposition tube?"

Megan stirred, and so I held my retort. She turned fully toward us, settled again. I joined my sister in gazing at her, at the lovely line of throat, the deep curve of hip, the slim leg drawn up ... She stirred once again, awakening; and sat up, rubbing and blinking sleep from her eyes like a child. She looked at me and smiled, and glanced at Venus; but Venus had turned Mother's chair and was staring at the viewscreen as if fascinated by the slowly revolving vista of coral cloud and ocean below. Megan raised the back of her chair and turned her attention to the data on the screen before her.

Much as I love my sister, I am secretly glad that this young woman with her rare gifts and pure beauty has somehow managed to escape her all too expert hands. Venus's face seems drawn, her eyes troubled ... But my sister has loved a great many women in her lifetime, and so I cannot truly gauge the level of her distress ...

We have assembled, the command room crowded with us—the Inner Circle and all the members of the exploratory teams—some seated on the floor, others finding room along the walls and under the crystal windows near Kendra's command chair, all of us facing the viewscreen as Megan has instructed. As we sit talking among ourselves, Megan walks to the viewscreen and stands under it, arms crossed. The room abruptly quiets.

I have seen her among small work teams, amid meetings of committees where she was easily in control; never have I seen her formally before a group so large as ours, nor so formidably constituted. Mother and we of the Inner Circle possess the mystique of our position and years, the expertise of our specialties and the acquired knowledge of decades. Others of us are highly trained in our fields, many with achievements noteworthy enough to accrue some degree of fame on the world we have abandoned. All have in common singular independence, strength, and assurance.

If she is apprehensive about confronting such a gathering, it is not apparent. Silence has fallen and still she contemplates us, standing very straight, her long legs set slightly apart, dark hair tousled as always from previous absent-minded strokes of her fingers. Her remarkable eyes are calm as they survey us; their emerald meets my gaze for an instant, then seems to look into the eyes of each of us. Our own eyes are riveted to her as if she is possessed of a current that magnetizes us.

"The choice of where we will settle was made by you." She speaks in her normal tone, her voice reaching us with bell-like clarity. "The choice indeed has been an easy one because of your knowledge, your talent, your ability. With the wisdom and expertise you have contributed, each of you has made the choice."

There is a pleased murmur. Her understanding of leadership has deepened yet further, she has even greater command of her gifts. I glance at Mother, who leans back in her big chair stroking the whoofie asleep in her lap; she watches Megan with a half-smile, looking very pleased indeed.

"With Kendra's permission we have temporarily linked our ship's computers with the viewscreen so that we may see most of the factors that combined in our decision. First, we will see why certain sites were eliminated."

On the viewscreen images form and swiftly vanish: vistas of ice fields and grinding glaciers; harsh mountain ranges of barren, twisted rock; sharply etched giant earthquake faults; boiling calderas; thick towering forest.

"All seven continents, no matter how formidable the terrain, are of course within our capability for settlement—with appropriate terraforming. But consultations with our cosmogonist Patrice, as well as many others of you, have resulted in certain convictions about the manner in which we must approach our new home planet."

If any of us is slightly puzzled as to how Megan has synthesized our various contributions, we hold our peace;

we all exchange pleased glances and smiles.

"We are not traditional colonists. Indeed, with our superior awareness we have the most profound philosophical obligations as we choose among seven biomes—seven ecological regions—with evolutionary processes very different from each other because of the barrier to common evolution presented by the oceans. And our obligation to the future compels us not to interfere in the ecological balance and evolutionary process of our world. On this basis, the decision has been taken that no terraforming shall occur on Maternas."

The murmur that passes through the room is one of approval.

"The decision not to terraform narrows our search to climatic and topographic regions most naturally friendly to us. These conditions are most ideally found on the continent we have named Femina—and it was by no accident that we landed there."

Megan smiles as several familiar vistas of Femina appear on the viewscreen—high waving grass, ivory-colored coastline. "She is our third largest continent. On her land mass of six million square miles, there are many specifics to consider."

The viewscreen shows the extensive earthquake fault we had flown over, an irregular stitching in the earth, a spine along the eastern side of the continent.

"Our planet is young and geologically volatile—we'll be subject to earthquake tremors wherever we settle. And further, a million square miles in the northeast of Femina is a vast plain where forest cover is rapidly breaking down and changes are occurring. Augusta is responsible for these remarkable magnifications of detail you see now."

We stare, murmuring, at armored creatures lacking horns, and huge elephant-like creatures without tusks. They graze peacefully on grass and shrub. Another squat long-necked spotted mammal delicately strips berries from a bush. We watch a small sabre-toothed cat leap from a tree and streak across the plain; we start in surprise as an ivory-spotted animal with a thick flat tail materializes from the grass to leap onto the back of an armored creature which promptly, if ponderously, rolls in the heavy grass to dislodge it.

"Dominance is still being resolved here. We will not—must not—intrude where we would interfere with such highly specific life-forms. Which brings us to the southwest area of Femina."

High waving grass flutters on our screen; low flowering shrubs in yellows and golds; trees sculpted into torturous shapes by the wind. Then we look at jagged mountains descending to the sea.

"Erika informs me that while all the mountains on our planet are young, these show much evidence of exfoliation and other indications of moderate rainfall, and the soil continues to break down to fertile elements."

The screen shows fruit-bearing trees, shrubbery adorned not with flowers but berries, pods, seeds.

"Venus and Miri inform me that all of what they test so far is edible, some quite edible indeed. Vesta has experimented with one of the pod-like fruits with most interesting results." She pauses, grins at Vesta.

"It makes the most wonderful wine!" Vesta cries enthusiastically.

When our laughter and applause finally die down, Megan continues, "Much remains to be tested, but all empirical evidence is highly promising. There is ample food, varied and interesting and safe for our consumption. Again, consider this mountain range that reaches to the sea."

We watch in silence. Hundreds of miles of rugged mountains perhaps six to ten thousand feet in height descend to humble peaks of less than a thousand feet, enclosing a system of lakes and streams and inland valleys.

"The fresh water lakes are part of an integrated drainage system which Jolan tells me provides artesian conditions for an ample water supply. This lovely land," Megan continues softly, "is very near the sea . . ."

She remains silent. We watch other vistas slowly unfold:

polished obsidian faces of mountainsides, dramatic water-
falls, sparkling coral lakes, gentle sloping foothills, wide
valleys of trees and flowers and high waving grass.

Megan speaks again. "We have the problem that Astra
first warned us of, and then Erika. Wind. And wind is a most
serious problem. From an analysis of probable wind patterns along the coast and out of these mountains, I have
produced my own contribution."

We stir in anticipation as she pauses.

"In this area of Femina, the mountain range presents a
formidable barrier to the many large life forms in other
sectors, and will protect us from them and them from us.
But while we must be concerned with our effects on the
varied life on our land, we need have no such concern about
the sea. Jolan advises that all our oceans and lakes teem with
life, and that evolutionary paths are well established in all
the waters of our planet. Sea life is so bountiful that to
impact negatively upon it is an impossibility. It is a certainty
that a vast variety of foodstuffs from the sea and protein
plants from the land will be available to us without drawing
on any animal life—"

"Meat-eating is barbaric," Vesta says with a shudder.

"Not if it's necessary," growls Erika.

"Argue later, dears," Mother says.

Grinning, Megan continues, "As for where and how we
might live, when I determined that our precious synthesizers
must be placed well inside a hollowed-out mountainside to
protect them from climate and from earthquake tremor, an
idea glimmered then. And when we first experienced the
violence of the nocturnal winds, I realized then that this is
how we also should live."

I exclaim, dismayed, "You mean in *caves?*"

Megan says gently, "Not in any sense that you imagine,
Minerva. Foothills must be at least a setting for our homes,
our main colony. Living amid the hills will minimize the
effect of earthquake by absorbing seismic tremors. And will
also protect the basic ecology of Femina. Our synthesizers
must mine for minerals and elements we need, but as we

carve ore from these mountains and hills, we can at the same time carve our homes. Erika, will you assist?"

"Gladly, Megan." Erika strides to the viewscreen, picks up a laser pointer and faces us, her face animated, her eyes intense. "Megan has discussed her plan with many of us, sought our collaboration."

She circles an intricate grouping of foothills partially enclosing a gently rolling plain. "Consider this as a central building site. The curve of mountain would somewhat deflect the nocturnal wind, and carved rock homes would further—and completely—protect us from both wind and rainfall, which will be more than ample in this temperate zone of Maternas. Megan has already made preliminary renderings of the beautiful structures that could be our homes, homes that will combine architecture with art and individuality, will give us flexibility of location. Megan's ideas are in all ways brilliant. And most of all—" Erika's voice drops dramatically, "her plan will allow us to be ecologically one with our world."

"Erika is totally correct," Patrice interjects.

"These nearby streams descend to run over flat land, minimizing land erosion from down-cutting. And on this grassy and fruitful plain we may accomplish any cultivation necessary. As important as anything else to us, this land is beautiful. And all of us will have considerable choice. All of this area of Femina—a hundred thousand square miles in total, a thousand square miles of fresh water, five hundred miles of coastline without factoring in the inlets and other permutations of our coast. Those who choose to live away from our main colony will have many nearby hillside sites to choose from, near lakes or streams, beside the sea."

"I ask this question not for myself but for others," Astra says. "What if some wish not to live in this area of Femina at all? On a continent other than Femina?"

Megan replies. "Astra," she says quietly, "I fully expect that some of us will not live here. A colony of four thousand—which will rapidly grow—will have sizeable impact on whatever area we choose to settle in. But the small number of us who choose to live elsewhere can do no conceivable ecological harm. Anyone who chooses not to remain with us will be given every assistance we can provide. We came here to live freely. And all of us shall be free."

Megan, smiling, holds up a hand to interrupt the applause which greets these words. "One other matter remains. To Mother has fallen the decision for the name of our colony."

"Simple, quite simple," Mother says, gently stroking her sleeping whoofie. "Our colony will be called Cybele. Explain, Minerva."

I reply: "In antiquity, Cybele was the symbol of universal motherhood. She was a Greek-Roman deity known as Great Mother of the Gods, and special emphasis was placed upon her maternity over wild nature. She was also known as Mountain Mother, and her sanctuaries were on mountains and in caves."

"Excellent," Mother says. "Simply excellent."

"Lions were her companions," I continue.

Mother pats the head of the furry creature in her lap. "I suppose whoofies will do as well."

"And," I push on, "her special affinity with wild nature drew rabid followers, their worship manifested in highly orgiastic behavior."

Mother looks around at us with glittering eyes. "That seems also fitting. Enough of this palaver," she says tartly. "Let's get down to Cybele and go to work."

I myself lead the cheers.

XVII

1.8.28

It has been many months . . .Record-keeping, visual and aural recording of our history, have kept me far too occupied to analyze and place events into perspective.

We continue to create our homes. Create—rather than build or construct—because never have such extraordinary structures come into existence, never such a flowering of architectural artistry.

The majority of our homes are in Cybele, but many of us have settled nearby. At our insistence one of the first houses to be crafted was Megan's—because she is our leader, and to give her rest, privacy, and solitude from her labors. We carved her own design into the hillside site she chose very near Cybele, on an isolated spit of land jutting into the sea which she has chosen to call Damon Point.

Her house is soaring planes and angles of weathered gray and brown striations that meld with the rocky mountainside, blend with the rugged coastline. The interior is an artful series of interconnected curves; fleece covers the floors, the tapestried walls conceal the myriad data and monitoring equipment she has installed throughout.

Our houses have been created and furnished by all of our artisans. Enhancing colors have been added to obsidian and igneous rock, and our incredible homes, glazed and polished, glow in the blaze of our two suns and under the light of our brilliant night sky.

A singularly noteworthy contribution has been made by

Zandra, the sculptress. Using Astra's comprehensive studies of the winds coming off the water and down the mountain passes, she has carved into each house an individual series of artful hollows. When the winds blow, these carvings play like flutes; glorious soaring harmonies warn us of oncoming nocturnals. They add unique beauty and charm to our houses; I have made many recordings when the wind has come up and our homes begin to sing . . .

Our homes are no two alike. Mother's is high on Cybele's main hill, and overlooks Radclyffe Falls and Vivien Lake, sparkling in the distance. My history chamber is in a complex of structures bordering Cybele's main square; but my house, a small simple square of peaceful grays and gray-blues, is beside the Woolf River.

Venus has chosen to live in Cybele. "Privacy is of course lovely, Minerva dear," she has told me. "But I prefer . . . the passing scene."

She is still with Miri—an unusual length of time for my sister to remain with anyone, and I doubt it will continue much longer. Old habits, especially the amorous habits of a lifetime, are hard to break. I suspect that Venus is attempting to justify to herself the miscalculation that cost her her tenuous hold on Megan, whom she continues to gaze at with ill-concealed desire.

Demeter also resides in Cybele, her skill in the medical arts on call every hour of the day and night. And she watches over and cares for Mother. Diana, quiet, gentle Diana, lives happily within the tiny artists colony which has formed along Stein Lake. More of Diana, later . . .

Vesta and Carina have settled near Diana on the Toklas River, their modest home one of the first we created; Vesta requires privacy in her work as a psychologist. Many of us, suffering from homesickness and other adjustment problems, needed to consult with her when we first landed on Maternas, and so we created a place affording peace and solitude. More of this later, also . . .

The previous denizens of Cybele, a reptilian population and a vast number of marsupials—a most comical cross

between kangaroo and primate—have been carefully en-
couraged by various non-lethal means to relocate outside
our borders. Whoofies, which inhabit the foothills in goodly
numbers, of course have the run of Cybele. Venus's studies
have determined that the overall reptilian population of
Femina is insectivore—only four species are poisonous.
And we have learned to contend with the mildly toxic
stings and bites of our myriad insect life. Therefore, in
spite of Megan's warnings, most of us including myself had
chosen to wear no protective devices, trusting to our security
teams and our wrist beacons and the forcefield barriers that
protect our settlement.

Until early this morning. Vesta was collecting from the
banks of the Toklas River a fungus which we have discovered
to be a rich meat-like delicacy, while Carina was keying in
her sector assignment and food quotas for this day. Then
Carina heard Vesta's faint scream. And at the same time
received, along with the rest of us, the distress signal on
her wrist beacon. She rushed from the house in a state of
alarm that can only be imagined.

She found Vesta backed against a tree by three small
but armored and razor-toothed Crocodylia camouflaged in
ivory and blue striping. They had crawled up from the
depths of the river to ravage the fungi, and now meant to
make a snack of little Vesta. Carina tore a limb from the
tree and beat the creatures across their snouts; they retreated sufficiently so that Carina picked up Vesta and
carried her to safety. Then over Vesta's shrieks of protest,
she returned to further inflict a furious pummeling upon
the creatures which had dared threaten her precious Vesta.
And so it was that Danya and her security team, summoned
by Vesta's wrist beacon, found Carina pursuing creatures
which scuttled about in panic, dodging her blows and seeking
only to return to the peace of their river bottom.

After this incident with Vesta, and until the mysteries
of our new world are fully unravelled, we have been ordered
by Megan to wear the device designed by her—no larger than
my little finger and emitting a non-fatal current of adjustable

strength which will repulse small creatures and seriously discourage larger ones.

Several mild earthquakes have rumbled through Cybele, causing dismay but producing no damage. A more severe one flung us about and frightened the children, and generated a seismic wave which roared inland, crashing over Megan's house—harmlessly—and reaching almost to Stein Lake. The children were counseled so successfully by Vesta that I believe they now almost enjoy our occasional tremors. Erika proceeds with the work on seismic prediction, and assures us it will soon be completed.

We continue to discover the vagaries of our weather. Clouds come in over the mountains so swiftly that Astra's rainfall predictions are of limited benefit. Waterspouts whirl in off the ocean, rising over the hills to deluge us; they delight the children as much as they exasperate us. Rains are brief if frequent and drenching, and are moderate, warm, never unpleasant. All our clothing has been made impervious, and since few of our Unity care to wear hats, hairstyles have shortened. We no longer take shelter from the rains; we simply go on about our work, afterward drying our hair with a few strokes of a warmcomb. We have assimilated the rain into our lives.

Our year has been calculated at precisely 336 days, a fact which is convenient as well as mathematically pleasing. We can divide everything perfectly, our days into twenty-eight day months and seven-day weeks.

We have now passed nine of these twenty-eight day months. "We've had summer, fall, and winter," Erika claims.

There seems little difference in the seasons to me. More frequent rains in the winter, perhaps; and spring seems to be bringing an increase of wind. Venus is oddly concerned about the oncoming season, muttering about pollens from burgeoning growth and the increased force of our winds. We shall soon see. Spring is fast coming upon us . . .

Our attire has become utilitarian, yet more artistic. In

the warm humidity of our climate our children and youngest women wear bright belted tunics and light sandals. The lithe beauty of their young bodies is better shown in our visual recordings than in any poor recounting of mine. The strong and athletic among us seem to prefer shirts and pants and boots; but one piece trouser-suits, brightly patterned, some belted, some flowing, are again popular now that sufficient time has passed since the days when we had no choice in our apparel. Others of us dress in long pullover tops with body stockings, or rough-cut tunics and leggings. Many of us older ones, including all of the Inner Circle, wear soft light robes.

Megan is always clad in black pants and mid-calf boots, a white shirt. All of us on Maternas wear off-whites, deep greys that come close to black, but not those two exact colors, it has become an unspoken rule that these are Megan's colors alone.

Soon after we had begun to build on Maternas, our fabricators synthesized select grasses into fabric, and Diana somehow found time to make the first clothing for Megan—perfectly fitting black lustervel pants and a white silk shirt. Then later she fashioned black velvet pants and ornate white shirts for ceremonial occasions—our first birth, the completion of Mother's house, certain of our Joinings . . .

One of the first Joinings I recorded on Maternas was Diana with Janel. Diana's emotion, once given, is firm; and entwined with her deep love for Janel is unceasing gratitude to Megan that she saved Janel. Diana fashions all of Megan's clothes, and Megan wears many subtle and beautiful variations of her simple attire.

Diana's time for creation of apparel is hard-won; she is fully occupied with the genetic testing and gene-blending necessary prior to the administering of Estrova to those who wish to conceive. Our first birth occurred two weeks after planetfall—Vita, Amber's baby, which she had carried while on board *Amelia*. Although births can be safely effected within four to five months of conception, almost all of us have previously chosen full term birth—to perform this act without any degree of efficiency. I am hardly being critical; years ago I too enjoyed every month of my own giving of life . . . But there have been 419 births in our nine months here, and a great many more of us—hundreds—are pregnant. "Short term," Diana has told us incredulously. "Every woman who desires pregnancy chooses short term!"

But Vesta has explained: "There is uncommon urgency within us," she says, "to plant our presence securely upon this vast and empty new world."

And so I have been mightily occupied with my recording of vital statistics, our numerous Joinings and Births.

Beginning with Diana and Janel, ceremony has evolved when a couple comes into my chamber for recording of their Joining. We of the Inner Circle managed to arrange a small celebration for Diana in Cybele's main square—music by Thea on her crystal instruments, food, wine—a small gathering because Diana is shy, more reticent in the matters of love than most of us. Afterward, she and Janel went off for the single day Diana could spare from her work to one of the tiny houses in the conifers overlooking Barney Lake, which we had decorated and stocked with delicacies prepared by Vesta. And the custom has continued . . .

But there have been other uses for these tiny houses in their peaceful setting . . . all has not been joy . . . I have sadly recorded Deaths, weeping for two which I felt most keenly . . .

The first were among the phobics who had traveled with us under sedation, one a precious young descendant of mine, the others descendants of Selene, Isis, and Olympia. All four perished within a week of our landing on Maternas, finding the strangeness of our new world more than they could bear. They simply walked off into the mountains, and in spite of lengthy and thorough search in our EVs and on foot and by the drones which were released from *Amelia*, we found the body of only one—my Martine—at the bottom of the cliff over which she had fallen.

While these deaths grieved us all, they prostrated Vesta. Throughout the existence of our Unity, the prevailing cause of death among us has been the taking of our own lives.

Women so gifted as we are sometimes cursed with hypersensitivity; we are apt to be less than rational in some respects . . . Indeed, all of us are susceptible to dark ailments of the spirit . . . Vesta knew she risked greatly in allowing our troubled kinswomen to accompany us. Our nine other phobics have adjusted well, but even knowing this has not consoled Vesta.

And there has been a drowning—Cara, Patrice's daughter, at the tender age of sixteen. We had been sternly warned by Jolan that our seas are treacherous at high tide, but Cara, strong and proud of her athletic prowess, did not listen. A search party, weeping, carried her body from a cove near Damon Point. And we sent Patrice to Barney Lake . . . most often a setting for the consummation of love, but now a setting of serenity for a sorely distressed spirit . . .

And so we have had the first internments on Maternas . . . and our grief will never truly leave us.

If our days vary in atmospheric event, our nights are what only our poets can describe. And the nights are warming again with the coming of spring. It seems a beautiful season unfolding to us, Venus's forebodings notwithstanding. Each evening many of us watch the coral-gold drama of our sky as our double sun sets. And each night, after our homes sing the diminishing of the nocturnal winds, we come out to bathe in the beauty of our sky, the silver light and fluorescent hues which transform our world into blue velvet and silver-gray shadow. We gaze at the inexhaustible glory of our sky, at the drifting orbs of gold that are our three moons, at the riotous tapestry of stars spread over royal blue.

I walk every evening; how could I not? I see women walking closely together, an arm about each other, I see women together in the shadows . . . There is little public display of affection during our days; we are too busy with our work, and we seem reticent in that regard; an oppressive history continues to influence our customs. But the beauty of our nights calls forth need for sharing and physical tenderness . . .

Often I think of my long-dead Serena when I walk at night. I feel my aloneness keenly . . .

Several evenings ago I took a runabout down to the ocean to walk upon the exquisite seaside moss and to watch the great illuminated waves crash at high tide. I saw Megan in the distance, white shirt fluorescent in the night colors, standing tall and straight at the very edge of Damon Point, hands in her pockets, gazing at sea and sky. I did not disturb her, but I ached with the loneliness this solitary young woman surely must feel.

I have discussed her with the Inner Circle. Mother seems unconcerned, even indifferent—as of course does Venus—and my other sisters believe that Megan will choose a lover when the pressures on her slacken. But when will that be? Our days are volatile, every urgent decision falls to her. Her swift and flawless judgment is accepted by us all, we rely upon her for ever more decisions, not fewer. And when her unitary command is ended, then she must be a major part of the complex evolution of the rules that will govern how we shall now live . . . When or how can her work possibly slacken?

An even greater concern is that she has already become a paragon, has acquired too mythic an image. Our youngest women gaze at her in awe; our mature women are daunted, intimidated. Who will there be to love Megan?

I see shadows of her future: The mythology has already begun. Songs written of our departure and journey, her heroism. A giant mural is being created in Cybele's main square depicting Megan as she first stands upon Maternas . . .

I fear for her, that the coming years will bring only increased isolation, even as we all cherish her . . . That her loneliness will only deepen . . .

While none of us can forget nor wishes to forget those precious ones we have left on Earth, as time passes we make the transition from our own lives there with greater ease. Earth plants and flowers continue to flourish unattended and ignored in *Amelia's* closed greenhouse systems. Maternas has food for every conceivable need, and the decision was quickly taken without debate to effect no transplantation of any growing thing from Earth . . .

We are exhilarated by what we have accomplished. Eager for the future, to complete our building, to further explore all the varied lands of Maternas, to study, to learn. Our new world has added buoyancy to all our lives—literally and figuratively. Venus tells us that our slightly lower gravity and higher oxygen level will further slow the aging process. And the coral colors of our world are kind to us. We tan to gold as we work in our soft warm air, under the gentle rays of our double sun. I look at our Unity with pride, with pleasure, and say without prejudice that we women of Maternas are truly beautiful . . .

XVIII

1.9.25

Venus's foreboding has proved prophetic.

Kendra was first—and in her proud strength would not admit her increasing weakness until she collapsed; and Demeter was helpless to prevent the swift spiraling debilitation.

And so we have lost the strong wondrous woman who carried us so safely across the stars. Hera is beyond all consolation; of all her daughters, Kendra was her greatest pride.

Kendra continues to give to us, even in death, her tissues providing the cultures Demeter and Diana require to combat the parasitic spores that stalk us. But nine hundred are now sick, including Vesta's precious Carina; and more fall sick each day.

"It selects the physically strong among us," Diana has told us grimly.

The physically slight now care for the very strong, while Diana and Demeter hover anxiously over the cultures they nourish. Even with force-growth techniques they must wait for them to ripen fully into the virulent antibodies necessary to defeat our predator. Myself and my descendants are mostly untouched; we are all small of build and as yet of no interest to the parasite, which Venus says is a variant germination that blew in upon the wind.

Kendra's great-granddaughter Christa, at the tender age of twenty, has Kendra's marvelous body; she is tall and muscular—powerful and beautiful. But the strength and power have left her; she lies on a medi-adjust in my house, and I tend her. Her mother, her sisters also lie ill, cared for by others.

I talk to Christa, to distract her. She is fascinated by my work and the world we left that she knew so briefly. And so I have talked for hours, and days, more than I ever have about myself and my work.

1.9.27

Christa weakens, and I do not leave her; I sleep as she sleeps, awakened by a body alarm when she stirs. But she moves less and less as strength drains from her. And now she has lost use of her voice and can only listen and watch as I speak, and gaze at me with dark eyes that with each passing hour grow more fearful.

1.10.1

Sixty-three have died.

I am determined, determined that she shall live.

Demeter has told me that Christa now lives one day longer than expected, and needs to live but one more, when the cultures will be ready. But she hovers on the edge of coma, drifting in and out, and I whisper fiercely, "Christa stay with me, Christa . . ."

1.10.2

I am sitting beside her gripping her shoulders still whispering to her when Demeter comes with the injection tube. I do not know if Christa lives . . .

"She lives," Demeter tells me. "Barely, but she lives."

"Hurry," I tell her.

1.10.4

She awoke in such pain that we immediately sedated her,

but she awoke. And hours later spoke her first word: "Minerva . . ."

1.10.10

I could not conceal from her that seventy-one of us have died, among them her mother and two sisters.

Grateful only that Vesta's Carina has been spared, I am devastated by my own grief. And knowing I could not console Christa, I have let her be, and she has spent the days afterward in silence, in solitude, beside the sea. Now I have brought her into my history chamber to distract her from her grief.

1.10.20

She has asked to work with me. I need her assistance, and could not in any case refuse anything she asked of me.

Like an assassin, love has come to me. Unexpected. Unbidden. Hopeless.

Only the counting of the years has given me age—but I know that Christa must see not the vigor of my body nor the energy of my later life, only my calendar years. If age has always been a state of mind, so has it also been in the mind of the observer.

I know she is fond of me; perhaps even loves me. My caring for her when she was in peril of her life has forged a deep bond between us. The kinship on our world has helped somewhat to cover the void in her life after the death of her family, and I strive to cheer her, to entertain her, to make her smile, to hear her soft laughter.

She complements me in our work, shares my deep commitment to the importance of our efforts, as we record the history of our fledgling world. She works far more slowly than I, with greater patience, has organized me by completing with thoroughness the tasks that always before I had postponed until confusion resulted.

During our days together she is affectionate in her

respectful, deferential way, shy to touch me. But at the end of each day she holds my shoulders gently and touches her cheek to mine. And I have made that be enough ...

But there are other pleasures I take in her ... which I steal like a thief ...

When she was ill, there was no part of her that I did not see and touch as I bathed and fed and clothed her. I touched her then not with desire but with caring; but now, during my solitary nights I remember every detail of her. Her smooth golden skin. The softness of her short lustrous brown hair. The feeling of her broad shoulders within my encircling arm as she drank the water I held for her. The firmness of her flesh in my hands as I bathed her, the curved contours of her small breasts, the muscular beauty of her thighs ...

During my nights, warm with my love and desire, I remember every detail of her, and I fall alseep imagining her strong arms holding me ...

1.11.25

The days have passed, each with her beside me, each with that single brief moment tantalizing yet comforting, when she holds me and touches her cheek to mine.

Until this day.

This day I think I was weary, and lonely with the thought of the coming night. I simply bowed my head to her shoulder, that strong shoulder, as if I could absorb her strength; and when I lifted my head to receive the touching of her cheek, I received instead a brief sweet touching of her lips to mine.

"Minerva." Her whisper was stricken. "Forgive me, I'm so sorry—"

"Christa," I said, and returned her kiss. How could I not?

"You ..." Her dark eyes were stunned, unbelieving. "I have never dared ... hope."

"My dear," I whispered, more astonished than she.

"I never dreamed ... you would honor me with ...

with . . . Didn't you know? You made me live," she whispered to me. "I lived because I loved you."

"I . . . You had to live," I faltered, "I love you so . . ."

The arms I had imagined all my lonely nights were around me. In tenderness and sweetest passion we kissed again. I slid my hands inside her shirt to caress those strong wonderful shoulders . . .

She sealed the door; then looked around. Some places are not well suited to what happens spontaneously, and there were only the molded consoles, the hard floor, our two chairs.

She opened my robe, took it off me, covered my chair with it. Discarding her own clothing, she came to me.

I held her warm, muscular, beautiful body in my arms. I thought: If ever you are slow at anything, Christa . . . let us be slow together now . . . with this.

Her mouth came to mine, her hands on me were gentle and unhurried. I stood clasping her to me and scarcely breathing, weakening to helplessness from her caresses. Her mouth, her hands were so slow and tender in their intimacies that I was a glowing ember when she finally carried me to my chair, and knelt to me, and lifted my legs to those shoulders. Somewhere amid the excruciating pleasure that followed I realized that there was nothing, nothing that she did not do slowly, and fully.

We were together that night, of course. I prepared food for us, and then took her to my bed where we would be comfortable and where I could love her. Her young body was resilient; and having some skill in these matters after all these years, I prolonged certain things considerably; and she spent some number of hours in pleasures that frequently heightened to ecstasies. My joy in her continued until nearly dawn, when she lay in my arms exhausted and replete; and if she was surprised by my passion for her she did not speak it; she simply wrapped her arms around me, and slept.

That morning we returned to our duties late but as usual, and with questionable efficiency. Soon afterward our eyes met; and she left the chamber to return a few minutes later to set up an inflatacot, as I sealed the door.

Sometime later, my ecstasy ended, I lay held close in her arms, still moaning with my memory of her. She held my face in her hands and said, "Don't ever make me leave."

"I never will," I whispered.

And so our names are Joined in the history of our world. I cannot guess how long I will have her, how long she will stay. But I do have her, and love and cherish her . . . and whether that will be for another month, a week, a day . . . I care not.

PART TWO

MEGAN

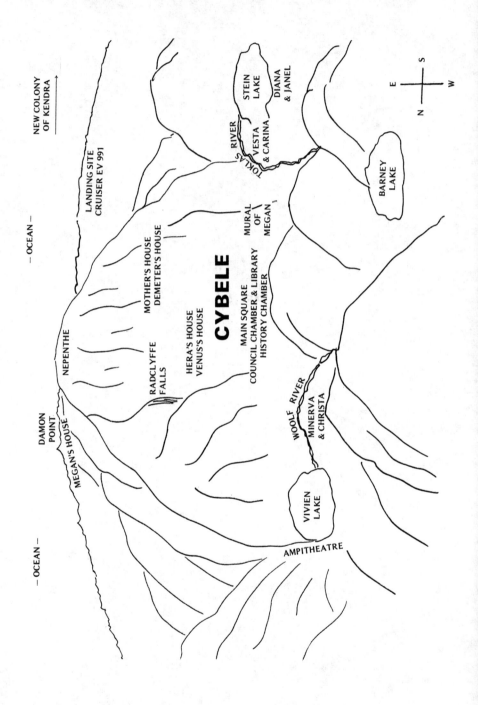

I

14.12.21

Megan has signaled an emergency meeting of the Inner Circle and the Council, the first such call in all our history.

We have rushed from our daily work to gather in the council chambers, and as we crowd around the crystal table we gaze at each other with expressions that range from anxiety to alarm. Only once before have so many of us assembled here—Anniversary Day exactly one year after we arrived, that joyous day when we voted to recommend to our Unity the Central Code we had fashioned to assure the peace and equality of everyone on Maternas.

Now Mother sits at the head of the table again, and wears her green cape and looks very somber indeed, which further unsettles us.

What could it be? A catastrophic earthquake prediction from Erika? A genetics discovery by Diana, with the gravest of implications for us all?

Hera sits next to Mother, tight-lipped, uncommunicative, acknowledging my greeting with a distracted nod.

Megan strides in bearing a receiving terminal. Standing next to Mother, she places the terminal carefully on the table and gazes for a moment at our motionless, silent gathering. Then she touches the terminal and stands with arms crossed as it glows to life.

Pulse pulse pulse . . . pulse . . . pulse . . . pulse . . . pulse pulse pulse . . . Pulse pulse pulse . . . pulse . . . pulse . . . pulse . . . pulse pulse pulse . . .

The rhythmic sound fills the room with its urgency.

Megan's cool green eyes traverse the table, meeting the stare of each of us. "*Amelia's* instruments picked up the signal before dawn," she says quietly. "From the general direction of Perseus. The signal has strengthened slightly, indicating it approaches our solar system." She falls silent again.

Pulse pulse pulse . . . pulse . . . pulse . . . pulse . . . pulse pulse pulse . . .

Demeter finally asks the question all of us instinctively dread: "What is it?"

Hera answers. "Morse code. The historical call for help—an SOS."

"In the event of implied danger to our Unity," Megan says in an uninflected voice, "I am empowered by our Central Code to take autonomous action only with your approval. Since this situation does not immediately imperil us, Mother has decided that I should not ask that approval, that the full Council shall decide what action we must take."

Mother makes no response, merely contemplates us.

"What is there to discuss?" Vesta asks. "We must help."

"Vesta dear," Hera says grimly, "the signal is clearly, unmistakably an SOS. Meaning a ship from Earth or one of her colonies."

"But I don't see—"

Understanding only too well, I interrupt. "We came here to be safe and free. To live in peace by living secretly."

"But still, why can't we—"

"We risk exposure," Hera says.

The dilemma has been crystalized—to all but Vesta, apparently. "Yes, but we can't just—"

"We don't know the nature or gravity of their distress," Megan says, "nor what kind of ship it is. It may well be an armed Cruiser. We detect no other transmission from them, but they may be in full contact with Earth."

"But Megan, we can't—"

"We are here to decide that, Vesta," Megan says gently. "What we should—or should not—do."

Mother, I notice, still has not spoken. A certain sign that she will not attempt to influence any decision in this matter.

"The stakes are very clear," Megan says softly. "We can help—and run the risk of exposure. Or we can choose not to help and perhaps—we can never know—consign an unknown number of persons to their deaths."

"They may already be dead," Danya points out.

"That is also possible," Megan answers, "but again we risk exposure if we investigate."

Pulse pulse pulse . . . pulse . . . pulse . . . pulse . . . pulse pulse pulse . . .

Demeter is gazing at Megan with stricken eyes. Her voice is almost inaudible: "Megan, what do you advise?"

"I choose not to advise." Megan speaks flatly. "It must be *our* decision, not mine. I recommend that we debate this further as we need to, then put the matter to ballot."

We talk quietly. But all has been said that needs to be said, and soon discussion dwindles.

Megan sits with Mother; they do not speak, only listen as we speak. When silence falls, Megan says, "All those ready to cast irrevocable ballot, please signify. Mother chooses not to vote unless there is a tie."

"As do I," Vesta says. Her voice is agitated. "I choose not to vote."

"Vesta," Megan says gently, "abstention except by Mother is not allowed under our Central Code. But you may take whatever time you need to decide."

I touch my bracelet; my blue-gray color appears on the holographic screen on our crystal table. Sixteen of our twenty signify readiness to vote.

"I require further time to reflect," Venus says.

"As do I," Demeter agrees.

"I too," Diana says.

"And I," Vesta whispers.

I am not surprised. The professions of my sisters have given them a most truly profound reverence for life.

We adjourn. Some of us gather in small enclaves to

converse. Sorely troubled, I choose the isolation of a meditation room, and remain there until, an hour later, the signal is given to reconvene.

Solemnly, we gather around the crystal table.

"All of you have signified readiness to vote," Megan says expressionlessly. "Please vote now on the question: Should we assist the ship that signals distress?"

I touch my bracelet hastily; then sit tensely and watch the holographic unit. Megan also touches her bracelet and gazes at the tally gauge before her.

"Nineteen have cast ballots," she says. "One remains before I can reveal the tally."

"I." Vesta sits with a trembling hand poised over her bracelet.

"Do you require more time, Vesta? If so I will void our current vote."

"No," she whispers, and jabs at her bracelet as if it would burn her.

"Our vote tally," Megan announces, and touches the gauge.

Eight for. Twelve against. I, Minerva, am one of the twelve who have pronounced a death sentence on other human beings . . .

"Our irrevocable decision is to take no action," Megan says evenly. "One other question remains. In the unlikely event that this ship finds Maternas, shall we then assist?"

"If they find us, there will be little possibility of maintaining our concealment," Hera states.

Megan nods. "The simplest readings would reveal signs of our technology. And we could move *Amelia* out of orbit and conceal her only with great difficulty. Is there further debate on this question?" We remain silent. "Please signify readiness to vote." We all so signify. "Please vote now on the question: Should we assist the distressed ship if it finds Maternas?"

The vote is twenty in favor.

Mother heaves a deep sigh and rises to her feet. "You are all my daughters," she says, her remarkable eyes softened to gentleness, "and I'm proud of both your wisdom and your compassion. And," she adds, "I'm grateful for no tie vote on question one. Or your poor old Mother would now be considerably older."

Mother takes her leave, tiny but indomitable in her flowing green cape. Megan says, "Except for the contingency plans if this ship should find Maternas, our business is finished. Danya, please remain, and also Jolan and Astra. And you also, please, esteemed Hera."

I am too dispirited to argue that I should remain in my capacity as historian, and take my leave with the rest of us, finding solace in the knowledge that their proceedings will be recorded automatically, that there are never any secret meetings of our Council.

Instead of returning to the history chamber, or going to my house, I visit the children's compound and watch Celeste in her linguistics class—unobserved by her. I long to hold her, but resist; I would communicate my distress to her. Soon I go to my house and gaze for a long time at the swift, soothing currents of the Woolf River.

Would I have voted so quickly and uncompromisingly, I ask myself, if this had been fifteen years ago and I did not have my dearest Christa and our own precious Celeste? Today I would suffer the flesh flayed from me before I would risk the slightest hurt to them. I would call death down upon any who would threaten harm . . .

How can I but question my wisdom? For years I did not, would not believe Christa's love—only the conventional expectation that if the young go with the old it is for a time and then they seek further, among their own age . . . All the years she did not leave I believed that soon she would; I refused to listen when she asked to bear our child . . . When she asked . . . And asked . . . Until she did a thing she had never done before with me . . . Cried . . . Only then did I see the depth of her love, the depth of my selfishness, my concern with avoiding my own pain at the expense of her happiness . . .

And so now I have my Christa and we have our Celeste . . .

Celeste, with my eyes but Christa's strength and beauty . . .

No, age does not automatically bring wisdom. And if it does, perhaps it also brings humility in equal parts . . .

Christa has come home. "I've been searching for you," she says softly. "Along with everyone in Cybele I watched the Council proceedings on the screen in the square. I knew I must find you, come to you—"

Needing her strength, the reassurance of her arms, I take her hand and lead her to our bed.

II

Journal of Lt. Laurel Meredith, SSA
2214.2.12

Perhaps the events of the past day are a preposterous dream—a delirium. Perhaps after six weeks of floating in death-like sensory deprivation my mind has also gone. But could even a broken mind devise events so improbable, so inconceivable?

I had risen from my vigil to stretch my legs. As usual we were all occupied with our individual obsessions: Ross and Hanigan tinkering with our life support computers—a shattered multi-thousand piece puzzle with no schematic from which to reassemble it; Coulter prowling the hydroponic room brandishing an instaweld gun, looking like a brawny thief, knowing full well that soon our precious atmosphere would leak out around his welds, and rasping curses as he welded the ominously hissing microscopic cracks. But then all of our compulsive tasks were hopeless, including mine—searching with the pitiful manual instrumentation left to us for a cloud-covered planet to give us shelter before our fatally damaged survival systems totally collapsed . . . It was hopeless, hopeless . . . as futile as our pulsing distress beam out here beyond the Einsteinian Curve, out here in this cold, achingly empty universe . . .

I had returned to my post and settled in again to monitor the EV scope when I saw it—misty, indistinct, vaguely coral. I narrowed scope and focused—and soon shouted for Ross.

Cruiser of the Americas 991, blind, deaf, partially paralyzed, retained enough navigational capability for Coulter to maneuver us into the star system—an optical binary, I noted—and then he muscled and cursed us into tumbling orbit around the coral planet, Hanigan and Ross punching at unresponsive stabilizer keys until Coulter said in his raspy voice, "Forget it. The gyros won't fire except in random pattern."

"I can't make consistent readings tumbling like this," I said, strapped into my module and concentrating on my gauges, on the rapidly shifting elements of surface data, the tantalizing glimpses of blurred landscape on the screen. "But there's no obvious indication of intelligent life."

"Who cares? What choice do we have?" Hanigan's red moustache was quivering as it always did when he was agitated. "We make it here or we don't make it."

"Let's go," Ross ordered, removing his restraint straps.

"Wait," I said. "What's coming over the IFC?"

The Interplanetary Frequency Channel was flaring with static that seemed—to me—rhythmic, repetitive.

"Must be something we reconnected wrong," Hanigan said impatiently. "Let's go."

We donned our EV suits and boarded the tiny craft poised in the launch pod—our final hope. I had taken all my exobiology instrumentation to quickly ascertain when we landed—if it was not already apparent—whether we would die in this alien environment, and if so how soon and in what manner, and whether I would die in that manner or in my own.

We had just taken off when our EV's short range radio crackled to life. ". . . acknowledge . . . Attention unknown craft, acknowledge . . . Attention—"

As we gaped at each other in astonishment, Ross managed to utter, *"Cruiser of the Americas niner-niner-one. Who the hell are you?"*

"There is little time and more pressing concerns." The voice was female, cool, bell-like in its clarity. And commanding. "Set landing coordinates on frequency one-eight-niner point—" The voice issued precise instructions, and soon we locked onto a directional beam.

Coulter said in a stunned voice, "Jim, this can't be one of our bases. Not out here. Jim—"

Ross, having recovered himself, demanded in his most resonant voice, "Who are you? Acknowledge."

"A representative of this world. Your questions must wait until planetfall."

Hanigan said excitedly, "Jim, a ship! On orbital path! I picked it up just before it went out of range!"

"Who are you?" Ross demanded over the IFC. He said to us, "We need to know exactly what we're getting into here."

Ross's dark eyes were baffled; and he doesn't like to be confused or frustrated. Under our circumstances I myself would not have pursued the matter of identification until we landed—but this was not the first time I'd questioned Ross's judgement.

Repeatedly Ross demanded, "Who are you, acknowledge."

But there was no reply. I was pleased with the apparently female personage on the mysterious coral planet.

"Distinctly uncooperative if not unfriendly," Ross said through tight lips. "Code four landing precautions."

I sighed inaudibly. This was lunacy. They were benefactors. They had not been hostile. They had contacted us, assisted with our landing. But our landing would be backed up by full electron power at the ready, with the real possibility of hostilities. After the sheer miracle of finding this world, we might never live to set foot upon it . . . But I maintained silence, as of course one of my inferior rank is required to do.

We landed on a flat perfect site, a wide clearing covered with waving ivory-blue grass and surrounded on three sides by sharply rising hills. "Perfect for them to cover us," Ross growled.

Quickly I took atmospheric readings while the others surveyed with telescopic probes.

"Nothing around but small animal life," Coulter pronounced.

"Breathable," I shouted. "Breathable air! Twenty-one point—"

"Full EV gear," Ross ordered impassively, as I knew he would. Commanders become commanders by being cautious, not adventurous or optimistic.

We donned our EV suits, Hanigan included, although he would remain on board for this code four landing and cover us with the EV's weaponry.

The clearing on all sides of us remained empty, vegetation stirring in vagrant breezes. The men scanned the clearing anxiously; I busied myself with taking further atmospheric and soil readings, increasingly elated as optimum figures registered on all my gauges.

"Attention *Cruiser EV niner-niner-one*," said the cool precise voice. "Our scanners detect electron-charged weapons on board your ship. You are required to deenergize these weapons."

Ross said, his lips thin and tight, "We come in peace. We will not disarm until we are certain of *your* intentions."

"We greet you in peace. This is our world and you will not be allowed on it unless you disarm your weapons."

I ventured to Ross, "They're not asking that we destroy them, Commander. Only deenergize."

"She's right," Coulter rasped. "We can bring them to power again in less than an hour, Jim."

"What choice do we have?" Hanigan, as usual, had gone to the heart of the matter.

Ross glared at Hanigan and said tersely into the transmitter, "Terms accepted." He said to us, "But first, for security I want all this grass around us burned off. Hanigan, burn it."

Hanigan had cut the first swath when we were momentarily blinded by the flash of a laser beam over our EV.

"The next burst will strike you. Cease fire immediately. Grass cover is vital to the ecological survival of this area."

"Space bilge," growled Coulter.

"Acknowledged," Ross said into the transmitter, barely concealing his fury. "We cease fire."

Working the switches in tandem, we disarmed the two electron guns. Ross seized the transmitter. *"Cruiser EV niner-niner-one,* we have disarmed as you demand."

"We pick up small weapons readings."

"Sidearms only," Ross protested. "Request we be allowed to retain these. We may need them for hunting, food-gathering."

The voice was flat. "Killing for food is not necessary and not allowed. Disarm these weapons."

"Acknowledged." Ross slammed down the transmitter. "Do it," he ordered us. "Damn them, we'll have our day . . ."

As I drained the power pack of the last weapon, a wide scope rifle, the receiver crackled, *"Cruiser EV niner-niner-one,* you may disembark upon Maternas."

Maternas. The word echoed in me as we donned our headgear and lowered the ramp. My mind was filled with the images I'd absorbed as we had descended to this coral world: great seas, continent masses covered with vegetation and magnificent mountain ranges and glaciers and volcanoes . . . a varied and fascinating world. I was consumed with curiosity about its inhabitants, hopeful that they would be Earth-like in these Earth-like conditions, like the inhabitants of Verna-III. With language synthesizers in existence for over two hundred years it was not startling that they communicated in our language—but out here? There could be no such undiscovered civilization out here. This corner of the galaxy had been sketchily charted, but indeed charted. I had detected no visible technology even as we'd descended to the surface. But then, as we all knew, the Service did have its secrets. Perhaps this was one of our military observation bases, camouflaged and clandestine, on this far distant outpost of the galaxy. But a woman, to command our landing? That wasn't possible . . .

Sifting these thoughts, I followed the men down the ramp and set foot on the lovely world of Maternas, and saw coming toward us six hovercraft.

We stood in our ceremonial row at the foot of the ramp and stared as the six craft landed in a semi-circle and only women debarked. There was no sign of weapons, no indication that this was either a ceremonial or military delegation. They wore pants and shirts mostly, a few trouser suits and tunics. A distinguished-looking older woman was clad in a blue robe; her fingers moved dextrously over the sensor-plates of a manual recorder. Another woman flung a silver cape imperiously over a shoulder and stood with hands on hips to contemplate us, her lips pursed disapprovingly.

They gathered around, staring at us as we gaped at them. They were handsome women, some much more than handsome. I can only speculate how we must have appeared to them, standing at attention in our white EV suits trimmed in navy and red, navy blue boots on our feet, oxygen helmets on our heads, our shoulders emblazoned with the flags of the Americas.

A gnome of a woman with enormous breasts stepped forward. She wore a green robe under a green cape which hung slightly askew; she pushed it back impatiently, causing the cape to hang even further askew. This extraordinary personage looked us over with wonderfully vivid green eyes and then spoke the first direct words uttered between us and the inhabitants of this world: "Take off those silly hoods," she said. "You look perfectly ridiculous."

I unsnapped my helmet; I would no more have disobeyed her than my own mother.

"Lieutenant!" Ross bellowed at me.

"Why not?" Hanigan said. "We'll have no choice eventually, Jim."

Glaring at me, Ross ordered, "All personnel shall remove their helmets."

A murmur arose from the women as my hair cascaded over my white-clad shoulders. I breathed in air that was sweet, warm, delicious. Then the gnome of a woman said to me, "Hello, my dear. Are you by any chance hetero-sexual? It would be so nice to have another on the planet."

Struck momentarily dumb by this question, I could only croak, "Who are you?"

She shrugged. "You, my dear, may call me Mother."

"Great Grimaldi," Coulter said in a husky, stunned whisper.

"Grimaldi?" The gnome who called herself Mother turned to the distinguished woman clad in the blue robe.

"Twenty-first century United States president," the woman said.

"Of course, Minerva," Mother said. "I must be getting senile."

Ross squared his shoulders and attempted to gain some control over this surreal situation. "Madam, I am James Ross, Commander of *Cruiser of the Americas nine-nine-one*, and this is my crew. Our navigator, Colonel Rolf Coulter." Coulter stepped forward and bowed awkwardly. "Our systems engineer, Colonel Roger Hanigan." Hanigan stepped forward, fumbling with his headgear, eyes darting over the women. "Our exobiologist, Lieutenant Laurel Meredith." I also stepped forward, irresistibly smiling at the gnome of a woman who winked at me as if this were a joke shared by only the two of us.

"It would be tiresome to introduce us all," Mother told Ross. "And there is only one name you need to know." She called, "Megan? Where are you, dear?"

A tall slender woman strode forward, dressed in black pants and a white shirt. I sensed immediately that she had remained at the rear of the group to scrutinize us, and I somehow also knew instinctively that she was the woman of bell-like voice who had commanded our landing and disarming.

Even among these women she was exceptional. She looked at us with rectangular eyes identical in color to Mother's, and to a ring I wore—emerald, my favorite of all Earth stones. Her eyes were interested and coolly curious as they surveyed me, lingering on my hair which is my one physical pride, its length apparently not the custom here; the hairstyles on these women—including her own dark hair—were simple, shoulder-length at most, utilitarian. I stared at her; she was the most arresting woman I had ever seen.

"I am Megan."

If Ross had also been affected by her presence, it was not now visible. Immediately his posture assumed belligerence; he also had recognized the bell-toned voice. Booted feet spread widely apart, gloved hands on his hips, he glowered at her and asked peremptorily, with a trace of contempt, "Where are your men?"

The green-eyed woman—Megan—crossed her arms and with an impish and attractive grin looked expectantly down at Mother. But Mother merely gave Megan's arm an absent pat; she was examining Ross.

Ross is not tall, but his burly swarthiness, his dark thin hair cut close to his scalp, his flat black eyes, have always reminded me of a portrait I once saw of ancient times, of a Tartar spurring a horse across the Russian Steppes. Mother's expression told me that she found Ross—for lack of another word—unsavory.

Ross repeated, "Where are your men?"

"We are of a species," Mother said slowly, her bright eyes fastened on Ross, "that devours the male after mating."

The women roared with laughter and so did I, irresistibly; until Ross—taken aback as were all the men—recovered himself. "Lieutenant!" he bellowed.

I found it difficult to stand at attention while all these women around me continued to laugh, but I did my best.

"Madam," Ross grated, "I see no reason for the levity of your—"

"Phosh," Mother said witheringly. "Did we ask you here?"

"Our ship," Ross protested. "A particle storm struck—"

"A particle storm?" Flinging her silver cape over a shoulder, the imperious woman I had noticed before strode forward, formidably handsome in her maturity. She demanded, "How could anyone be stupid enough to be caught in a particle storm?"

"The matter is complex," muttered Ross, his face dark and suffused with fury as the women again roared with laughter. "How could any of you possibly understand or—"

"Commander," Megan interrupted. Her glance had just left me; I knew that she had seen my amusement at Ross's helpless rage. "Commander," Megan said, "this woman who gives you honor by speaking to you is esteemed Hera, an astrophysicist."

"But if you were stupid enough to get caught," Hera continued inexorably as if never interrupted, "then proper precautions should have minimized your damage."

I heard this with bitter satisfaction; and I noticed that Coulter and Hanigan had focused their gazes carefully downward. So Ross's actions had been inappropriate, born of panic. As I had suspected.

"I took the decision which my best judgment—"

"Details," Mother interrupted, her hand raised in a command for silence. "Bore the girls with all that, not me. I've been trying my best to be civil but . . ." Pulling her cape around her, she said, "I know you girls can manage," and stalked off, a phalanx of strong young women surrounding her in a ceremonial if informal guard.

"Who are you?" Ross demanded angrily of Megan. "What are you doing here? Where are your cities? Your towns? Your—"

"You were not invited here," Megan said evenly. "We are under no obligation to answer any of your questions."

"Just a minute, you—"

"Food will be provided, also your other reasonable requirements. You may not leave this area without permission."

"Now just a minute, you can't—"

As Ross took half a step forward a dozen women surrounded him, silver rod-like objects in their hands trained on him.

Megan said easily, "I'm certain Commander Ross did not intend to be foolish."

Ross stepped back and squared his shoulders. "How long," he asked stiffly, "do you intend to keep all of us confined? And uninformed?"

"Until we decide. Lieutenant Meredith?"

I started at my name and rank as spoken by the cool and melodious voice.

"You may accompany us if you wish. However, if you do so you may not return to your ship until our decisions are made."

I said without hesitation, "My duty is to remain."

She nodded, and added to that a brief glance which seemed approving.

Ross said, "Decide what?"

Megan looked at Ross, and apparently felt no need to reply.

"To kill us? Is that what you need to decide?"

"We could have performed that act at any time," she said softly.

"We're your captives. Your prisoners."

"Until we decide the conditions of your release."

"How long?"

"Very possibly a long time, Commander." She turned from us and walked away, followed by all her companions.

The hovercraft soon departed, rising over the sharply canted hills. Ross watched until their craft disappeared. "Lieutenant, perhaps you'd want to . . . run further tests."

It wasn't a question; he hadn't called me Laurel as he usually did. The men boarded the EV and I busied myself with grass and soil samples. It wasn't the first time I'd been excluded from their discussions, but under these circumstances it was less infuriating. My separateness—my femaleness—had become even more visible, my allegiance suspect under the domination of female captors who had granted me permission, however conditional, to join them.

Also, I didn't mind this particular ostracism because I needed to sort through my own perceptions. But I couldn't extract much coherency from a turmoil of mind crowded with images of these confident women, especially the strong

and purposeful woman named Megan . . . Never had I conceived of women in ascendancy over men, much less with
such ease of control. My ostracism increasingly rankled as
I packed my samples; soon unaccustomed anger grew out
of my resentment. In defiance of Ross's implied order I
stalked aboard the EV.

As I'd expected, Ross and Coulter and Hanigan were in
discussion—heated—which abruptly halted as I entered.

"I'm a member of this crew," I stated to the scowling
Ross, "and if I'm not to be included in your discussions
and decisions under these extraordinary circumstances,
then advise these women that I accept their offer."

"Now wait a minute, Laurel," Hanigan said with the
facile smile I hated. "I was just making that very point to
Jim."

"He was indeed," Ross said smoothly. "And we're all
in agreement about it. Sit down, Laurel. Join us."

"We didn't want to worry your pretty head," Coulter
rasped.

For a thousandth time I reminded myself of Coulter's
rank, and held my tongue. Their sudden conciliation did
not deceive me; I cynically wondered what use they'd been
plotting to make of me. But I asked, "Who do you think
they are?"

Ross answered, looking at me shrewdly, "Stories circu-
lated some few years ago about a group of women taking a
ship and leaving Earth—"

"I heard all the stories." Coulter's voice rose, obviously
in resumption of an argument. "They were all officially
denied. And anyway, no ship could escape our pursuit
craft."

"So they told us it never happened," Hanigan sneered.
"I never believe anything I'm told by our sacred government."

"I saw filmed evidence, Rolf," Ross said to Coulter. "An
ore carrier—"

"Doctored film, a hoax."

"Rolf," Hanigan said, "there's a ship orbiting this planet

that looks big enough to be an ore carrier from what I could tell."

"They claimed they blew it up at the EC," Ross said. "And I did see the film."

"Maybe that's the part of the film that was doctored," Hanigan said.

I listened with interest to the continuation of the argument I'd interrupted. I too had heard these stories . . . and other stories. Among our Women's Officer Corps there'd been whispered discussions of recordings in existence telling of Earth's pursuit craft tracking a ship which had tauntingly identified itself as *Amelia Earhart* as it leaped to hyperspace. And there were more stories—gleeful stories—that the escaping women had been exceptional, highly gifted, vital to the professions they'd abandoned . . . and that they and their strange ship had outwitted their pursuers, had vanished among the star systems . . . And that their disappearance had caused turmoil—and somewhat more liberalized treatment of women in all the professions, including my own . . .

Ross asked, too casually, "Laurel, what do you know about this?"

I shrugged. "The same stories."

"But think about it, men," Hanigan exulted. "If it is these women, then we're on a world of—Damn, we've landed in paradise!"

I suggested drily, "Your enthusiasm may not be shared by the inhabitants of . . . paradise."

But Coulter slapped Hanigan on the back and playfully flexed his own muscles, puffing out his chest. "Come on, Laurel. When they have a choice . . . I mean, when women really have a choice—"

Ross said cautiously, smiling, "We'd better be selective. Some of these women, they're big. And look to be in as good shape as we are."

"Better," I could not resist saying.

The receiver crackled to life. Megan's cool voice inquired

about our comfort, whether we would prefer their food or our own.

Ross replied shortly, "Ours."

She went on to inform us of the limits of the confinement area within which we must remain—three square kilometers. Ross's face darkened with anger. We were less than a kilometer due west from the sea, she stated, and gave us its temperature and tide times, cautioning that we must not swim at high tide. In concise language she warned us of the suddenness and strength of the planet's nocturnal winds, and of the preparation we should make to secure our craft. Then she bade us a courteous farewell. Ross replied with a muttered obscenity; but Megan had switched off.

We made a meal from the EV's ample food store, and continued our speculations. Where were their settlements? The consensus opinion—underground. How sophisticated was their technology? From all appearances—formidably sophisticated. Would they eventually agree to assist us in repairing our Cruiser, and allow us to leave? Whoever they were, if concealment of their existence was so primary a concern—not very likely.

The men were still debating this after the meal. I asked myself: Since the circumstance wasn't forced on me, why remain in their company? I left them, ostensibly to perform more tests. With purely sensory perceptions, I explored our area of confinement, the tiny expanse of this lovely world allotted to us, making my way through the high grass, removing my gloves to stroke it. I strolled toward the hills, acutely aware of soft warm air that stirred my hair, the late afternoon sunlight of this coral world gentle on my face.

Near the hills I entered a wooded cove of small but defiant trees shaped tortuously by the winds like some of our cypress trees on Earth. One, long since uprooted, lay across the base of another, and I sat on it, straddling it, my back against the living tree.

For some time I watched the sunlight dance in dappled patterns on the grassy ground as the needle-covered branches swayed in the warm breezes. I opened the neck of my jacket to savor sun and air, conscious of the loneliness in me that could never be assuaged by any of the companions a kilometer or so from me . . . I longed to express the sweet sadness of my emotion in music, wishing I'd brought my crystal reed with me. But I did have my journal, and was recording these events when Coulter found me.

III

Journal of Lt. Laurel Meredith
2214.2.12

I'm exhausted . . . But I'll record these events as long as I'm able to . . . It's very late this night, my first night in the house of the women called Vesta and Carina. They are mates—indeed, lovers.

I'm having difficulty adjusting to this unsettling aspect of my surroundings. Even while knowing rationally that on this world of women they would of course choose love partners among themselves, that of course their lives, their homes, their art would reflect and glorify their own physical beauty and the physicality of their love, I am discomfited by it. Their love is forbidden on Earth, a taboo enforced in our culture by a proliferation of laws and by all the communication media.

But I am far ahead of myself, of what happened to bring me here to this house of Vesta and Carina on the Toklas River in the colony of Cybele.

As I sat peacefully in the wooded cove not far from the EV, Coulter had inflicted his unwelcome presence on me, greeting me and then staring at the small expanse of throat I'd exposed to this world's gentle suns, now beginning their descent to the horizon.

"I want to talk to you, Laurel."

How I detested that huskiness in his voice! Over the

months I'd learned enough in our close quarters about my shipmates to regard all of them with distaste. "There's nothing to be said," I answered, understanding his reference and therefore unconcerned with my rank or my obvious hostility.

His blue eyes narrowed. "You know how I feel, Laurel. You know it very well." He took my hands.

I tore my hands out of his. "Don't you touch me! I *forbid* it!"

"We'll never leave here. Never." He grasped my shoulders, tried to draw me to him. "You're what I want, none of these women here. Service regulations don't matter anymore. Or what Ross wants us to do—"

"Don't touch me!" Furiously I pushed him away, and stood to confront him. "I ordered you not to touch me, I'll put you on report to Ross, don't think I won't, you—"

"Fool, you little fool—" He leaped to his feet and came toward me and what I saw in his face made me afraid. I tried to run but he caught me easily, tangling his hands in my hair, pulling me against him as I struggled and pushed at him. His arms tightened powerfully, his mouth searched for mine.

We were both flung violently to the ground.

"Lieutenant, over here."

I lay dazed, but recognized Megan's voice, and realized that Coulter and I had been struck by an energy charge. I got to my feet, stumbled over to her; she stood on the fallen log, feet braced, one hand extended to me, the other holding a silver object trained on Coulter. I reached to her; she grasped my hand and with unexpected strength pulled me over the log and behind her.

Coulter got to his feet, came at her. And was again hurled to the ground.

"Colonel, don't be foolish. Leave us. Return to your ship."

But Coulter rose to his feet swearing and came at her again—with the same result. He scrambled to his knees and rasped, "Put that damn thing away just once you coward bitch—"

To my utter astonishment she did so, tucking the silver weapon into her belt.

"No!" I shouted, "he'll—"

Coulter, leaping to his feet, did not hesitate. As he charged she seized the tree branch above her and with a swift whipping motion of her body, drove her boots into his chest.

With an "Oof!" of surprise he staggered and stumbled backward, then regained his balance. Fists clenching and unclenching, a crouching beast of pure menace, he stalked her as she stood braced and waiting on the log. Arms extended, he rushed her again.

And was hurled to the ground. And this time hauled to his feet and secured, his arms pinioned, by two burly women. A dozen more materialized from the woods behind us, among them a handsome woman with short-cropped blonde hair and dressed in green pants and a shirt. She confronted Megan, hands on her hips. "Megan," she sighed in exasperation.

Megan said with an entirely attractive grin, "Danya, what took you so long?"

"You know very well we were a distance further from here than you." With a motion of her head toward Coulter, Danya asked with an amused smile, "What method of hand-to-hand combat were you planning next?"

Again Megan grinned. "I'd have thought of something."

And with that grin, humorous, prideful, I felt a stirring ... of something stronger than admiration, an emotion I could not identify.

"What business is this of yours?" Coulter snapped, pulling against the two women who held his arms secured. "We're Earth citizens, you have no right to interfere."

Megan nodded to the two women holding Coulter. "Adria, Paige, thank you. You may release the Colonel."

Coulter brushed at the grass and soil staining the pristine white of his EV suit. Megan waited until he finished and looked up at her.

"This is our world. You are subject to our standards. Not," she added contemptuously, "your own."

"Spying on us," Coulter snarled. "I should have known."

"You should have expected some kind of surveillance, Colonel, when you come here bearing military rank on a ship bristling with weapons. But still we had expected better of you. You were under random sweep surveillance only, and only by chance I monitored your . . . behavior."

She turned to me. Her voice was firm but her green eyes seemed wounded. "We cannot overlook or chance recurrence of . . . this. We extend to you again the offer of safe conduct among us. If you still prefer to remain with your ship, then we must sequester Colonel Coulter elsewhere."

I hesitated. Coulter's absence would only create further stresses between myself and the men, I decided. "I'll go with you."

"Laurel, let them take me. You know I never meant to hurt you." Coulter was calm now, his voice soft and husky. "But you don't know that about these . . . creatures. God knows what they'll do to you when they get their hands on you, they . . . they'll . . . they'll probably . . ."

Coulter faltered into obviously furious silence; the women were responding to his words with increasingly raucous laughter. "Lieutenant," Megan said to me, her eyes fixed derisively on Coulter, "is this a concern to you? I can give you no assurance other than our word."

"It's not a concern," I declared as bravely as I could, with a passing thought to Coulter's behavior should he ever be in a position to take female captives.

"We can provide for all your needs," Megan told me, "but is there anything you wish from your ship?"

After a moment I replied, "My crystal reed."

"Danya," Megan said, "would you escort the Colonel to his ship and then bring the Lieutenant's crystal reed to my house?"

"Consider it done." Danya spun Coulter around and sent him on his way with a far from gentle shove.

Megan led me to a hovercraft scarcely large enough

for two. I asked, "Why did you put your weapon away? You must have known—"

"My greatest weakness," she said seriously, "seems to be my inability to resist a challenge."

And then there was that grin again. I said awkwardly, "If I may call you Megan, then will you call me Laurel?"

She climbed into the craft, extended a hand and pulled me in with her. She smiled. "Very well, Laurel."

"I see why you were able to rescue me so quickly," I murmured. In scant seconds we had come upon her house which I did not immediately recognize as a house until the craft dipped into an alcove of it, so artfully had it been carved from the rocky coastline. So this was why their settlements were not observable from the air.

"I was nearest to you," she said quietly as we walked into her house. "When you had to push him away a second time I knew to come. And of course I signaled for Danya and our security team."

"Thank you. This is my first mission, all the men were a trial but he was the worst, he wouldn't believe or accept my invoking of the privacy regulations, he'd have been more of a problem except for Ross, he's a rules and regulations Commander, his lack of imagination almost killed us—"

I knew I was rambling like a fool, speaking with only part of my mind. I was staring helplessly at the house we had entered, struggling to absorb its searing simplicity and beauty. The wall tapestries were woven complexities, the fleece floor coverings of warm earth tones, the furnishings of contrasting brilliant blues. There were many art objects ... Her house itself was pure art, beautiful in all its elements, overwhelming in its totality, each element intrinsically compelling, yet blending into the whole.

Hypnotized by a soaring sculpture of silver that reflected in its angular planes the colors and designs of the room, I whispered, "Did you make this?"

"No, that was created by Zandra. I have only the capability of appreciating it."

I asked abruptly, "What is your function here, Megan?"

She hesitated. "I am . . . a coordinator."

I understood her hesitation. I'd joined them because of circumstance, not conviction. I said, "I believe that you're the women who escaped on the ship you called *Amelia Earhart*. And I'm happy you succeeded."

She smiled. And relaxed visibly. "That makes things much simpler, Laurel."

She touched a place on a crystal table; a large section of tapestry disappeared to reveal lumiscreens and data receivers. All the screens were active; I recognized our EV on one, the surrounding area on another, in slow pan. "Please be comfortable," she said absently, eyes scanning her message screen. "I need but a moment . . ."

Then Danya arrived, bearing the case with my crystal reed. "The officers were conducting a meeting in loud tones as I left," she said with a chuckle. "Commander Ross was most upset with Colonel Coulter."

"He would be," I said, visualizing with amusement Ross's apoplexy at this new complication.

"Shall I escort Lieutenant Meredith to her quarters?" Danya asked politely.

I looked at Megan; but her gaze was on the screens. "Laurel," she asked, "have you eaten?"

"No," I answered impulsively, curious about her and wanting to remain with her longer.

"Then we'll take you to Vesta's now, and later I can—"

"I require little food," I interrupted, attempting to correct my error. "I have no need—"

"Would you mind answering some questions, then? Perhaps sharing what food I have?"

"I wouldn't mind at all."

"Megan, security is fully functional," Danya said. "Relax and leave all the monitoring to us after your long day."

I had already seen that Megan was held in considerable esteem on this world. Danya's tone was entirely deferential, and she looked at Megan with admiring affection.

"With full confidence and gladness," Megan said, touching the crystal table. Tapestry again covered the walls. "I'll bring Lieutenant Meredith to Vesta's house shortly. Good night, Danya." Again that grin as she extended a hand. "And thank you."

Smiling, Danya grasped Megan's hand and clasped it in her two. "If I hadn't been there in time, do you realize what the Unity would have done to me?" She bade us both good night.

"You know nothing of our food, you'll simply have to trust me." Megan moved gracefully in preparation of our meal and I watched with pleasure, watched her fine hands pulling temperature tabs, arranging both steaming and chilled contents on two highly polished curved glassine surfaces which adjusted to tray height as she served us. She poured drink from a metallic flagon. I tasted it first: a most exquisite wine. We ate with a variety of implements which were strange to me and no more efficient than those I knew, but pretty, and interesting to wield.

"How much is known on Earth of our Unity?"

"Strong rumors. They persist stubbornly despite emphatic and constant denials." As we ate I related fully the stories I'd heard. She often smiled, and sometimes laughed, lovely laughter.

I ate very little of the wonderful and savory food; not only was I not hungry, but I was strangely unsettled by her, and by the green eyes that looked so perceptively into mine. She ate with good appetite, asking questions about events and places on Earth, obviously enjoying our meal together, her long fingers handling her implements with delicate grace.

"Not much has changed since we left," she mused, "but then it's been only fifteen of our years." She removed my tray. "You ate little. I so rarely have a guest . . . was the food not to your liking?"

"No, it was . . . I was . . . I—It was wonderful," I stammered like an idiot.

"If you liked this," she said, smiling, "Vesta's creations will enchant you. She's truly an artist with food."

I watched her place our trays in a disposal unit and pull down white shirt sleeves she had rolled to the elbow.

Obviously, she was planning now to take me to the person named Vesta.

"Vesta's house was built with room for guests," she told me. "She's a psychologist—sometimes patients stay with her for a time. We surely did not plan for guests when we built Cybele."

She looked at me then. "You have not seen our suns set, our evening come. It's always extraordinary here at Damon Point. Would you like to stay longer and see it?"

We walked less than half a kilometer over increasingly soft mossy terrain toward the water's edge where waves crashed and wheeling birds uttered shrill cries. An unobtrusive coral marker was fastened amid the ivory-colored moss. Megan opened a container secured into the ground and drew out a fleece which she spread over the moss. "I keep this here," she explained. "I swim most mornings depending on the tides."

We sat, her with legs drawn up, fine hands clasping her knees. She did not speak; the silence between us was comfortable. The coral sky swiftly, swiftly darkened; and then no words seemed appropriate.

The air had become suddenly chill; I felt it keenly on my ungloved hands and uncovered head. She rose and drew the fleece fully up around me, saving only a corner for herself to sit on. "I am well accustomed to our climate," she said, and gazed again out to the horizon. She was now in my line of sight, part of the beauty I viewed, her shirt very white against the royal blue sky, rippling against her slender body in the breeze, her collar fluttering around the smooth ivory sculpture of her face and throat, the dark tendrils of her hair. She turned and looked at me, eyes deep luminous green in the silver light.

"We must leave now," she said. "The nocturnals will soon begin."

We returned to the warmth and security of her house. There she served me again from the flagon of wine and explained about the carvings made in her house when it was built. I listened in amazement to soaring tones and random melodies as her house sang in the rising winds . . .

I heard the winds die . . . Now she would surely take me away from here. And she picked up the case containing my crystal reed and gave it me. Then paused. "This instrument, will you play it for me?"

I don't reproduce conventional music on my reed. Rather, I create harmonic patterns similar to the singing of Megan's house in the wind—except that my patterns are structured, emotionally shaped, and seek the purest tonalities to express emotion. I was about to explain this to Megan as I lifted my reed from its case, then decided that I wouldn't, that it wasn't necessary.

I sat across from her on a teal blue chaise, and with my eyes closed, I played the composition most personal, most closely held to me, one I had never played for anyone . . . the melancholy and grieving harmonies I had composed two years ago at the death of my mother. I breathed into my reed purest notes of this emotion and did not open my eyes until I had finished.

And looked into eyes wet with tears, at cheeks streaked with tears . . . In great distress I put my instrument down and knelt to her and took her face in my hands and stroked the tears from her face as tenderly as I could. "Megan, I did not mean for this."

Her hands took mine. "It was not the grief of your music, but my pleasure in its beauty."

Her words gave me intense pleasure; and to make her smile, I smiled. "Do you always cry when you receive pleasure?"

"I don't know," she said seriously, "you are the first to give such pleasure."

"The first?" I asked with a feeling of shock.

"The first." She released my hands. "I must take you to Vesta's."

I spoke my wish boldly: "Can I not remain here?"

"That . . . would not be . . . appropriate."

It was the first awkwardness between us. And I realized that this was indeed a world of women, and what that ultimately—shockingly—meant.

We flew in the hovercraft without speaking until our landing. Then she turned to me. "If you have any difficulties with your situation here, I urge you to talk to Vesta. She's a dear and wonderful woman. Tomorrow I would like you to stay with her and also see Minerva the historian who will be most interested in talking with you."

"Will I be seeing you again?"

"The day after tomorrow is significant to us," she said softly, "our Anniversary Day. A day of celebration and event. Would you like to attend as my guest?"

"Yes, Megan. I would."

And so I went off to stay with Vesta . . .

IV

Journal of Lt. Laurel Meredith
2214.2.13

Vesta, a tiny woman of puckish humor and quiet yet bustling energy, has kind gray eyes that reflect a gentle and sensitive nature. She seems every woman's wish for a sister, a friend. Carina, considerably younger, is a big silent woman who hovers about Vesta with anxious awareness, loving concern.

They made me comfortable in a main room soothing in its warm tones and filled with low and well-cushioned furnishings to encourage reclining. They served me wine. I sipped, and said incredulously, "This is even more wonderful than what Megan served."

"Hers has aged beyond best drinking time," Vesta said in distress. "She has neglected to ask for replenishment." She sighed. "Megan will not take the time to enjoy even simple aspects of the goodness of our life. She keeps only prepared foods at her house, as if she were on visitation to another continent. Nourishing and healthy food, yes, but hardly . . ." She sighed again.

I asked carefully, "What keeps her so busy?"

Vesta's answer was entirely unsatisfactory: "Everything."

I was curious about Megan, especially after the tender moment with her following my playing, but lacked a convenient method of asking questions. Who was Megan, exactly? What work, exactly, did she do? What were the personal circumstances of her life?

"It's late," Carina said firmly, one of the few times she had spoken that evening.

I slept restlessly—my kaleidoscopic dreams filled with images of a coral world, of confident women, of emerald eyes and a tear-streaked face.

I arose to find Vesta and Carina breakfasting.

"My Carina is captain of a hydroflit," Vesta told me proudly as I gazed at Carina, who looked very strong and capable in slicker pants and a form-fitting jacket stretched over her broad shoulders, her soft hair tucked up under a cap. "She fishes the ocean with her crew."

Carina glanced at me with shy dark eyes, smiled adoringly at Vesta, and resumed eating her breakfast. I soon understood her undivided attention. There was sweet-tart fruit juice, tiny berries of varying tastes, a hot and delicious main dish composed of I know not what, bread that crunched like toast but melted on the tongue, a hot bracing liquid that far surpassed coffee. I can't really describe tastes and textures—but each mouthful was exquisite sensory delight.

I said to Vesta in awe, "Megan told me of your cooking artistry. May I observe you sometime?"

"Today, if you wish. Food is simple, it's just good ingredients. The complexities of preparation are greatly exaggerated."

Like music, I thought in amusement, my affection for this dear woman increasing.

As we finished breakfast a gray-robed and quite lovely older woman named Diana arrived. She nodded absently when we were introduced, surveying me. "I think blues and browns," she said mysteriously to Vesta, and went briskly out to her hovercraft to return with swatches of fabric in her arms. "Come with me, dear."

Scarcely surprised any longer by anything on this world, I followed her into my quarters.

Selecting among her fabrics, she asked distractedly, "May I measure you? For clothing?"

I replied, bemused but pleased with the prospect of wearing something other than the enveloping EV suit, "This is very kind of you."

"Not at all," she said in the same distracted voice, as she held a bolt of pale blue cloth up to me. "We cannot allow you to wear white or black on Maternas."

"You can't?" My mind wrestled with possible reasons for such an arcane custom—and that Megan had worn a white shirt and black pants.

"No, dear. Only Megan wears those colors."

"Megan—white—black—" I stuttered stupidly, stripping off my suit.

Diana surveyed me impersonally, as if I were a field to be planted. Then she said, "That hair of yours is far from your only asset."

"Thank you, but why those colors only for Megan?"

"She is our leader."

After I heard those four words I stood mute and allowed Diana to do what she would. In only a few minutes I was draped in a knee-length ice blue tunic, my arms bare, the material gathered softly over my breasts and belted at my waist.

"It's quite lovely," I said, considerably understating the beauty of my dress.

"I'll just make a few more while I'm at it," Diana said, assessing me once again. "With that hair you should also wear . . . browns, yellows. Vesta will get you some sandals . . . You'll look like one of us now, except for that hair . . . And I have a feeling long hair will come into fashion very soon in Cybele. Off with you now, Minerva is chafing to see you."

Carina took me to Minerva's history chamber by hover-craft, thus allowing me only tantalizing glimpses of the contours of Cybele.

Minerva, slim and straight, stately in her deep blue robe, greeted me softly, and then disarmed me by kissing my cheek; then she charmed me with a gentle manner and her insightful grasp of the history of Earth; and soon afterward further disarmed me with quicksilver humor. She had been informed by Megan of my knowledge of the escape from Earth, and therefore had no concerns about what she should reveal.

I soon asked, "You keep all the records of this world's history?"

"Yes, both image and verbal history of important events. And I record vital statistics and our Joinings."

If I had not already suspected during my time with Vesta what was meant by Joinings, I would have guessed from observing Minerva with the young woman named Christa— tall, brown-haired, handsome, her body so magnificent in its size and strength that she might well be a living model of heroic sculpture. As I arrived she was quietly consulting with Minerva, and when Minerva appeared agitated, Christa had taken her hands and gazed at her lovingly; Minerva's face had softened to tranquility, and she had lifted Christa's hands briefly to her lips . . .

I pushed this image forcibly from my mind, uncomfortable with its strangeness. But I asked curiously, "If you record Joinings, then you must also record . . . partings?"

She answered with quiet emphasis. "We share gladly in the joyfulness of a Joining, but the sorrows of parting are matters not for public notice or comment."

"But there must be problems to be solved, disagreements," I protested, vividly recalling the rancorous parting of my own parents, finally adjudicated by binding decree of the marital arbiters.

"We have no concerns here about property," she said, "and our children are little damaged by our partings."

This was a subject of compelling interest to me. I long to have my own children—but single women are forbidden the use of Estrova by Earth law, and I have not yet found a suitable husband and father. "The children here," I asked, "how are they raised? Educated?"

"In the most fertile environment we can provide," she answered simply.

I asked tentatively, "Minerva, how can you say your children are little damaged by your partings? How can that be?"

"It does not damage them greatly," she said gently, "but unhappiness between the birth parents is always felt by the child—"

"Yes," I murmured, remembering.

"—And healthy development of the personality comes only from exposure to many individuals and situations. Our child—Christa's and my Celeste—very early learned to spend time away from us, she soon learned the kinship of our Unity, that other adults value and care for her as well. And we all share in her teaching—"

"You do? How?" I had already considered that I might leave the Service after this mission, perhaps to teach young children. "Teaching is so specialized a profession—"

"And we do have specialists. Highly skilled women who organize our knowledge and determine its dissemination. But the dissemination itself is simple—almost all electronic. And since each child is given comprehensive education until a distinct field of interest emerges, we all have opportunities to contribute our own experience, our own presence. Tomorrow you'll see many of these things yourself. Megan will show you."

"Megan," I asked casually, "how did she become your leader?"

It was then that she allowed me to see and read the records of the journey to this world of Maternas. It was then I learned of Mother and the Inner Circle, of the choice of Megan . . . and that she had assumed the mantle of leadership at the age of twenty-three, the same age I am now . . . It was then that I learned the full scope of her leadership, her brilliance, her courage . . .

"Minerva," I murmured, "I suppose you've recorded Joinings . . . for Megan?"

"None," she replied sadly. "Her life has been taken up fully with the lives of us all. She has accepted a life of loneliness for our sake."

I thought again of Megan's tears at my music, and her words: *You are the first to give such pleasure . . .*

I will be seeing her tomorrow . . . Perhaps I could bring my crystal reed. Perhaps I could play for her again . . .

V

Personal Journal of Megan
14.12.28

The crisis of the Earthmen, while continuing, has eased in urgency. Commander Ross this morning requested permission for him and his men to explore Maternas at low-level altitudes while we pursue our discussions about their presence among us. I did inform him that repairs have begun on their Cruiser, and that he should not take this to signify any decision on our part.

As a condition of their departure, we required surrender of the electron cores of their weapons, offering in exchange charge rods which will be sufficient for their personal safety. Commander Ross agreed. Then, in an act of pure, even comical, irrationality, he and his men spent many hours separating the cores from their weapons. The Commander is surely aware that now that we have these cores, no conceivable circumstance could persuade us to return them, and their weapons are therefore worthless. But the symbolic act of actually surrendering them seems contrary to some deeply rooted instinct.

I am suspicious. I believe they have a plan . . .

They have left, however, and will be gone two weeks on their circumnavigation of Maternas—observed, of course; drones have been programmed and released from our faithfully orbiting *Amelia.*

Since tomorrow is our Anniversary Day, it is good to have the men gone, even temporarily, from our consciousness.

Of course there has been vociferous discussion about them in the Council. The decision not to aid a distress call was difficult enough, and very different from the reality of their presence. Proposals have ranged from outright release to re-settlement of them on another continent. Colonel Coulter's behavior with Lieutenant Meredith has not enhanced their case nor their welcome. All of our discussions have had decidedly uneasy undertones.

It was my decision to repair their ship, but agreement from the Council required maximum use of my personal prestige. It is clear to me what must eventually be done, although I do not speak it . . . I have today involved myself with the repair crew, enlisting the quiet and trustworthy Carina, temporarily reassigning her from her chosen activity. She speaks little, this big gentle woman, but her strength and wisdom exceeds that of many of us, and she, along with me, understands what must be done. We work together in unspoken communion.

Laurel is a disturbing complication. It gives me anguish to consider her months in space . . . her tender and sensitive nature amid her crew . . . I hear her quiet voice telling me that this was her first mission, that the men were "a trial," that Coulter would not believe or accept her invoking of the privacy regulations . . . When the Council speaks of releasing the men and their ship, I think of her back in space with them, especially Coulter . . . But if they have formed a plan as I suspect, this may very well decide the problem.

She is so young. I remember her standing at attention below the ramp of the EV as we arrived, the contours of her uniform already suggesting to me that she was a woman . . . Then she took off her helmet and that hair cascaded over her shoulders—thick and soft, luxuriant waves of rich browns and golds—and I saw how very young she was . . . It seems weeks, not years, since I was her age. I am suddenly so aware of the part of my life that is gone forever from me—my youth . . .

That she drew tears with her wonderful music does not disturb me. Had she been any of the women on this world, it would have disturbed me profoundly. I must always be strong for them, always in command of myself with these women of Maternas—it is required. I could only have shown the weakness of tears to her, and somehow I knew I could trust her.

I look forward to the relaxation of a day spent with her, I am eager for tomorrow to come. But she concerns me. She is among us but not one of us, and must be kept under informal surveillance; she has done nothing to warrant more. The best solution is to find an activity for her over the next weeks, or until the crisis is resolved . . . It is my intense hope she will express a desire to remain with us . . .

Venus will return tomorrow from her sojourn to the continent of Nin to celebrate Anniversary Day with us. The obvious choice would be to assign Laurel, an exobiologist, to work with her. But the prospect gives me considerable unease. It is impossible to gauge Laurel's overall attractiveness dressed as she is in an EV suit, but she is young and pretty, and that hair alone will be sufficient to draw Venus's attention. If Venus so chooses, she will focus all of her many charms on Laurel, regardless of any objections of mine . . .

I shall have to decide about Laurel. But in the meantime I look forward to tomorrow with her . . .

VI

Journal of Lt. Laurel Meredith
2214.2.14

For this day I'd chosen the pale yellow tunic Diana had created for me, its color as delicate as a sunbeam. Self-consciously, I extended a hand to Megan.

She took my hand, hers firm and cool. She informed me of the excursion of my shipmates, her voice subdued; oddly, she wouldn't let me see her eyes.

I looked at her boldly—and with acute pleasure. For this ceremonial day she wore a white silk shirt with puffed sleeves, her dark hair curling over its high collar. Her close-fitted black pants were tied at the waist with a coral sash. Knee-high boots were softly gleaming black. She looked at me then with her green eyes and it was I who looked away, heat rising to my face as I remembered the meaning on this world of one woman's glance lingering on another.

She said lightly, "Vesta was at my house yesterday personally delivering both a new supply of wine and yet another lecture on my deprived way of life."

I looked at her, trying not to smile. "Will this latest lecture have any good effect?"

"Probably not." She grinned. "It would be helpful if you would not bring me to her attention."

"If I speak too freely," I retorted, "you don't talk enough. I had to find out from Diana who you really are."

"Does that create . . . difference between us?"

I was astonished by the concern in her voice and the

sudden shyness—yes, shyness—in her eyes. I answered, "I've looked forward to this day with you, Megan. Do you have many special duties? Will you be able to show me Cybele?"

"I have duties. And I must open the games now." We were walking toward the hovercraft as she spoke. "This was once Mother's prerogative which has fallen to me. Mother becomes less patient and more irrascible with the years."

I nodded, remembering Mother's greeting at the EV and how she had so confounded us.

"Mother and I both make awards to the participants in the games. But I will have an opportunity to show you anything you wish to see."

We flew over a tranquil coral lake and into a huge natural amphitheater formed by high but gently shaped grass-covered mountains on three sides, the lake on the fourth. An audience of thousands was gathered along the canted slopes of the amphitheater, some in sheltered areas carved from the mountainsides, others taking their ease in the open air, on small plateaus. It was a casual, festive gathering of these thousands; most were lounging on fleece, with much evidence of food and drink.

Megan flew into the very center of the amphitheater, which I could now see was sectioned and shaped for athletic events. She landed and leaped from the hovercraft, assisting me from it amid a rising crescendo of sound.

I said impishly, "All that cheering is undoubtedly for me."

She grinned and led me to a cordoned-off area in which were assembled Mother and the six robed women I now knew were the Inner Circle. She presented me to Mother, who was draped in a green cape edged in gold and sat resplendent on a gold chaise.

Mother took my hand and patted it. "Welcome to our festivities, my dear. Now that you've shed that white sack, you're really quite lovely. Isn't she lovely, Megan?"

"Indeed she is," Megan said easily.

As I stood tongue-tied under the gaze of these two women with their identical eyes of emerald, my awkwardness was eased by the arrival of a member of the Inner Circle whom I had not seen before, a woman of remarkable beauty, her features sensually shaped perfection, her azure robe suggesting equal perfection of body. Her eyes were a more true azure than her robe, and rivaled Megan's in beauty.

"Megan, I have not met your guest."

"Nor have several other members of the Inner Circle," Megan replied. I noted the testiness of her tone. "Venus, I present Lieutenant Laurel Meredith." I also noted the formality of the introduction.

"I learned of your landing only this morning." Venus gazed at me with eyes hypnotic in their beauty. "I was on the continent of Nin on an expedition with . . . a friend."

"I know what you accomplished with your friend," Mother said tartly, "but did you do any work?"

Venus said with dignity, "Farica and I will be making our presentation to the Council, Mother. Perhaps you will be interested in our discoveries of—"

Mother waved a hand. "You know very well your poor old Mother isn't a bit interested in new bugs or strange shrubbery. Megan dear, let's get on with the games."

"Leave your guest to me," Venus said, smiling.

As Venus murmured something I didn't hear, I watched Megan mount a small platform amid rising applause; she stood with feet braced apart and said in a clear voice that echoed throughout the amphitheater, "On our fifteenth anniversary on this world which we chose, this beloved land which is our own, let us celebrate ourselves and each other." She had slowly raised her arms as she spoke, and she turned to all sides of the amphitheater as cheers thundered down, as hundreds of young women clad in bright coral warmsuits streamed onto the arena floor, clapping their hands joyfully above their heads, running along the perimeter to the reverberating homage of their audience. It was a colorful and stirring sight, and I was watching with great pleasure as Megan returned to us.

"There are others I must have Laurel meet," she said to Venus.

Venus smiled at me. "May I also call you Laurel?"

"Of course."

"Will I be seeing you at the fete tonight?"

Megan said impatiently, "Excuse us, Venus. There is little time before the games are underway."

And indeed there was scarcely time to be presented to Demeter, and the formidable Hera whom I remembered well from the time of our landing; then applause began again, signifying the beginning of the events. We lounged comfortably on luxurious chaises covered with thick soft fleece, a holographic unit before us. I gazed at several women nearby who were stripping off their warmsuits. Then I gaped. They were totally nude.

Megan had apparently observed my shock. She said quietly, "Part of the aesthetics of competition is the total beauty of the athlete. We enjoy athletics in its fullest aspect."

"I see," I murmured, staring at a gloriously tanned, perfectly formed girl of no more than sixteen, staring at the blonde triangle of hair between her legs, at the white-blonde hair that whipped about her face as she practiced a toss of a crystal javelin which glistened in the sunlight. At her young age she was already full-breasted; I saw that her breasts were held by a transparent band of material that did not diminish their beauty.

"These seats on the arena floor may be prestigious," Megan said in an amused voice, "but they offer the poorest views of our games. I suggest that you watch the holograph, as I do."

I took my eyes from the blonde girl to see that the unit had been switched on; tiny three-dimensional nude figures were performing an elaborate ritual that seemed partially composed of dance steps. "What game is this?" I asked, fascinated by the subtle rhythms of the players as they blended and flowed together in energetic and intricate patterns, a series of small balls floating among them.

"We call it Criss-Cross. It's a ball game, but based on chess principles, and it makes intellectual demands as well as physical ones. It's very popular. Would you like me to explain it to you? Or would you like to see other events?"

I said reluctantly, impelled by curiosity, "I think other events."

"You'll find our other games more familiar." She touched a color-coded key on the unit.

Naked runners crouched in a still tension of waiting, then exploded into flashing limbs and flying hair; a lithe dark-skinned woman broke the beam seconds later, arms raised in triumph, her competitors close on her heels.

"Vardis," Megan said. "She's perhaps our finest runner since the inception of the games." She touched another key.

Two women, both small-breasted and with dark glossy hair and delicate Oriental features, leapt high and in unison from a raised platform composed of a material which lent additional spring to their legs. They somersaulted and spun in breathtaking synchrony, then landed softly and perfectly together.

"Pairs-spring ballet," Megan said. "A lovely sport. Points are given for the difficulty of the leaps, the coordination between the performers." She reached for the keys.

"Please wait," I asked, compelled by the grace of the two figures. They had leapt again, hands joined, to perform an artful somersault away from each other, then a spin back to link hands for their landing.

"You will surely enjoy our ballet this evening," Megan commented as I continued to be absorbed in an increasingly intricate succession of leaps and spins. The two women, hands joined, finished their final leap and bowed to a crescendo of applause. Megan touched another key and played back their performance, slowed to further distill its beauty—faultless to my untrained eye; but she said, "Slightly flawed, but quite lovely."

Next we watched women swim in the coral lake that formed one side of the amphitheater, their bodies assuming different angles in an ever-changing variety of graceful strokes.

"Terpsichorean swimming," Megan said as I gazed in pleasure.

"Skin pigmentation varies so among all the women,"
I remarked. "Are some differences due to atmospheric
factors?"

"No," she answered, "purely genetic. Many of us come
from various racial backgrounds and when we gene-select
for our births we do not interfere with this. We enjoy all
the differentiations among us. Genetic change is of great
concern to us on this new world and we do continuous
genetic analysis, especially on those born here. Diana says
that if changes occur it may be only after several generations."

She touched a key. "The pentathalon is beginning. The
blonde girl you saw earlier is Cytheria, one of our finest
pentathletes."

This event was taking place so close to us that I looked
up from the holograph to see Cytheria running with long
fluid strides, crystal javelin poised; then the taut bracing
of her nude golden body, the smooth powerful throw; then
her steps—delicate, dancing—her body teetering, leaning
perilously forward with the force of her throw, her eyes
fixed on the glittering flight until her implement struck
and stood quivering in the earth as applause swelled around
us.

I murmured, "May I see that again on the holograph?"

"I also would like to see her again," Megan said.

We followed her through all her events, leap-and-vault,
ten-kilometer run, skim-discus, five-kilometer swim. She
was a feast to my eyes, she above all her nine glorious competitors, my absorption in her scarcely distracted by Vesta's
serving of another feast, for the palate—a lavish tray of
delectable bite-size morsels, no two alike, and a lovely com-
plementing wine.

The pentathalon events concluded and Megan declared,
"Cytheria will receive the victor's award. She has undoubtedly won."

I asked happily, "What has she won?"

"A garland. Fashioned of crown-shaped leaves from a
most regal tree that grows in profusion far north of us.

She'll wear it with pride at the fete tonight and be celebrated by all of us, she and all the athletes."

The marathon had begun, a fifty kilometer run over a grueling course laid out in the foothills, with several hundred women of greatly disparate age competing. "This is the best time to show you Cybele," Megan told me. "The dynamics and challenges of the marathon are fascinating, but the event is several hours in duration."

We made an unobtrusive exit. Megan smiled at my frown of concern as we took a hovercraft near the entrance. "These craft are our main means of local transportation and we have a great many. None belongs to anyone. Someone may take the one we came in."

We landed in what I soon learned was the main square of Cybele. As Megan assisted me from the hovercraft my eyes were taken by an immense mural forming one entire curving side of the square. The figure of a woman stood next to an EV in waist-high grass—a heroic figure with raised head and proud straight shoulders, confident and splendid in a white shirt and black pants, standing with hands on her hips, her dark hair tousled and blowing in the wind, her eyes of emerald . . .

Megan did not speak nor did I. For some time I gazed at what I knew to be the depiction of the landing upon Maternas, without necessity for asking its subject, the woman who stood beside me with white shirt susurrous in the light breezes of this fine warm day. Finally I looked away to the structures carved from the foothills forming Cybele's main square, buildings simple in design and apparently purely functional. My eyes followed the curves of hills upward, taking in a labyrinth of dwellings, glazed and burnished jewels in the sunlight, long balconies and rock bridges interconnecting the whole into a unity of great delicacy and beauty.

I asked in amazement, "Do all of you live here?"

"Most. Some live beside lakes and streams nearby, like Vesta and Carina. Several dozens are scattered all over

Maternas, preferring to live in isolation and seeing the rest of us only occasionally."

"How many of you are there?"

"In fifteen years we have increased from four to ten thousand. I'm currently occupied with the design of a new colony, necessary because of our growth. It will be on the coast not far from here. We have decided to call it Kendra."

"I know of her," I said softly. "Minerva showed me some of your history. She was a very great woman."

"Yes. She was."

Still I gazed at Cybele, stunned by the artful, symmetrical, logical design of it. "Who created this?"

"It is my basic design. Colony design was my specific training on Earth. But all of us worked to create it."

"Is there anything you do not do well?" I murmured, looking at her.

Again there was shyness in her eyes, but her smile was pleased. "Let me show you our council chambers."

"What form of government do you have?" I inquired as we walked toward this structure.

She answered first with a chuckle; then said, "Very little. We believe each of us is the best judge of her own interests. We place highest value on self-reliance, privacy, respect for each other, and instinctively we oppose authority, uniformity, any kind of fixity . . ."

I was listening with concentration, trying to absorb her words along with my surroundings. The essential element in the massive main room of the council chambers was simplicity—in the pillars and walls and all of the furnishings: a long crystal table, smaller tables apparently for discussion groups, functional chairs. Soft grays and blues and greens were conducive to reflection; no bright color intruded, no cleverness of line distracted the eye.

". . . Our primary function is simply protection of the colony," Megan was saying, "and preventing any individual from interfering with another, which happens even in a rationally based society . . ."

Then my attention was taken entirely from her words. Between two pillars stood a life-size sculpture, ivory-colored, smooth and warm, sensuously carved, of two slender nude women coming together in embrace; they leaned toward each other on tiptoe, one's hands clasping the other's shoulders, one's hands circling the other's waist. Their small lovely breasts were just lightly touching at the nipples; their parted lips were also just lightly touching . . .

I gazed at the sculpture, struck by the grace and tenderness of the two figures. Then I became aware that Megan had stopped speaking and was observing me.

"Are you displeased?" she asked as I looked at her.

"Displeased?" I repeated in surprise. Then I realized that I hadn't felt any sense of shock or even slight discomfort at the sculpture; I had simply enjoyed its aesthetics.

"I should have remembered," she said apologetically. "There is much public art in Cybele that celebrates the love among us. But the art in these rooms where only the adults assemble—"

"Let's go on," I said firmly, and asked as we walked, "Since you don't have formal government, you must have laws, surely?"

"We have a Central Code and a yearly vote to determine if any part of it needs to be changed, and—"

I halted before a huge painting, its background the soft coral hues of this planet, its foreground a woman with dusky skin and burnished black hair, her nude body voluptuous, her mouth avid on the full breast of a slender blonde who lay arched, arms flung up and concealing her face, luminous thighs parted, pale hair curling up around the dark cupped hand and fingers that lay curled intimately within.

Disconcerted, I walked on, and blurted the first question that came to mind: "Do you have courts? There must be criminal acts here, even occasionally."

"We have occasional . . . errors in judgment or deed—which need to be atoned for. Then we have an informal tribunal composed of six, chosen by lot to decide the nature of the atonement."

I'd noticed that she remained curiously undisturbed by the art which had had so opposite an effect on me. Perhaps she had simply grown accustomed to it. "Minerva tells me that you have no arbiters to settle disputes among you when your . . . Joinings are dissolved."

She said quietly, "We have no equivalent of divorce arbiters or courts. We recognize no contract between two people arising from passion or sentiment. And most disputes are caused by property considerations, and we have no transferring of property here, no bequeathing of it. There is too much on this world for all of us to share."

She led me to a series of small enclaves. "These are areas for individual contemplation, for those who wish a period of solitude before they assist with the decisions of our world."

I walked into one of the enclaves, into a blending of soft warm whites through deep grays, the colors of the mind, I thought, just before the drifting into sleep. There was a piece of sculpture in this room, smooth curves of silver; and I gazed at it for a long moment before I realized that it was two women, featureless and with highly stylized limbs, bound together in a passionate knot of consummation. I stared at the inextricably twined limbs and said with a smile, "Is that physically possible?"

Megan was also looking at it, hands on her slim hips; she cocked her head to one side and said seriously, "Zandra's interweaving of arms and legs needs some deciphering, but the physical position is possible." She added with a grin, "With a considerable degree of athletic ability."

Laughing, we walked on, into a high-vaulted chamber of small interconnected rooms well lighted and with lumi-screens and other optiscan equipment.

"This is a most interesting place," Megan told me. "It was designed by me but constructed under the direct supervision of Minerva. It houses all knowledge we accumulated to bring with us, all that we've acquired since coming here. It's an electronic-storage historical archive, but Minerva chooses to call it . . . a library."

She led me to an inner room warmed by fire-grottoes and covered floor to curved ceiling with rows of objects I had seen only in old films and photographs. She said, "Minerva has revived the ancient art of bookbinding. Only in the past few years has she had the time. She and Christa have taught themselves penmanship, have taught it as well to several of our children who expressed enthusiasm for learning it."

"May I look at . . . a book?" I spoke the word with reverence.

She hesitated, then chose. "This is poetry by Selene, one of the Inner Circle I never knew, she died many years ago. Before we came here we acquired a number of rare works, some with great difficulty—they had been suppressed for hundreds of years. Such as this newly bound book of poetry by a legendary woman named Sappho."

I held the books in my hands with awe, first hefting them, then staring at shaped print I'd never seen in such form in a lifetime of lumiscreens. "You must come here very often," I said, returning each book carefully to its shelf, knowing I would implore Minerva for permission to return.

"Seldom," Megan murmured, "I lack the time, and must do my reading by lumiscreen." She took down a large book which lay upon its own shelf, the cover of rich coral and gold brocade. "In this book Minerva records by hand our Joinings."

Again I stared, the first time I had ever seen interconnected writing thus formed. Megan turned back pages to find the entry:

Christa and Minerva

Joined in their Love

1.11.26

"How wonderful," I whispered, deeply moved. "How very beautiful."

She closed and returned the book to its shelf. "There are other books," she said, "which record our births. And our deaths."

Reluctant to leave, I gazed behind me as she led me from the room.

"Let's go into the adults' discussion room," she said.

"Zandra's latest sculpture is there and Minerva tells me it's magnificent. I haven't had the . . ."

Her voice trailed off and she stood rooted as did I in the entryway of a room whose contents I didn't see; my eyes were riveted to the figures on a fleece-covered platform between two permanently burning torches.

Compelled, I walked toward the sculpture. The heat that slowly rose to my face had nothing to do with the firelight that played over the two golden figures, one standing, one kneeling. The standing figure had risen to the balls of her feet, slim legs apart and rigidly braced, slender body arched, head flung back so that the curve of throat was full and the shoulder-length hair hung suspended; her arms fell straight down from her shoulders, the tendons in her hands revealing tension as the frozen tension of her features revealed her rapture. Her body seemed both to yearn toward the figure kneeling to her and to strain away, as if to delay the greater ecstasy to come from the lover who fiercely clasped her hips, the fingers of both hands deeply sunk into the soft flesh. Tendons stood out on the kneeling woman's wrists, her arms, across her shoulders, down her neck; her eyes were half-lidded in a face austere in its hunger, and she stared in her own rapture between the parted thighs as if straining, herself, not to end this moment before she would press her lover forward the final distance onto her waiting mouth, her tongue.

Waves of heat continued to pass through me as I stood hypnotized by the two rapturous figures. Never had I dreamed that eroticism could be so purely and powerfully captured in stone. Megan, I eventually saw, was also transfixed, her color heightened. She had perhaps become accustomed to the other art we had seen, but she now appeared as stunned as I.

Our fixation on the work broke simultaneously; and without a word we left the room. And I realized as we emerged from the council chambers into sunlight that I hadn't seen any other contents of that room Megan had called the adults' discussion room . . .

After a while I spoke into the bemused silence between

us, asking about the subject of so much interest to me. "The children here, may I see one of their schools?"

Megan landed the hovercraft on a wide grassy knoll overlooked by rock homes built high in the hills. Three-sided structures were laid out over the knoll, seeming casually built, almost haphazard in placement. We strolled across the grass which was strewn with playthings and held the presence of children so strongly that I could almost hear their laughter.

Megan gestured to the structures. "Of course our children are all at the games today. Our classrooms, such as they are, are open always to surrounding playgrounds. We begin teaching in infancy, as soon as awareness begins, but at every age our children play constantly in full development of their physical capacity, in the full joy of childhood."

"Minerva tells me that all of you have opportunities to contribute your experience, your presence." I asked, smiling, "Is Megan also required to contribute her presence?"

"No woman on this world enjoys doing so more than I."

This answer was given with such simple honesty, the voice contained such effort to hold its even tone, that I turned away from this proud and gifted woman so that she would not see my anguish at her loneliness.

She helped me into the hovercraft. "There is one other place I would like you to see," she said softly. "We have enough time. I must be back at the games in fifteen minutes."

She'd made this statement without a glance at the placement of the suns or at any chronometer. I asked, "How do you know what time it is?"

"I always know, even asleep. An inner clock tells me."

Bleakly I wondered if anyone had ever broken through that solid wall of discipline to cause her to forget what time it was, however briefly.

The hovercraft soared high over Cybele, coming to land on a peak that overlooked both the colony and the sea. I sat for a moment gazing at the large square shape cut from the mountain, with rounded edges and no seam anywhere and covered with intricate carvings. Then I stepped onto a granite mountaintop deeply etched by a sighing wind that whipped my tunic about my legs and whirled my hair into my face.

Megan stood beside me; her voice was bell-clear in the mourning wind: "In this place are mingled the ashes of all the dead of our Unity."

I walked to the structure, passed my hands over some of its carvings.

"Having no time, we made it hastily." Megan's voice was uninflected. "For the first dead of our planet. Then a plague struck us down—"

"Yes, I read of it in your history." I had been moved to tears by Minerva's eloquent account of the pain of that time.

"Those deaths devastated us all," she said, "and Zandra came to this mountain and remained here alone, refused to leave for the ten months it took her to make these carvings."

Wishing to be with my own thoughts in the windswept grandeur of this place, I turned my face from her, my eyes sweeping the vista of coral ocean and the hills of Cybele, its homes indistinct save for the creative art that had shaped their beauty into the land.

I reflected that the colonists who had first come to the American continent centuries ago had created a brilliant time in history, when the very best of a person was called upon, courage no less than wisdom. But in the centuries afterward on my quarrelsome and strife-torn birthworld there had never again been a time like that, or kinship such as this, on this new world where a great artist would isolate herself for months in her grief at the death of many, to make this a more fitting place . . . I caressed the carved stone that held precious contents within, as melancholy as if I too had known these dead . . .

Megan broke into my thoughts. "We must return now."

I told her, "I am honored that you brought me here."

We flew in sober silence to the amphitheater, landing beside an entryway. I reached to her then. "You should look like a leader," I said gently, and rearranged soft strands of her dark hair which had been put into disarray by the mountain winds.

She smiled. "I suspect I rarely look like a leader."

You always do, I thought. Always.

"Great Geezerak," Mother muttered to Megan. "I thought you'd abandoned me to all these athletic paragons." She turned to me. "My dear, would you be good enough to assist me with the presentations?"

I soon learned what that assistance would be. All the athletes received medals, the event winners a wreath—half of the athletes receiving their awards from Megan, the other half from Mother. The first athlete, a dark-haired girl no more than thirteen, approached Mother with all the enthusiasm of a fish swimming toward a shark. But Mother took her hand and smiled warmly. "You were lovely to watch, my dear. And you performed very well."

A very nice speech, I thought; and the young girl bowed gracefully, smiling shyly. "Laurel," Mother said, "be a dear and fasten the medal around this child's neck." I did so, and the girl bowed again and fled back to her companions.

The next athlete, a much older woman, was given the identical speech and medal; and also the woman after her, who received a wreath as well, which I fastened upon her head as efficiently as I could.

"Don't ever become important, Laurel dear," Mother grumbled as the next athlete approached, "it's such a dreadful bore."

I glanced over occasionally at Megan who was seated on a chaise quite near us. Taking their hands in hers, she spoke warmly to all the athletes, and she made her own presentation of award. I smiled in my own pleasure as she affixed the wreath onto Cytheria.

I noted that those who received awards from her stood in various attitudes of acute self-consciousness. Some shifted from foot to foot, some ducked their heads in embarrassed acknowledgement of her compliments, the youngest ones blushed furiously. Megan had one singular effect on these graceful athletes: she turned them awkward before her. And when she took their hands in hers they gazed at her with expressions that ranged from awe to adoration.

There was something else I noticed about some of them, and I mentioned it to Megan when the award ceremonies concluded. "The youngest girls have similar hairstyles," I said teasingly, "Megan hairstyles."

She looked uncomfortable, almost distressed. "It's a recent practice. I don't know what I can do about it."

We dined at Mother's house, myself and Megan and the Inner Circle, on delicacies prepared by Vesta. The formidable Hera sat with me, pinioning me with impatient and searching questions. I observed Megan; she spoke for a considerable time with Mother, sitting at the foot of her chaise and gazing at her with the same reverence I had seen in the faces of the athletes for Megan. Megan also spent time with each member of the Inner Circle, at ease with all of them except, apparently, Venus, who sat with Vardis, the wreath-crowned, lithe runner I remembered from the games. Megan's slim shoulders seemed tense as she passed a few courteous minutes with Venus, who lounged on a chaise and sipped wine and somehow always managed to meet my eyes whenever I happened to glance at her.

Mother's house was singing in the nocturnal winds when Venus finally made her way over. "Hera," she said, "you're monopolizing our guest shamefully." As the scowling Hera began a retort Venus continued, "Vesta and Minerva tell me that Laurel and I have our profession in common. It seems therefore that I should have an opportunity—"

"Very well. Of course." Hera rose and nodded to me, then stalked grandly off with a swirl of her cape to join Mother and Demeter.

But it soon became evident that it was not Venus's intention to discuss biology. "Tell me," she said with a disarming smile, her azure gaze enveloping me, "have you been with women before?"

"I—" I was mesmerized by her eyes. "You mean . . . No."

"Is your preference restricted solely to men, then?"

Taken aback, I stammered unintelligibly. Never before had I thought of considering alternatives to what I had always known and been taught to accept.

But she smiled, a bewitching, dazzling smile. "An answer is not required," she said. "Since your response was not immediate, your mind is still open."

"I—well, I suppose—" I could not prevent my stammering; I felt heat in my face.

She smiled again. "Your hair is glorious, simply extraordinary," she said softly. "And you wear our clothes beautifully. You're a lovely, lovely young woman."

"I—thank you." I was no less flustered than before.

"It is now time to begin the evening's festivities," Megan said in a clear even voice from behind me.

Cybele glowed with light. Light from its homes, from torches outlining the main square. I sat with Mother and Megan and the Inner Circle before a newly erected platform flooded with brilliance from a source invisible to me. Women crowded the square, the balconies, the bridges of Cybele. The night air was soft and gentle as it had been during the day, warmth radiated by inconspicuous solar units on the colony's structures. There was a continuous murmur of expectancy, and I myself waited eagerly.

The brilliance dimmed; the stage was illuminated only by the silver night and flickering ribbons of gold from the torches around the square.

Figures draped in head-to-foot shapeless clothing shambled onto the shadowed stage, their features dark cavities in ghostly white faces. Light came up slightly to reveal coarse heavy cloth garments, dark dismal gray. Each figure lurched about in isolation, yet with an odd poignant grace. Two figures moved tentatively toward each other, only to scuttle away; two others brushed together, stumbled apart, looking back lingeringly, yearningly . . .

Light narrowed, focused: one figure tremblingly raised an arm. Ugly gray folds fell away to expose a bare arm, round and white, and, in so somber a context, dramatically beautiful. The mouth in the face upturned to the naked arm was an O of wonder. The arm was hurriedly lowered and covered again; the figure lurched painfully off to the shadows. But in the shadows the arm was raised again, exposed . . .

A deeply shadowed corner of the stage gradually lightened. Two gray figures peered at each other. One exposed a white arm; the other hastened to cover it and then turned away . . . and turned back . . . and reached to the other, pushed the grayness aside and gazed at the naked arm, and with trembling fear and need placed a hand upon it . . .

Shadowed sections of the stage lit up one by one. Figures lovingly stroked each other's bare arms . . . Suddenly from center stage a figure cast off her confining garb. Shockingly nude amid all the shrouded figures, she leaped, head back, arms flung high in exaltation. She was pulled down, encircled, hidden from view as figures crouched over her . . .and she was dragged, again fully clothed, into the shadows . . .

But figures began to adjust their garb so that they might constantly reveal their limbs, raising and fastening hems to reveal bare legs . . . In narcissistic absorption they performed individual dances of self-discovery, dances of fascinating intricacy and grace . . . Then all stopped as at an internal signal, and gazed at one another. One figure held out her hands . . .

Applause began, startling me; I had been immersed in a drama performed thus far to an utterly still and silent audience. Applause swelled as the figures joined hands and began a dance of compelling grace and inventiveness in their confining clothing . . .

The dance stopped, and the dancers turned and looked at the sky.

The stage abruptly darkened. For the first time, music began. Sonorous music from woodwinds, strings. Into a single spotlight stepped a figure; there was but a microsecond to see a white shirt and black pants before the spotlight vanished. Then the stage flooded to brilliance as dancers clad in bright-hued single-piece trouser suits danced in ecstatic abandon around and through a gigantic holograph, a spaceship identified by luminous lettering: *Amelia Earhart*. This dance had comic elements—pantomimed quarrels and acrobatic shoving—which brought much laughter, from me as well; I remembered from their history the miserable months in their crowded ship during the journey across the stars.

Darkness abruptly descended again, even the torches outlining the square were extinguished. When light came it was not on the stage at all, but strobe-like upon the mural of Megan standing on Maternas. Amid the wild cheering I felt Megan stir beside me, and knew I should not look at her.

Bright stage lights came up. The dancers opened and stepped out of their trouser suits, flinging them into the shadows. They stood before us, their nude bodies dusted with diamond-like particles that shimmered with slightest movement. Each was a single glistening shade, in hues ranging from bronze to diamond white, and areas of their bodies were enhanced: a greater radiance decorated each breast and pubis and one other feature of distinctive beauty on each dancer.

They leaped—and floated in an antigrav field. Holographic images formed among them. A dancer the color of warm sand pantomimed strokes on a holographic lyre, her slender wrist and hand outlined in brilliance. Another, the lovely sweeping line of thigh enhanced, shaped holographic pottery; another stood upon the prow of a hydroflit navigating choppy seas, her bright delicate feet dancing for balance; another, the smooth powerful muscles of her arms outlined, hoisted and carried a woven basket of fruit; another, of sensuously rounded hip, created furniture; another, of finely shaped calf, laid mosaic . . . Scarcely breathing, I felt the joy and pride of the women on this world in their daily work . . . and knew their beauty . . .

The holographs vanished. In the slow-motion of antigrav the dancers glided, and arched and spread and shaped their glorious bodies into magnificent glittering statuary, breaking and reforming into new friezes of exultation.

They turned to each other. An interweaving of bodies began, fluid and sensuous. Pairs formed, each performing separate *pas de deux*. Some playfully somersaulted in slow motion tumbling grace around each other. One dancer formed her body into a circle, fingertips touching toes, slender body slowly revolving around her lovingly imprisoned partner. More and more erotic elements emerged: dancers caressed the outlined features of their partners, and they soon embraced, briefly at first and gently, separating to stroke a glowing breast, a thigh . . . coming together again with shimmering limbs intertwining . . . The dancer of broad strong shoulders carried the tiny dancer of slender wrist and hand, using her strength to treasure her partner's delicacy as she brushed her lips over an exquisitely formed breast; the tiny dancer ardently caressed the broad shoulders of her partner, glorying in her strength. In a slow dimming of light each dancer also slowed, her body gradually fusing in love with her partner's. Locked in embrace they floated in a circle, and out of that circle each extended a hand and took the hand of a sister so that the circle was joined . . .

The stage lights extinguished.

No less than any woman on that world I was on my feet applauding, tearful in gratitude and pride. To a thunder of love the twelve dancers arranged themselves, forming an arrow that pointed to us, Mother and Megan and the Inner Circle; and as one the dancers bowed. The arrow shape broke, the dancers formed a line and joined hands to acknowledge the continuing homage of us all.

The fete began. The platform that had held beauty and enchantment now was taken up by a lavish presentation of food and drink on numerous tables, and by three musicians, one strumming a multi-level, multi-stringed instrument, the other two electronically producing graceful melody and vibrant percussion.

The lights of Cybele had been extinguished. To the

pulsing rhythms of the music women danced all around me, danced on the balconies and bridges, danced under the light of the gold moons and the torches that themselves danced with flame in the night breezes.

Mother had told us, "I'll leave you dears to your silliness," and had gone off to her house. Other members of the Inner Circle were availing themselves of food and drink, or were dancing. On a fleece-laid chaise before a small table with wine and a tray of fruit, I sat with Megan. This place had been made ready especially for her, positioned between two torches and with a fine view of the square and the activity.

Only one thing seemed strange to me now—and that was myself, not these women who danced in joyous embrace. How could the love among them, their loving relationships, have ever seemed strange to me?

I watched the dancers, thinking that of all the beautiful women I had seen this day, none was more beautiful to me than the woman whom I sat beside . . . thinking that with her straight slender shoulders, her slim hips and long legs she would be a willow-graceful dancer, beautiful to watch . . . to dance with . . .

I asked Megan, "Do you dance?"

"It would not be . . . appropriate."

Again the isolation, from the women on this world who so adored her . . .

Minerva and Christa danced nearby, Christa magnificent in dark brown flowing silk shirt and pants, Minerva equally striking in an elegantly draped full-length sapphire tunic. All the women I could see around me wore fine and ornate garb for this night. Hand in hand, Minerva and Christa came over and sat with us, and I expressed again my great pleasure in the ballet.

"Historically," Minerva said with pride, "achievement in the arts has always occurred late in the development of a new society. But we have come very far in only fifteen years."

Christa smiled. "Think of our accomplishments if we hadn't been so occupied with the problems of settling."

Christa and Minerva had left us to dance again when Venus sauntered over, startlingly beautiful in satin turquoise pants and jacket with lapels edged in silver. She held out her hands. "Dance with me, Laurel."

Automatically I took her hands and as if obedient to a hypnotic command began to rise—then caught myself. I love dancing, but knew now that Megan would be displeased if I danced with Venus. And so I released her hands and murmured, "I think not, thank you. I . . . I'm tired. It's been a long day." And truthfully I was tired, drained by the emotion of this day.

"Will you sit with us, Venus?" Megan asked courteously.

Venus accepted this invitation with a nod. "Laurel, you'll be with us at least two weeks, I understand. Until your crew returns and decisions are made. Perhaps part of that time we could work together?"

I looked at Megan; this was not my choice to make.

"Plans haven't been made yet about Lieutenant Meredith's activities," Megan said stiffly. "I must consult—"

"But perhaps she could work with me?"

"Perhaps."

Vardis came up to us then, held out a commanding hand to Venus. Venus said coldly, "I wish to remain."

"I'm taking Laurel back to Vesta's," Megan said easily, rising to her feet. "As she said, she's tired."

I hadn't intended to cut short this evening with Megan, but I was helpless to prevent it. And so I wished Venus and her friend a good night. I felt isolated, cut adrift.

"Will I be seeing you tomorrow?" I asked disconsolately as Megan assisted me into the hovercraft.

"I'm fully occupied tomorrow. But perhaps . . . I'm fully occupied, as I said. You may enjoy spending more time with Minerva and Vesta, and among the books in our library."

I had heard her hesitation, had heard very clearly the regret in her voice. As we landed at Vesta's house an idea struck me and I blurted, "I wish to be useful here. I want to earn my way, contribute."

She frowned slightly. "What would you like to do, then?"

"Be . . . of personal service to you?" I suggested, my idea still forming itself.

Her frown deepened. "I have no need of . . . personal service. Whatever that may be."

"I'm well informed about advances in my field since you left Earth," I said, searching my mind for any notions of how I might acceptably offer her my companionship. "I could perhaps give you information helpful to this world."

"Whatever information you're willing to give us in your specialty would be more appropriately directed to . . . others."

"Fields other than my specialty," I pushed on. "Perhaps not in technical depth, but even general information may be useful."

"Any such information would be welcomed by our specialists in those fields."

"Perhaps then I could assist you in personal matters you lack the time to—"

"Never. Never would I permit that. No woman on this world has such . . . assistance given her."

I played my final card, uncertain of its value. "Then I wish to work with Venus until my crew returns and decisions are made."

After a moment she parried, "There are many other occupations on this world you could assist with. Time away from our fields of expertise can be beneficial, restful."

"What occupation do you suggest, then?" I asked with immense satisfaction, seeing that my final card had value indeed.

She looked at me musingly. "Obviously, food gathering would not be suitable . . . Pottery? Metalworking?" I shook my head. "Clothes making," she said hopefully. I shook my head vigorously, enjoying myself. "Music," she said in triumph. "You can spend your time working on your wonderful music."

"And contribute nothing to this world. Unless you allow me to play for you in the evening."

She smiled. "That I would permit."

"Composition soon exhausts me, and will take only a small part of my day. But cooking is interesting and enjoyable." I spoke firmly, seeing that I was on solid ground, planning my strategy as I spoke. "For that part of the day I can assist Vesta. She prepares the evening meal for Mother and tells me she's often hard pressed for time. I could at the same time prepare the evening meal for us both."

She looked at me dubiously, considering.

"I'll work with Vesta," I stated, "work on my music, bring food and play for you in the evening, spend whatever spare time I have in the library. And that's how I wish to use my time." I opened the door of the hovercraft. "Or you must allow me to work with Venus."

"We'll try it," she said, "for a day or two."

Personal Journal of Megan
15.1.10

I clearly remember that first evening with Laurel . . .

I had come home after the kind of day that tires me most, a day of contentious discussion with Erika and Jolan over structural engineering of our new colony, and with Miri about appropriate ecological safeguards. I entered my house wearily, to find on a table next to my chaise a flagon of chilled wine and a tray of fresh vegetables crisply cooked in some manner—I know nothing about cooking—hot and delicious to my sampling. The message screen stated that in twenty minutes Laurel would bring my dinner. Smiling, I leaned forward expectantly on my chaise, enjoying the wine and tasty light snack.

She was wearing a blue tunic and managed to be lovelier to my eyes than the day before. So unlike me with my spare flesh stretched over a tall frame, she comes but to my shoulder and is womanly, with womanly fullness, rose-tinted skin and swelling curves of breast and hip, small hands and feet . . . hands of great delicacy and grace as I had discovered when she played her reed, and of astonishing softness, as I had learned when she brushed away my tears at her music, and when I took the hand she offered, surprised and awkward before her loveliness, the morning of Anniversary Day . . . She had worn yellow then, enhancing the golds of her gold-brown hair; but on this day the dark blue of her tunic drew notice to her eyes, light blue and so clear and direct in their gaze that they seemed transparent, taking mine into a limitless depth . . .

She came in with two containers that opened into trays, their contents permeating the room with intoxicating aromas. She said softly, placing a tray before me, "I understand that earlier today Farica and Venus presented most interesting discoveries on the continent of Nin."

I had planned to call up their presentation from information storage that evening. I asked, "Would you like to view this with me?"

"Very much," she said eagerly.

We sat companionably, I enjoying a meal even more delicious than its aromas suggested, she sitting with her legs curled up under her, the folds of her blue dress gathered around her, bare arms resting on the sides of her tray; occasionally and absently she ate her food as she raptly watched the lumiscreen. Afterward, as I took the trays away, she said that she would enjoy nightfall and then return to play for me.

I called up coordinates for the drones tracking the path of Laurel's shipmates, and scanned Danya's surveillance reports. Nothing unusual. Then as is my habit I walked down to Damon Point, and found Laurel seated with my fleece drawn up around her against the chill, watching the night deepen. We both sat in silence as the waves crashed, as the moons rose into a clear sky limned with brilliant stars and gauzy fluorescent stardust, until regretfully I broke the silence, knowing that the nocturnals would soon begin.

At my house she sat on the floor, her gaze distant, listening to the winds play over Zandra's carvings, smiling at tonal qualities that pleased her. Then she played for me . . .

Her appeal lies not so much in her loveliness—she is doubtless no prettier than many women—except for those eyes . . . and that hair . . . It is her nature that pulls me to her, a nature that extracts the goodness, the sweet essence from what she sees. She has somehow managed to set aside her Earthly upbringing to enjoy the beauty of our world, to joyfully watch our games, our ballet, our art—even the sculpture in the adults' discussion room that so took me aback with its erotic impact, for which I was so ill-prepared . . .

It was this nature in her that led me to bring her to Nepenthe, treasured place of our beloved dead, because I knew her response would endow that place with a full degree of honor.

From the beginning she has seemed at ease with me, displaying none of the gravity and veneration of our women that is so discomfiting. She regards me as I have always wished, with the respect due my responsibilities—as I respect others in their responsibilities—and with informality and comradeship and humor. Especially humor.

Our second night together, as I set up the trays for our dinner, she asked if I had ever seen Vesta cook. When I nodded, she mimed the dreamy manner Vesta acquires as she concocts her dishes, as she adds and combines ingredients in trance-like slow-motion, aware of nothing but the culinary vision in her head. I found myself laughing. Then, during the nocturnals, after we had returned from watching the nightfall, she mimed Hera, her haughty walk and disdainful manner and flamboyant gestures. And even though Hera is my deeply revered kinswoman, I could not prevent my laughter.

The third day, I came back to my house after my usual morning swim already anticipating Laurel's presence that evening, only to see her waving to me from a parapet of my house, a hand shading her eyes against the morning brilliance. She had brought breakfast. I set up a table and chairs outdoors.

"This was not part of our agreement," I said, immensely pleased.

"I came on another errand," she said mysteriously, "which I will explain after breakfast."

I sat in contentment, savoring the varied tastes and textures of a fine breakfast, and her unexpected company. She gazed off into the horizon, only sometimes remembering to eat, watching storm clouds gather. Soon those clouds hurtled toward us and I hurriedly removed our meal indoors before the rains drenched us. But when I called to her she gestured for me and took my hand, preventing both of us from taking shelter, and laughed in sheer delight as the warm rain pummeled us.

She warmcombed her hair, soon restoring its soft curl, its warm colors and sensuous texture. Knowing I should be tending to my own hair and then off and about my duties, I instead succumbed to the pleasure of watching her.

"I'm going to dress your hair now," she told me firmly. "You said you were disturbed by young women wearing similar hairstyles. A way to change that is to change your own hair, at least somewhat. Let me try. If you don't like what I've done, you can easily change it back."

I had worn my hair in the same fashion all my life, but curious, I submitted. She used several settings on the warm-comb and lingered over my hair, her fingers stroking through it, a soft hand cupping and upturning my face as she inspected the effect she was creating. Then warm gentle hands held my face for a long time as she gazed; and so intense was my pleasure in her touch, so held was I by the transparent blue of her eyes that I had to close my own eyes.

Finally she murmured, "See how you like it now."

I inspected her handiwork in a reflective edge of the angular sculpture Zandra had given me many years ago, which I proudly keep in the very center of my house. To the crown of my hair Laurel had added fullness; she had pushed the waves back from the side of my face giving my cheekbones more prominence and revealing the lower curve of ear.

"I like it very much," I said truthfully. Aware of my deficiencies in such matters, I added ruefully, "I'll never be able to duplicate it."

"I'll come each morning," she said promptly. "With our breakfast, and to dress your hair."

I would have argued, had I not been still so weak from my pleasure in her touch.

It is ten days today since Anniversary Day. Five days before Laurel's shipmates return. Laurel knows she may remain here on Maternas but thus far has kept her own counsel, and I will allow the full five days before I ask. If she voices a desire to live among us before her crew returns, I will no longer have even scant justification for continuing to indulge in the pleasures of her "services." But she must be allowed maximum time to reflect whether happiness is possible for her with us, whether she can leave Earth forever behind as we have—and whether she can love and be loved by a woman. Happily, she has never spoken of any binding tie with Earth. But if she chooses not to remain . . . I retreat from thoughts of the anguish I will suffer, my utter and inconsolable desolation . . .

Precious few days remain to me. If she joins us, she will then belong with the women of this colony, in her own occupation or another of her choosing; she will begin a new life without me. No longer will I be able to protect her from the acquisitive Venus . . . And there will be no lack of other enticements . . . On Anniversary Day she was oblivious to the many glances that lingered on her in interest and admiration.

Our evenings have lengthened. Selfishly, greedily, I have kept her with me late into the nights. Mostly we talk, and read, or she watches holograph recordings of classes involving the children. Her love for children is great . . . Perhaps if she remains among us she will teach them her profession . . . That would effectively remove her from Venus's presence. I keep Laurel with me until her exhaustion is evident; then I send her off to Vesta, and filled with anticipation for the next day, go off to my own bed.

With difficulty I extract from my duties the time to be with her. Having to condense activity into even lesser hours, I have learned something unaccustomed to me: delegation, a discretionary judgment that tells me when I do not have to decide something myself. I have always acted whenever my judgment seems required, but the talented women of our

Unity are more than competent—and willing—whenever I delegate my decision-making.

Strangely, I sleep longer. It is as if a balm has settled over my spirit and eased my restlessness. I sleep for several hours at a time—a pleasure unknown to me before—and rise to perform tasks until I become weary and return to my bed to sweetly sleep again.

Five nights ago I awakened and did not know the time and had to place the positions of the moons to reset my internal clock . . . Such a thing has never happened before . . .

I become increasingly disoriented when she sits beside me in the mornings and begins, with those gentle fingers, to brush the hair back from my face. I sense that she lingers more and more over my hair—but I am uncertain, so great is my disorientation. There is always silence between us at this time. She concentrates on her task, I suppose, and I—I simply cannot speak.

On Anniversary Day I knew that she had entered my heart. And I also knew that I had never conceived of love, that what I had felt for Venus so many years ago was but a foreshadow of this piercing sweetness, this joy at the sight of her, this quiet exhilaration in her presence, this desolation when she leaves me.

I have looked at the art in our council chambers many times since viewing it with her. It affects me profoundly, as never before, warming my body . . . But I do not need other images to suggest how I would love Laurel. I hold one central image in my mind: Laurel, in my bed, in my arms, her hair spread over my throat and shoulders.

Last night she fell asleep before I realized her exhaustion. I came to where she lay on the chaise, a graceful arm extended above her head, a hand resting lightly where I longed to place my own hand . . . on her breasts . . . I gazed for a time at the creamy smoothness of her brow, the tender set of her lips, the sweetness of her sleeping face. As I reached to awaken her, involuntarily I took strands of her hair into my hand, the silken curls caressing my fingers . . .

She awoke and caught me like a thief. "I was . . . just awakening you," I said lamely, and released her hair and moved quickly away from her—because she had looked at me with those eyes and in another instant I would have taken her into my arms.

My love for her will be forever the treasure of my heart, a love that will never be given, or spoken. Many years ago I gave my word—no less sacred now than then. And I have greater responsibility than to my own happiness. I owe a greater allegiance.

But I love her so . . .

VIII

Journal of Lt. Laurel Meredith
2214.2.28

Megan will ask my decision tomorrow. I could have told her before, but had no doubt that her sense of duty would compel her to send me from her.

I shall be forever lonely for my family, but little else ties me to home. Alienation from Earth has increased during my months in space and during my time here. But I must be here, on this wondrously unfolding new world. I must be near the person I've grown to love with all my being.

Loving her has come so easily. This proud woman with her sophisticated grasp of even most complex problems has in her the simplicity and tender nature of a child. Her mind with its keen hard edges has won my respect and admiration—but her innocence has melted my heart. And like a child she needs caring for, needs tender loving.

One evening after we'd enjoyed our meal together, the message screen blinked with a request from Erika to consult her. For some time she and Erika discussed a schematic of bewildering dimension displayed on the lumiscreen, part of the plans for the new colony of Kendra. As she spoke, Megan touched the flower I'd placed on her tray, her long fingers stroking its stem, its petals. Afterward, we went down to Damon Point to watch the nightfall, she tall and straight beside me, walking with her confident stride—and I saw that she'd placed the blossom in the pocket of her white shirt.

How very much I love her . . . How could I not grow to love her?

Often I've been at her house when she's gone—to feel her presence there, to feel near her. All the houses in Cybele are open—there's no reason to be otherwise—but all have privacy shields. A shield is frequently up around Vesta's chamber where she treats her patients, and around the bedchamber next to mine when she and Carina make love—a shield which may prevent entry but doesn't muffle Vesta's sounds. But shields are never up in Megan's house, and I wander freely, often going into her bedchamber to gaze at the place I most long to be.

I dare come no closer to this proud and revered leader of the women of Maternas, no further than I already have; only she can take us beyond. And it was quite by accident that I discovered her desire to do so.

When I play my reed I turn slightly away from her because her beautiful eyes disconcert so, they so easily disturb my concentration. It was four nights ago that I sat turned away from her as before, but in a different place—facing the great sculpture in the center of her house. And I saw her reflection in one of its many lustrous sides, a side so intricately angled that her reflection was visible to me but not to her. And I saw her look at me. Look at me in such a way that I faltered and almost stopped playing. But I did play—surely dissonances—and my body turned to hot liquid under the emerald gaze that caressed me, caressed my hair and throat, lingered for many moments on my breasts before slowly drifting down to my thighs . . .

And so I know she wants me.

Why won't she let me give her my nights—even if only one night? It would grieve me if there was only one—but at least there would be the one.

I've never felt for another this desire to give, not take, pleasure. To give her my breasts that she stares at with such desire. I long to hold her slender body to mine, to love her body with mine . . .

There was an opportunity. I'd fallen asleep, and feeling

her hand touch my hair I awakened; but she released the strands as if they burned her, and murmured an excuse, her face stricken. I gazed at her, reached to take her into my arms—but in a single instant she'd risen and was gone from me.

These past four days I've tormented her. Because she torments me. Because our time together is ending. And because I don't understand why she won't come to me. And I don't know what else to do—only to make her want me more, to make her reach out for what I long to give—before she must send me away.

I've grown pitiless. As I dress her hair I caress her as lovingly as I dare. Always she sits with eyes closed, but now she sometimes catches her lower lip between her fine teeth as, supposedly to inspect my handiwork, I allow my fingers to stray over her throat before cupping her face. I clasp a slim shoulder lightly as I brush through her hair; trace her delicate ears with my fingertips as I shape her hair there; caress the soft nape of her neck; finally cup her beautiful face in both hands and gaze at her, yearning to draw her to me, to bring her lips to mine.

Pitiless, I'm pitiless. Tonight I played for her the composition I've worked on these past days—the tonalities of my love for her. I played from my depths, seeing in the sculpture her want of me, pouring out through my reed the love I can't speak. Afterward she rose, her face averted from me, and murmuring something so faint I couldn't hear, she walked from her house. After a time I searched for her at Damon Point but couldn't find her. An hour later she returned and did not speak when she came in, but went to her chaise and only then asked wearily, "Do we have wine?"

On this, our last night, I would not take pity on her. I gave her wine and sat beside her and asked, "What you wear around your neck, may I see it?"

She reached, but I was too swift for her. My hand was inside her shirt. Slowly my fingers slid down and searched lingeringly, caressingly over small firm breasts and between . . .

With equal slowness, reluctantly, I drew out the object I sought, and then stared at a crystal streaked with coral and gold, and warm, warm from her skin.

"It is the first object I picked up when we landed," she said huskily, her voice almost inaudible, her eyes closed. "Janel polished it and created this for me."

"It's truly beautiful," I murmured, forgetting for a moment my purpose in seeking it.

"I give it to you."

"No," I exclaimed, astonished. "No, I—"

"Allow me the pleasure of giving it to you," she said, reaching to take the chain over her head.

I stopped her hands. "You honor me," I said, deeply moved. "But I could never accept anything with such meaning to the history of this world. Its value is inestimable. Please understand that I can't accept it."

She nodded, but as I took my hands away she clasped one, and traced a fingertip over the emerald ring I wore. "This also is rare. No such stone has yet been found on our world. The color green is a great rarity."

"Yes." I gazed into the eyes that matched my ring, that had so utterly bewitched me.

She looked at me with a childlike wistfulness that closed my throat with love. "I'm so tired," she whispered.

Defeated. Defeated, I had no choice but to leave, and I was suddenly exhausted myself. I said as I rose, "Tomorrow, Megan . . . the men return."

"Yes," she said, her voice a distant murmur." A day of . . . decisions."

IX

Journal of Lt. Laurel Meredith
2214.3.1

I was desolate with the knowledge that a short time earlier my shipmates had landed not far from here, and that Megan would now ask my decision and end our time together. But she was silent, her face closed, her thoughts distant from me as she unfolded the trays for our break-fast together.

Then her bracelet buzzed and she leaped for the hover-craft a few steps away from us on the parapet. I rushed after her without a thought to my act, scarcely reaching the craft as it began to rise, Megan's hand grasping mine, dragging me in with her.

"What—" I sputtered.

She'd touched a key that now blinked rhythmically; the craft was being directionally controlled. "One of our Unity has called for help," she said grimly, eyes narrowing as the craft swooped low and slowed to land by the sea, very near the landing site assigned to my shipmates.

Other hovercraft had landed all around us. A group, perhaps six or eight women, circled a figure writhing on the ground. I pushed my way in, and gaped. Hanigan was being flung about from the force of the charge rods trained upon him.

"Stop," Megan said from beside me.

The women either did not hear, or would not obey.

"Stop," Megan commanded in a voice of granite.

Hanigan's body halted its spasmodic jerking; he groaned and lay still, insensible.

Danya had arrived; she strode up to a small blonde woman who still held her charge rod aimed at Hanigan, her arm trembling. Danya gently took the arm, lowered it. "Diantha," she said softly.

"She was running along the seashore as she does each morning," Diantha quavered, gesturing toward a figure who lay prone, a knot of women crouched around her. "He . . . accosted her. He . . . seized my daughter. He . . ." Her voice, which had dropped to a whisper, disappeared.

"How has she been harmed?" Megan's voice was clear, even, penetrating.

"She is unharmed," another woman answered. "When we arrived he was much the worse for wear."

I saw two things then. The women around the prone figure shifted so that I could see she was Cytheria, the golden athlete from the games. Clad in a brief tunic, she lay curled in the fetal position, hands covering her face. Then Hanigan groaned again and sat up, and I saw that his EV suit was torn, his nose bloodied, that a bruise was emerging from around an eye. Undoubtedly he had been very much surprised by this young athlete's physical skill.

"Colonel Hanigan." Megan's voice was a whiplash.

Hanigan jerked and stared at her, gingerly touching his face and wincing. "I did nothing! You understand me? Nothing! All I wanted was to talk to her, I've never seen anything like her, I just wanted to—"

"Why did you put your hands on her?"

"I meant nothing by it!" Hanigan shouted. "All I wanted was—that's all, just—" He spied me. "Laurel! Explain to them! You know me, you know I don't mean anything when I just touch, you know I'd never—"

Cytheria began to sob.

"Laurel," Megan said evenly, "please take Cytheria to Vesta."

"Laurel! No! They'll kill me!"

I said to Megan, "Will you kill him?"

"No," she answered, her eyes remote. "But please leave us. This is now our affair."

"Laurel! You've got to help me!"

Cytheria had risen to her feet and stood with hands still covering her face, gold hair disheveled, her body shuddering as she sobbed. Remembering the magnificent athlete who had so gloriously flung her javelin, I turned back to Hanigan and stared with hate. Then I circled Cytheria's shoulders and led her to a hovercraft.

As we climbed in, I heard Hanigan scream. And as the doors closed behind us, I heard him scream again.

After I surrendered Cytheria to Vesta's soothing care, I returned to Megan's house. As I waited for her I saw the message screen receive Ross's demand for a conference, the blinking print seemed to pulse with fury.

Megan strode in, and after a distracted greeting to me, keyed in coordinates. Ross filled the lumiscreen, his thick body bristling with anger as he leaned forward, his dark eyes piercing.

Megan said quietly, "Yes, Commander."

"What kind of barbarians are you!"

"What kind of barbarians are you?" she countered.

"Hanigan," he said heavily. "Every bone, you broke every bone in both his hands."

"It was the least punishment the women on this world would accept, Commander. If it had been left to some of them, especially Cytheria's kinswomen—"

"You—you—" Ross sputtered furiously, "he didn't *do* anything. He didn't—"

"If he had," Megan interrupted, "he would be in the process of dying, and begging to do so."

Ross recovered in a moment. "Barbarians!" he exploded. "All this because a man merely placed a hand on one of you!"

"Forced a hand on one of us," she corrected. "No such behavior has ever been known by Cytheria or any of our children. She is but fifteen. And has never seen an Earthman. To her you are strange beasts. And she is unaccustomed to the sexual aggressiveness practiced by men of Earth, Commander. Our finest psychologist advises me that it will require months to repair the damage that has been done."

Ross cleared his throat. "I regret any . . . damage. It was not intentional. But you must realize we have no knowledge of . . . the nuances of your culture. My men have been many months in space. And you are women. However you live, you are *women*."

She did not reply to this contemptible statement that choked me with rage.

Ross continued, "But we do respect your culture. As you must respect ours. And therefore I demand the return of Lieutenant Meredith. She does not belong among you. She is a loyal Earthwoman—"

I stepped to Megan's side. "I do belong here. I choose to remain."

He protested. Shouted. Argued. Cajoled. Threatened. I listened indifferently to this man who had so recently commanded me.

Conceding defeat finally, he said to Megan, "What is the decision about me and my men?"

She replied, "I will contact you within the hour from our council chambers." She switched off before Ross could respond, and touched another key. Mother's face filled the screen, scowling with annoyance until she saw who it was that disturbed her. Megan said quietly, "Mother, may I see you immediately?"

Mother's eyes scrutinized the image of Megan on her screen. "I'll be expecting you, my dear," she said softly.

Megan took the bracelet from her own wrist and molded it to mine. "You're one of our Unity now," she said. "You have only to press this indentation to summon us. This will keep you safe." She walked from me.

"Megan," I said.

She turned to me.

"What is the decision?"

She would not answer, only looked at me before she walked to the hovercraft. And her eyes were eyes of winter.

X

15.1.16

Megan has signaled an emergency meeting of the Inner Circle and the Council. Unlike the last such call we know very well the subject at hand: a decision about these men from Earth can no longer be delayed.

Megan has sent word that she meets at this moment with Mother and will join us shortly. And so we wait; and discussion continues of the matter that has occupied our thoughts since the dark day when these men found our world. And now, after the harm done to our Cytheria, the talk is rancorous.

"They must be sent away," Erika says angrily, "to the farthest place from us where they cannot possibly do harm. Perhaps to the treacherous continent of O'Connor."

Astra responds in a bitter voice, "They would manage to do harm even there."

Janel places a calming hand on Erika's arm and suggests lightly, "Perhaps we could send them on an outing to Schlafly Lake."

We all chuckle; Schlafly Lake is where the creature GEM lives which almost took the life of Janel and others of us when first we came here.

Patrice speaks; she is kinswoman to Cytheria. "Perhaps," she says hopefully, "they could be castrated."

"Symbolically satisfying as that would be," Hera states, "it would accomplish nothing. It would not even eliminate the possibility of assault since men do not necessarily require that exact piece of apparatus to accomplish their deeds. And further, they would spend the remainder of their days devising a method of savage revenge."

"They are a contamination." Augusta's dark face is grim, her deep voice heavy with vehemence as she repeats, "They are a contamination. They contaminate our world."

Megan strides in. Strangely, Mother is not with her. But Megan immediately switches on the lumiscreen that dominates our council table, and Mother gazes down upon us all. She sits on her chaise and wears her ceremonial green cape, a symbol that in these circumstances chills with its gravity.

"Mother's presence is not required," Megan says evenly, "and she has chosen to only observe our proceedings. I have discussed this matter with her and she has approved every act I now take."

I stare at Megan in wonder. She stands blade-straight, booted feet apart, her face a still tension of steely decisiveness. Never has she been more commanding.

She touches a key and on the lumiscreen next to Mother a section of the Central Code appears. "Our Central Code grants authority to me, with your approval, to act autonomously in the event of implied danger to our world or to any of our Unity."

She allows us a few moments to read through the several paragraphs.

"I require from you a vote that the event of today has given me this authority to act independently of you—mindful that I have heard your debates over the past days, that I have consulted with Mother. Signify your readiness to vote."

Our readiness is unanimous.

"Please vote now on the question: Shall Megan have authority to act independently in the matter of the three Earthmen?"

We have all entrusted our lives to her before; how can we not do so again? Our vote agreeing to her authority is unanimous.

She acknowledges the vote with a distant nod, and opens

an optical channel. We see the EV, a menacing insect on our lovely land.

"Commander Ross," Megan states.

"This is Ross." He is on aural channel only; Megan well understands that none of us wishes to see him.

"Your ship has been repaired, Commander." Megan's voice is precise, uninflected. "You and your men are ordered to leave our world immediately."

All of us including, apparently, the Commander, sit in stunned silence. Then he says, "I don't trust you. Or this decision. Not after what you did today to my crewman. I don't believe you'd simply—"

"Commander," Megan interrupts in a voice of galactic chill, "you are ordered to leave our world. You have one minute to comply. Or the lasers trained on you will destroy you where you sit."

There is no response from the Commander. But in fifteen seconds the dark insect rises from the soft colors of our land.

Hera says, "Megan, you can't just—"

"Hera," Mother says from the screen, "do shut up."

Only Mother could speak to Hera in such a manner and further, have her obey. Hera subsides into infuriated silence, staring at Megan with eyes both baffled and angry. I take my eyes from her and watch the EV—to see it veer sharply from the vector that will lead it to the Cruiser.

Ross's voice crackles over the Interplanetary Frequency Channel: "We're not the fools you think. It's not difficult to guess how you've repaired our ship. But since you've ordered us to leave," he says, his voice taking on an overtone of smugness, "it shouldn't matter to you which ship we take. Particularly since you have no further use for yours."

"As you wish, Commander." Megan stands with arms crossed, eyes fixed on the dark craft that closes in on our *Amelia*.

For some minutes, in total silence, we watch; and then *Amelia* eases from her faithful orbit of all these years. Suddenly she becomes a vanishing dot, and I hear a muffled moan—I believe from Hera, who had been responsible for much of *Amelia's* redesign. A moment later a stream of numerals appears across our monitoring frequency.

"Coordinates," Megan confirms as we stare. "They are attempting to transmit their position to Earth."

Hera whispers, "Why this? Megan, they give us away . . ."

Her voice has trailed off because Megan is looking at her, and as I see Megan's eyes I understand along with Hera what has been done. That she has made the decision the rest of us would not make, a decision all of us retreated from, failing in our courage.

"The transmission will travel in a loop, esteemed Hera. As will all their transmissions. They will be received by no one, not even ourselves in seven more minutes as we move out of range of the loop."

A movement catches my eye; it is Mother, on the screen. Her face is etched with pain as she stares at Megan. And she is reaching to the dials in front of her. Her image vanishes from the screen.

"The Commander was correct about the manner in which his ship was repaired. But he erred in assuming we would not have similarly modified *Amelia*—which was accomplished before he and his crew left on their journey. It was my estimation that they had planned their excursion to attempt escape. Our rigidly programmed surveillance drones could never have tracked them, not with the evasive capability of an EV. But apparently such a stratagem never occurred to them."

She is looking at none of us as she speaks; her eyes are fixed on a point somewhere above our heads. We all sit in frozen tableau, listening to her.

"In five hours, when they are in an area which can absorb the force of so enormous a blast, *Amelia's* power drive will implode. An hour before this they will know it is going to happen—and that there is insufficient time to escape in their EV."

There is absolute silence. I draw shuddering breath into me.

"Esteemed Hera," Megan says, her eyes gentle upon my

sister, "I regret this ending to a noble ship so beloved by us all."

"It is a fitting end." Hera's eyes glitter with tears. "Her destruction is for the protection of us all."

Megan nods. But her eyes are remote. "I require some time," she says softly. "At least . . . a day. Perhaps more. For . . . contemplation. I wish to be disturbed only for an emergency."

"Megan," Erika says. "Megan, it was . . . right."

Megan is walking toward the entryway as we chorus agreement with Erika.

"It was not right," she says, leaving us. "It can never be right."

XI

Journal of Laurel
15.1.17

The evening sky darkened, became a carpet of stars and stardust. I stood between Carina and Vesta on the balcony of their house as the time drew near, Carina's arm gentle around me. My eyes ached with my staring. Then it seemed to me the sky lightened briefly—just briefly—in a tiny corner above the horizon.

"I'd like to be alone," I whispered. They left me—the single mourner of my shipmates on this world. I contemplated the sky, sorrowful and remembering the men as generously as I could, melancholy that the events that had so opened my life to me had meant the ending of theirs.

After a while I went in and Vesta came to me, took my hands. "Laurel my dear . . . will you talk to me in my chamber? Please let me help you."

I nodded and followed. But I had no need, did not intend, to speak of my dead shipmates.

After Megan had left me, I could not be alone. I had gone to Cybele's main square. But all the women I had grown close to on this world were in the momentous meeting in the council chambers, and I went into the library to watch on the lumiscreen.

In the company of several other women of Maternas—my sisters now, but strangers to me—I watched Megan send my shipmates to their deaths; and I wept silent tears for them, for my own pain, and most piercingly for hers.

As she left in her hovercraft I followed, but she had already activated her privacy shields and my craft would not land at her house. All that day her shields were impervious to my siege, her message screen rejecting all transmissions save those over the emergency channel, a frequency which accepts only a specific signal, not voice communication. She had effectively and completely withdrawn from all of us. From me.

This I revealed, and all of my heart, to Vesta. Confessing my love, I asked what I should do.

Vesta listened intently, gray eyes softening in compassion. She took my hands. "Dear one, does Megan return your love?"

Clasping her hands, I told her about the reflection in the sculpture, how Megan had looked at me. "And so I don't know if she loves me, Vesta," I concluded. "But it's enough that she wants me."

She smiled. "You understand a distinction many who are well beyond your twenty-three years never grasp. Dear one, I suggest several possibilities why she would not approach you. First, your status among us. As a guest of our world, all of us—she no less—owed you certain obligations of conduct until you declared your wish to stay. Second, Megan undoubtedly faced immediately what none of us would contemplate, what the inevitable decision about your shipmates must be. She may believe her decision has irrevocably cost her your affection."

I sat thunderstruck. "But how can I—She's cut off all communication—"

"You can only wait. And then tell her you are as one with our Unity about her action. She knows her decision can never be justified. And truly, such a decision can never be right. But it was correct—if you understand the philosophic difference." She sighed. "She believes she must have this time alone."

"It's not good for her to be alone now. It's not good, Vesta."

She sighed again. "No, it's not. She suffers greatly, she

carries a burden alone not understanding that we all share it. And all we can do is wait."

But suddenly I saw that I would not have to wait. Knowing how I would be able to see her, I went to my bedchamber and slept fitfully.

I arose very early, stepping into my hovercraft as the suns hung just above the horizon. I landed as close to Megan's house as her privacy shields would allow, and walked down to Damon Point.

Early as I was, she'd preceded me for her morning swim. Her fleece was spread over the moss, a towel and warmcomb laid upon it, white shirt and black pants folded neatly beside her boots. I sat down on the fleece to wait for her.

I didn't wait long. A distance away I saw her cutting through the water, swimming toward shore with strong strokes. When she reached the breakers, she body-surfed almost to the shoreline, then stood and walked from the sea.

Why hadn't it occurred to me that she would swim nude? Of course she would swim nude, my numbed mind told me.

She saw me, paused but a moment. She walked toward me, her ivory skin, her breasts wetly gleaming in the strong morning light, streams of water coursing over her thighs, water running down her arms and dripping from her elbows as she pushed wet strands of dark hair from her face. She was long lines and slender curving planes, and the dark triangle between her legs was small, delicate, as I'd thought it would be . . . Then our eyes met, and held. She sank down upon the fleece.

I came to her, knelt to her, and wrapped her in the towel; and as I felt her shiver I enveloped her in it, wrapping her hair, turning the towel setting fully up. I took her into my arms. Her arms were pinioned in the towel and she could not have prevented me had she wanted to.

I held her for a long moment, pressing my face into the

quickly warming towel that swathed her hair. Then I said softly, "You knew long ago what had to be done about your visitors from Earth, didn't you."

"Yes," she said, still shivering against me.

I tightened my arms, drew her face down to my breasts. "If I had chosen to be with them you would have made the same decision, isn't that so?"

"Yes." Her voice was muffled against my breasts; I could feel the warmth of swift breaths through my tunic. "Much as it would have . . ." She did not finish.

"To fully protect this world you would've done whatever you had to. Isn't that so?"

"Yes." Her shivering had begun to ease. "But that does not make it right."

"Some lives are more valuable than others."

"There can be no justification for taking life. The taking of *three* lives—lives that can never be replaced."

"Share your pain with all of us. Because all of us agree with what was done. Agree and love you still more as our leader."

She lifted her head from my breasts and looked at me; her eyes seemed defenseless, as if the events of yesterday and her time alone had broken down a barrier in her. But she tried to extricate herself from me. I further tightened my arms, unwilling to release her.

"Laurel," she said, and with effort smiled. "You'll cook me in this towel."

I had to smile then, had to release her; I'd turned the control up full and it was indeed very warm to my touch. She tossed the towel aside and pulled on her clothes. I watched with only little regret. I knew—simply knew—that we would touch again. That she was vulnerable, open to me now.

I picked up the warmcomb. I dressed her hair efficiently, with none of the caressing delays of before, except that I cupped her face afterward and gazed at her, as before.

"Thank you," she said, her voice husky.

I released her face and did not reply, only looked at her.

We sat still, gazing at each other, her eyes increasingly help-less as we leaned closer, ever closer.

Our lips met. Mine softly pressed hers, so softly . . . her lips more tender than I had dreamed . . . I reached for her, but her hands grasped my arms. Our kiss became hers. Her lips were tenderly possessive of mine, sweetly savoring mine . . . Again I tried to hold her; her grip only tightened. My body sought hers, yearned toward hers, my lips yielding, parting under hers, and I heard the sound in her throat as my seeking tongue met, stroked hers . . . Her hands on my arms were a vise, and I moaned my need to hold her as her tongue thrust and thrust into me . . .

And then her mouth was torn from mine, and her hands, trembling, held me away from her.

She sat with head bowed, hands still clasping my arms. Then she lifted her head and looked at me, her eyes con-taining so much pain that I couldn't bear them.

She whispered, "I . . . cannot."

I stared, struggling for voice.

"I . . . have given my word."

And she released me and was gone, running over the moss, fleeing from me.

I took longer to recover from the shock of her words than to interpret their meaning. So this was why she'd lived her days and nights in solitude here beside the sea. Why she had resisted, fought her desire.

Only one person possessed sufficient influence to extract such a vow. The one person on this world whom Megan revered, the one person to whom she would have given such a vow.

Having determined this, I sat on Megan's fleece and gazed out to sea, carefully considering what action I should now take.

Of course I could go directly to Mother. Even to this intimidating personage I was certain that I could convincingly plead my case—the strength of my love giving me both courage and conviction. But what if she decided that I was simply a fool, an impertinent upstart new to their world and their Unity who presumed—who dared—to love the great leader of them all? What recourse would I then have?

No, I thought as I folded the fleece and towel and packed them away under Megan's coral marker. Going to Mother would be my final recourse, not my first act. And there was a person of wisdom and prestige and influence whom I could trust to plead my case with Mother.

I set off over the moss to go to my hovercraft, to go to Vesta.

XII

15.1.17

All my privacy shields were up. Despairingly, I sank into my chaise. I knew now that I would require more time—considerably more than I had thought yesterday—to reconstruct my strength and resolve. To regain the solitary peace of my life.

Again I was stabbed by memory of the flash in the evening sky—a shattering of my soul. The flash of death, caused by me.

The pain was great again, so terrible that I assuaged it with forbidden memory of Laurel's arms. The flowery scent of her skin. The pliant softness of her breasts beneath the silky fabric of her tunic . . . The soft lips parting under the hunger of mine, the tender touching of that delicate tongue to mine . . . My body heated with forbidden memory.

For some time I lay on my chaise, sinking, it seemed to me, ever more deeply into despair.

Then I received a signal on the one non-emergency channel unaffected by any privacy shield. Composing myself, I opened the channel. I said as calmly as I could, "Good morning, Mother."

Mother did not immediately reply, merely looked at me with shrewd narrowing eyes. "Good afternoon, Megan dear. But it was indeed a lovely morning."

"I misspoke," I said quickly, stunned that so much time could pass by me unnoticed.

"Dear one," she said in the tone that permitted no discussion, "would you come immediately to my house?"

Tiny in her green robe, Mother paced rapidly, a whoofie scampering at her heels in pursuit.

"I've asked much of you, Megan. Because I, better than anyone, knew what was required for the Unity to survive. When I came to Earth—misled by fabricated stories, I assure you my dear, entirely unsuspecting what a backwater place it really was—I soon discovered that I had to protect myself and my precious baby daughters with every resource at my command. Every resource," she emphasized, "never knowing what next to expect from a planet with so irrational a history, so bizarre a culture."

Mother halted so abruptly that the pursuing whoofie tangled itself in the hem of her robe. She scooped it into her arms and soothed its mournful whoofs with gentle pats as she resumed pacing.

"My responsibility was enormous and terrifying. But it was a blissful Vernal day compared to the fearsome responsibility of your leading our four thousand from Earth—and the perils of assimilation on this new world as forbidding to our presence as Earth was to mine."

Mother released the whoofie which ran two or three steps, skidded to a halt, leaped back into her arms.

"You've done everything I have asked. More than I could ever have asked." She gazed at me with wise and compassionate eyes. "Perhaps we've all used more of your strength than was right."

Mother sat on the chaise next to me, placing the whoofie gently beside her. "I've raised nine precious babies I would have given my life for. I love none of them more than I love you."

She took my hand, patted my cheek. "The work is not finished, Megan—but the danger is over. We're safe. Safe, dear one. We've carved our foothold, and we'll soon have carved another in the new colony."

She drew my face down to her, kissed my forehead "If there is someone now who can give you a happiness you desire, then go to her, dear one. Go to her."

Vesta's soft voice was almost inaudible over the hover-craft's transmission channel: "Megan dear, she said she would be at Damon Point."

Unobserved, I approached her. She wore her yellow tunic—the one of Anniversary Day—and from a distance she was a bright mote on the vast mossy shore. She sat on my fleece gazing at wheeling crying birds that dipped and swooped and dove into a school of leaping fish just below the horizon.

She glimpsed me long before I reached her, and I dropped onto the fleece gratefully; my knees had weakened from her gaze as I had walked to her. Clumsy in this unimagined freedom to give, speak my love, I groped for words, and found that capacity for speech had vanished. Helplessly, I took her hands and looked into her eyes. A word came to me then, the only word I now knew. "Laurel," I whispered.

Never had I known such gentleness as Laurel's soft arms winding around my shoulders, my neck. And as she took the too-brief sweetness of her lips from mine to kiss my eyes, never had I heard such a breathing of my name.

I trembled; again she had breathed my name as my arms enclosed her. Then her tender lips were warm, warm against mine, parting under mine; and my tongue met her delicate one . . .

My fingers touched her throat; of themselves and un-bidden my hands opened her tunic, caressed satin shoulders, cupped the full breasts that had haunted my thoughts . . .

She gazed at me; she traced my face, brushing back strands of my hair. She caressed my throat, she opened my shirt . . .

I slid the tunic from her shoulders. Then my body was angles and simplicity against the richly curving nakedness everywhere under my hands . . .

She sat touching me, again stroking my face with tender fingertips, smoothing my hair, running her hands across my shoulders. She circled my breasts with those fingertips, created fiery trails down my body, over my thighs. Gasping, I reached for her.

There was the flowery scent of her skin amid the sharp salt fragrance of the moss; I do not know if I drew her down or if she lowered me. Her hair was spreading silk over my throat, my shoulders, her body was curved over mine as again she kissed my eyes. Again a breathing of my name and more: "So beautiful, beautiful Megan . . ."

Then softness, the soft curves of her body everywhere melting into the angles of my own, her mouth melding with mine.

I took her silken hair into my hands, filling my hands with it as I kissed her face . . . My fingers, my lips explored the velvet of her throat . . . my lips returned to hers . . .

Her arms were warm around me, she held me close into her as we kissed; but as I took my lips from hers to kiss her face, her throat, she caressed me, slowly stroked her soft hands over the planes of my back and down over my hips; and as my mouth came back to hers I felt her arms again slide around me to gather me closely into her . . .

She kissed my body, pouring waves of her hair over me, sighing as I gasped my pleasure . . . She covered my breasts with her warm hands; and then I writhed as my nipples hardened and tingled to the brushing of her hair, as they ached and throbbed in her mouth . . .

Irresistibly, I took her breasts into my hands and kissed them, my tongue stroking and loving each taut jewel . . . I reveled in her breasts, fed on them, endlessly kissed them . . .

My hands on her were hungry . . . careful, gentle, but hungry . . . Her body arched in my hands and she breathed Megan against my throat, but my hands were awkward . . . and soon I would touch her tender places only with my lips . . .

I feasted. A long slow feasting . . . When her soft thighs opened to me I brushed the golden softness between with my lips, the most delicate softness of all, softer than the moss covering the earth beneath us, her moss damp to my most gently stroking fingertips; within the moss the moist velvet flower of her . . .

The sweetest feasting of all . . . Passionate feasting; her sounds, her quivering shaping and feeding my passion . . .

Her cry blended with the cries of the wheeling birds, and her quivering ceased . . . but I bathed my face, all of my warm face in her . . .

She dried her wetness from my face with her hair. Then she put me under her and began sensuous loving of me, her lips tender and warm, her hands a feathery caressing. She sighed her own pleasure as she stroked my thighs . . . Soon she parted them gently and her fingers began another feathery stroking that turned my breath to gasping.

Soon I could not breathe from her fingers and I took them away, groaning. Blindly I pressed the throbbing center of me into the still-wet moss of her. She clasped my hips and pressed up into me, undulating, her legs enclosing me, and I groaned again, my sensations escalating as my body moved in involuntary rhythm with hers. Pleasure became urgency, and I buried my face in her shoulder, moaning as pleasure swiftly rose and sharpened . . .

"Megan." Her hand grasped my hair, lifting my head.

Our bodies pulsing synchrony, I looked at her and fell into an endless depth of transparent blue . . . I closed my eyes.

"Megan." Her whisper a command.

She held my hair and forced me to look at her as my body writhed with hers in an ever more fierce fusing; she forced me to look into her eyes as the tide of pleasure crested to its fullest height . . . Then for a moment I saw nothing, as my blood turned to silver . . .

My body slowly stilled; and only then did she close her eyes and let go my hair; she held me in her arms and I lay with my face in her breasts, wetting them with my tears . . .

When my heart had slowed she asked very softly, tenderness in her voice, "Do you always cry when you receive pleasure?"

I smiled at this question she had asked before. "I don't know," I answered as before, "you are the first to give such pleasure."

She was silent a moment. "The . . . first?"

"The first."

She took my face in her hands and lifted my head and gazed into my eyes so gravely that I said, to draw a smile, "Do you always speak so many variations of oh when you receive pleasure?"

And she did smile. "Only when I receive it from you." Her arms encircled me as her smile deepened. "Is there anything you do not do well?"

Speechless, shy and tongue-tied with pleasure at her question, I buried my face in her hair and murmured, "If there were but one thing I could do well . . ."

She brought my lips to hers. I heard—felt—the crashing sounds of the sea as desire rose in me so sudden and sharp that each nerve end seemed to burn with it. I felt all of her tender body with my own, I knew her fingers separately on my skin, the lovely friction of her palms. I had new perceptions of her that I had been too overcome before to comprehend. As I savored her mouth, I found that I could do other things simultaneously . . . I kissed her throat and shoulders as my hands embraced her waist, my palms caressing the curves of her stomach and back; and as I kissed and loved her breasts, I clasped the smooth curving of her hips, delighting in the rosy hues of her skin. As I kissed her thighs, the blended golds of the place between, my hands explored the shape of her legs and feet, I breathed in the scents of her . . . Inflamed beyond all forbearance, I then did only one thing, needing, wanting only that, feasting on her again, and she uttered many new variations of oh as I gave us both longer pleasure . . .

When her hands in my hair drew my lips away, she whispered, "Hold me."

I had taken her into my arms, I was gazing into blue eyes heavy-lidded with contentment when a downpour came. The day had darkened, the clouds had come over us unobserved, and we lay for a moment astonished as the warm rain drenched us. I tried to cover her body with mine but she laughed and pushed me off her. Then I began to laugh and we wrestled and rolled around on the fleece together like gleeful children as rain pelted our bodies and streamed through our hair.

As I playfully pinned her hands she smiled up into my eyes, her own eyes seductive; then she worked a hand free and pushed dripping locks of hair from my face. "You're so beautiful wet," she murmured, pulling me down to her.

"So are you," I answered against her lips . . .

The downpour lasted only a few minutes; the clouds blew off toward the horizon and our suns reappeared. I took my thermal towel from under my marker and knelt to tenderly dry her. She sat up and patted me dry.

Slowly, loving the task, I dressed her hair, watching, feeling it turn to silk in my fingers. She took the warm-comb from me and I sat looking into her face and savoring the warm hand that caressed my face as she tended my hair . . .

She drew me to her and we knelt together, rocking slowly back and forth; and then our mouths joined in deeper intimacy. As her soft body yielded in my arms I thrust in increasing passion, my hands moving over her, feeling her tremors, feeling her arms tighten and her hands flutter on my back. I cupped her sweet moss; her hands fluttered and fluttered as my tongue stroked in velvet, as my fingers stroked in velvet . . . She stiffened, would not allow me to lower her; her arms would not release me to give her greater pleasures . . . and so I discovered her with my fingers as we knelt, her hands on my back becoming ever more frenzied in their fluttering . . . She gasped her ohs next to my ear . . . Her cry was muffled against my throat.

She was limp in my arms; I felt her rapid heartbeats.

Gently I lowered her, and gathered her into my arms. Ex-haustedly she pushed our towel into a pillow on my shoulder and lay her head on it and curled herself into me and soon breathed the deep even breaths of sleep.

I could not keep all of her warm with my arms, and so I pulled the fleece, dried now of the rain, around us. To the placid, rhythmic sounds of the sea she slept quietly in my arms, endearingly, breathing deeply, her hair spread over my throat, my breasts, my arms. As if a tightly wound spring in me had fully released, I too slept, a brief lovely sleep, my awakening euphoric: Laurel, sweetly asleep in my arms.

A freshening breeze had risen when she stirred, and she pressed into me, further seeking my warmth; I tightened my arms and she sank again into sleep, but only a few minutes longer; she stirred again and awakened. She plucked at the fleece around her, gazed at me with sleepy, startled eyes.

"It's turned very cool," I murmured, shivering as a vagrant breeze chilled me. I drew the fleece more closely around us and stroked her hair.

"What time is it?"

"I don't know," I said, disoriented, glancing helplessly at the sky. "Perhaps . . . four."

"Good." Smiling, she rose onto her elbows and settled her body onto mine.

Sometime later she murmured, her voice a pleased purr, "Did I make you warm?"

I could only smile in answer, and as she still stroked my face, my hair, I asked with a suddenly dry throat, "Would you . . . be with me . . ." Then, fearful of what I would suffer if she did not reply as I wished, I said merely, ". . . tonight?"

"Yes," she replied, and as this beautiful word rever-berated in me she added, "Of course."

I pushed on as bravely as I could, "Would you be with me . . . after that?"

She gazed at me and again spoke the beautiful word.

"Laurel," I blurted, "I need you so, I love you so much—"

Tears welled, spilled down her cheeks.

"Dearest one," I whispered, stricken. "Laurel don't, I love you so—"

She held my face so that she could look into my eyes. "I love you more."

I murmured later, my lips pressed against her hair, "Take whatever time you wish to reflect, but I want Minerva to record Laurel and Megan as Joined."

"Yes." And to this most beautiful of all words she added, "I wish it too, Megan. Now. Right now."

We dressed and returned to the house, where I signaled Minerva in her history chamber. Standing with Laurel, our arms about each other, I informed her of our intention. She seemed surprised, as I had expected, and also somewhat distracted.

"Of course, Megan dear. But you must surely come here in person for so momentous and symbolic an occasion. Could you come in . . . half an hour?"

As Minerva's image faded from the lumiscreen, Laurel said, her face puzzled, "Given your stature, why would she ask you to wait?"

"I don't know," I said, not caring at all, leading her to a chaise where I pulled her down with me. "I only know we have half an hour in which . . . to find something to do." I kissed her then, and soon opened her tunic.

A brief time later she took my mouth from her breasts and whispered, her words coming between swift breaths, "It's time . . . to go to Minerva."

"It can't be," I protested.

"It is," she said. "Never would I stop you for any lesser reason."

And so I joyfully stepped into the hovercraft with the woman I loved with all my being, to whom I would soon be Joined.

XIII

Journal of Laurel
15.1.17

My hand in hers, Megan and I ran into Minerva's history chamber. And stopped in surprise. A solemn group confronted us—the Inner Circle.

"Minerva," Megan said reprovingly, her face tensing in displeasure.

"I had no choice but to reveal your plans," Minerva protested. "To have such an occasion as your Joining accomplished in commonplace and quiet fashion would have cost me my head."

"At the very least," Hera emphatically confirmed.

Megan walked to the group and confronted them with hands on her hips. "No," she stated.

"Megan dear, only a small celebration," Vesta protested, her eyes coming to mine and beseeching. "Certain things have already been made ready. Food, wine—"

Megan said sternly, "This is ours, and private." She turned to me for support. "Laurel?"

Diana had broken away from the group, had come to me. Before I could speak in agreement, she leaned to me and said in a low voice four words—the same four words she had spoken days ago to first reveal Megan's status on this world: "She is our leader."

I swallowed, and then said, "Please allow them, Megan."

Her green eyes widened. "You want that? You truly do?"

I hesitated, seeing her distress. But Diana had said: *She*

is our leader. "Please allow them," I repeated. "Only a small celebration, for this very special day of our Joining."

She said, her eyes softening, "If you wish it."

"Come with me, dear," Diana said, taking my arm.

As Diana led me off, Megan looked at me yearningly. "Soon," I called, wanting—as she did—nothing in this world but to be together in these moments of our unfolding love.

Diana held up several swatches of white fabric and quickly selected lace. "This, most assuredly," she said.

"It is Megan's color," I objected.

"And now yours as well." She wrapped me in a section of it. "Trust us, Laurel. We love her, we wish only to make you beautiful for her." Head cocked to one side, she studied me, lifting my hair from my shoulders. "Yes, yes," she said distractedly. "I'll be but a few minutes. Venus will dress your hair."

Her blue robe swaying gracefully with her walk, Venus came to me, arms filled with a variety of short-stemmed blossoms. She smiled perfunctorily and set to work, holding locks of my hair this way and that before beginning to insert and pin flowers. The silence between us was constrained, awkward. I finally said, "I have never . . . worn my hair in this fashion."

"It becomes you, and will become the dress which is being created for you," she stated in a tone forbidding argument. Then she posed the most extraordinary question I can ever conceive of one person putting to another: "Orgasm with her," she asked, "is it wonderful?"

Utter astonishment bludgeoned voice from me. Then memory ambushed me. Most vivid and intimate memory . . .

Venus had been scrutinizing me. "A reply is unnecessary," she said softly. She pinned one additional blossom and then walked from me. "Make her happy," she said in a manner that made her words not a wish and much stronger than a command.

Vesta came in. I embraced her, kissed her cheek. "Thank

you," I said fervently to this benefactor who had so successfully pleaded my case with Mother.

"Make her happy," Vesta said, the same words Venus
had spoken, but this a tender wish given lovingly.

"Vesta," I said uncertainly, "now that our Joining has
acquired some formality, is there behavior—are there customs
the women of Maternas—"

"Not really, Laurel dear. Most often the two exchange a
gift of symbolic or sentimental value, but even that is not a
formality."

"Thank you," I said, knowing that I had something of
both symbolic and sentimental value to give to Megan.

Diana dressed me. A knee-length white lace dress fitted
closely over my breasts, opening at my throat; lace sleeves
clung tightly to my arms, flaring open at my wrists into a
delicate nebulous fabric that reached to my fingers.

"It is time," Diana said, fitting sandals to my feet as I
stared at my reflection, the reflection of someone who
seemed very young and more than a little frightened.

They took me to Cybele's main square. Flaming torches
lighted the early evening sky. The platform used for the
ballet on Anniversary Day had again been erected, and held
flower-banked banquet tables and musicians—and also
Mother, resplendent in her green cape. All around me on
the balconies and bridges of Cybele were the women of
Maternas. Diana led me—so stunned I could scarcely
walk—to the platform, to Mother.

"It was to be . . . a small ceremony," I stammered to
Mother.

Mother waved a hand. "Phosh. If there must be ceremony
what does it matter whether large or small?" She indicated
a place on her chaise. "Sit down and talk to me, my dear.
Megan will be right along."

Obediently I sat, but it was soon clear that it was Mother
who wished to talk. "Of those I have loved in my long life,"
she told me, "I love Megan more than any. You will make
her happy, won't you?"

"I'll try with all my heart, Mother."

Mother patted my hand. "It would annoy me greatly if you didn't, my dear. And when I become annoyed—"

There was a rising murmur from around us and I glimpsed Megan and quickly stood. I knew that Diana had indeed dressed me well when I saw Megan's eyes come to me . . .

Her white shirt was of brocade, with a high collar, her boots of sculptured design, rising just above the ankle; close-fitted lustervel pants, tied with a white sash, burnished her long legs as she walked to me.

"You're so beautiful," she said, taking my hands and drawing me to her; but there was a tumult of sound from all around us, and only then did she become aware of the preparations that had been made, the women gathered on the heights and tiers of Cybele.

"Be as gracious as you can, Megan dear," Mother said serenely, as Megan's face tensed and her eyes narrowed in displeasure. "Be grateful you don't have to endure what I did." Minerva had come up to us and Mother said to her, "Did I ever relate the story of when I married your father?"

"Yes Mother," Minerva answered, "and it is time to—"

"I married him in the pleasure capital of Vega," Mother continued inexorably, "and nothing but the best would do. Which consisted of the ceremony taking place in a cavernous monstrosity of gilt rococco stuffed with grotesque statuary and lined with fifty incompetent musicians, who played an appalling ditty which I was told was Earth's traditional wedding march."

"Mother," Minerva said with a gesture signifying that everything was in readiness.

"A moron swathed in white from head to foot for Geezerak knows what reason chanted words over us, accompanied by a lachrymose violin and deafening drums, cymbals, and tambourines," Mother said. "Then he threw a switch that released a collection of terrified doves that swooped down on us, and another switch that sent a torrent of flowers hurtling down at our heads, and still another that unfurled a roll of red carpet over which I fled to the door, closely followed by your father."

Megan and I were laughing heartily, and Mother said to Minerva, "What are you waiting for, my dear? Let's get on with it."

Mother rose from her chaise and took my hand and Megan's, escorted us before a table with a high slanted top. As Minerva took her place behind it, lumiscreens around us glowed to life. She opened the book of records I had first seen in the library on Anniversary Day.

I watched Minerva's hand form words with a writing instrument I had never seen, the words appearing on the lumiscreens for the women of Maternas to see as she inscribed them:

Laurel and Megan
Joined in their Love
15.1.17

As she finished, the lumiscreens extinguished; and Mother joined my hand with Megan's. Through my tears I could see nothing, not even Megan. I could only hear the thunderous sound from all around us.

Blinking my tears away, unable to speak, I released Megan's hand to take the emerald ring from my finger. Then I took her hand again and slid the ring onto her finger, forming it to fit. "I love you," I whispered.

She lifted the chain from around her neck, the chain holding the precious crystal she had found first on this new world, and lowered it over my head; the crystal rested between my breasts. She took my hands and kissed them, drew me to her and kissed my forehead. "I will love you forever," she whispered, her arms enclosing me.

I slid my hands over the irregular surface of her brocade shirt until my arms fully embraced her shoulders. Uncaring of the witnesses to my love, I kissed her . . .

Music began. Megan's arms tightened around me. We danced, her arms holding me close into her. I lay my head on her shoulder, aware only of her, her arms, her slender graceful body in my arms.

After a while she told me in a low, pleased voice, "I have never danced before."

I asked with a sigh, "Is there anything you do not do well?"

She chuckled softly. "My hair. Demeter prepared it for this moment, took great pains with it. I don't like it nearly so well as when you dress it."

"It will be my beloved task every day from now on," I promised. I caressed her slender shoulders, feeling her warmth through the ornate fabric. "I've been threatened with dismemberment at the very least if I fail to make you happy."

She laughed. She had danced us into a shadowed corner, and her arms tightened . . . When she danced us from the shadows again my head lay once more on her shoulder—from necessity; I was weak from the sweet passion of her mouth.

Vesta brought us food, wine. I tasted nothing except the morsel Megan told me was delicious, feeding it to me with her fingers . . . We danced again. If I could not be alone with her, I was content holding her, being in her arms.

Mother came up to us. "You two might as well leave," she grumbled, "since you'll have nothing to do with the rest of us. Take the hovercraft beside the council chambers. The controls are set. A place has been made ready at Barney Lake, supplied with everything you need." Mother reached for Megan, kissed both cheeks. "If I see you before many days from now, I will be most seriously annoyed."

She turned to me, took my hands, kissed me as well. And whispered, "Make her happy."

XIV

Personal Journal of Megan
15.1.17

Each with an arm around the other, we stood at the window watching Barney Lake become dark coral rippling, our world become silver. I took Laurel into my arms and touched my lips to her forehead, and began to take the flowers from her hair, cascades of silk tresses spilling over my hands.

"Perhaps it doesn't seem the time to talk of it," she said hesitantly, her lovely face upturned to mine and solemn, "but . . . Megan, will we have children together?"

"Yes," I whispered, kissing her forehead, "yes."

With a pleased sigh she lowered her head to my shoulder, her arms drawing me close. "But not for a while," she said. "We'll enjoy each other for a while before we begin having them."

"Them?" I murmured, smiling. "How many did you have in mind?"

"I think . . . three."

Tears in my eyes, I tightened my arms around her.

She murmured, her lips close to my ear, "Three beautiful little girls with dark hair and green eyes."

"Two will have blue eyes," I said firmly, "and gold-streaked hair."

"One can have blue eyes. The other two—"

"We'll have four then, two of each," I said, and stopped my reply with my lips.

Kissing her throat, I opened her lace dress to kiss her shoulders. She stepped away from me and pushed her dress off her shoulders; it fell in a soft heap around her feet. I gazed, not attempting to touch her yet, treasuring her loveliness in the silver light, all curves and contoured shadows. She turned for me, slowly, standing for a moment with the full, swelling curves of her hips to me; then she stepped to me.

I reached for the gleaming crystal between her breasts to take it off her, but she stopped my hands. "I wish to wear it always," she said. I nodded, knowing that never would I take off her ring.

She opened my shirt—but in tantalizing increments, her hands and lips exploring each exposure of throat and shoulder. She pushed the shirt from my shoulders but not off my body, so that my arms were pinioned in its sleeves; she kissed down to my breasts, her lips circling them, her tongue stroking.

"Laurel," I whispered, eyes closed, my body warm, weakening.

"Let me," she murmured against my breasts.

My body was a fine network of filament ever more glowing as each nipple was exquisitely, repeatedly, taken.

She released my arms from the shirt and discarded it, then knelt to me, running her hands caressingly down my legs; she took off my boots.

Slowly, she slid clothing down, then off me, her lips inflaming me as they also descended, to my thighs ...

I clutched at memory to control my weakening and the trembling of my legs ... memory of how I had commanded escape from pursuing Earth ships, how I had confronted the monster GEM with so many lives at risk ... But as her lips traced the triangle of hair within my legs I further weakened; and when her lips began to brush through the hair all sensation left my legs and I sank to my knees, and finding no strength there, further collapsed onto the fleece-cushioned floor.

She bent to me, hands gentle on my thighs. "Let me," she whispered, and lay down between my legs.

Slowly, her lips brushed me again . . . And then she turned my bones to water.

Never at any time in my life had I been out of control, and as my legs acquired quivering life of their own from this inconceivable pleasure, I fearfully put my hands in her hair and took her sweet mouth away.

Her hands took mine. "Megan dearest," she whispered, "let me."

I gripped her hands; I clasped her in my legs. Her warm mouth again took tender possession of me. In my deepening ecstasy my legs trembled uncontrollably around her, my hands tightened vise-like around hers amid pleasure as pure as a note on her crystal reed. Able only to take swift breaths into me, my body an ever more rigid arch of ecstasy, I approached a dazzling edge and hovering there, tried to speak her name and could not. And within my stilled body it was as if our planet's two suns had fused.

She cradled my head in an arm as she dried my tear-streaked face with her discarded dress. She held me close for a long time, then took my face into her hands and smiled and told me softly, her blue eyes merciless, "If you cry each time this night, you'll have no tears left long before morning."

I closed my eyes for a moment with the thought of that, then rose and pulled her to her feet, led her to our bed-chamber—to discover it banked with flowers.

Laurel playfully tucked blossoms behind my ears, laughing at me; laughing together we removed the blossoms covering our bed. I took her into my arms, pressing my naked body into hers, caressing her body with all of my own. "Megan," she soon breathed, eyes closed. I lowered her to our bed.

Entwined in her soft limbs, I kissed her face, her throat, in unhurried loving of her . . . The wind came up and played its tune as again my mouth came to hers, my tongue parting her lips to stroke the velvet within, an act so suggestive of another that I was suddenly impaled with desire. As her body surged into mine with each stroke of my tongue I heard the sounds in her throat and knew no more of the outside world then or throughout that night—only our own sounds of joy, of love.

XV

20.1.1

On this, our twentieth Anniversary Day, Christa and I swell with pride—our beloved Celeste competes for the first time in the games, and in a most difficult event, the pentathalon.

Megan has opened the games as usual. As is now her custom, she does not remain with Mother and our Inner Circle, but goes to a tiny plateau overlooking the amphitheater to watch the games with her dearest ones. As the games begin, I bring Megan in on my scope . . . She lies on a fleece with her head in Laurel's lap, smiling at the antics of their second born as she struggles to walk, a lovely blue-eyed child of less than a year whom they have named Crystal. Laurel, even lovelier in these past few years in the fullness of her womanhood, sits stroking Megan's hair. Their first born, a restless child displaying extraordinary intelligence at the age of only three, is raptly watching the game of Criss-Cross on the holograph, determined to comprehend its complexities. She has Megan's coloring and those green eyes, and they have named her Emerald.

Megan has changed so these past few years . . . Although her advice is constantly sought on many problems of significant scope, she is less involved with the affairs of our two colonies and we must seek her; she is not freely available to us as she once was. And while she is no less a personage, no less revered among us, she seems softer in manner, younger—less Olympian. Happiness has come to her. And

changed her. And no one of us would wish that to be different.

I ruminate over events of these past years, trying to
calm myself as our dear Celeste prepares to compete . . . She
is so like my Christa, the beloved woman to whom I am
Joined, who has brought such joy all these years to my days
and nights . . .

The pentathalon begins.

Celeste has finished fourth, a highly creditable performance for a first appearance in the games, considering
that she is but fourteen. All the members of the Inner Circle
are gathered around us in congratulation.

Mother has joined us, has kissed my cheek, and Christa's.
"Hers is a medal that will give me great pleasure to award,"
she says, beaming.

Then she pulls her green cape around her and examines
each of us with those extraordinary eyes. "Dear ones," she
finally says, "honestly now, how much more of this peace
and quiet and happiness do you expect me to endure?"

We greet this with astonished silence.

Mother looks at us impatiently. "You mean to tell me
that none of you is bored?" She adds hopefully, "Even a
little?"

"Perhaps we could arrange a trip for you, Mother,"
Hera suggests drily. "A month on the treacherous continent
of O'Connor."

"Phosh," Mother retorts. "Volcanoes? Earthquakes?
In a week I'd be bored again. Dear girls," she says so softly
that I have to strain to hear, "I find myself thinking more
and more about . . . my other girls. I know better than to
worry, but I do wonder . . ."

We all stir uncomfortably; I exchange glances with
Demeter and Diana. Such thoughts have never been far from
any of us, and only yesterday we had again spoken of our
sisters, speculated about that part of our Unity that has been
separated like an amputation from us.

Suddenly Mother turns to my beloved and says, "Christa, what do you think about returning for a visit to your birth-place?"

"Whatever Minerva would wish," Christa says carefully, in a low voice. "We would have to consult." But I have seen the surge of eagerness and excitement on the face of my beloved to whom I can refuse nothing. Mother's cleverness is, at times, not to be borne.

"We would all have to consult," Venus murmurs, gazing at her latest companion, a pretty young woman with Oriental features and dark glossy hair.

"It would be so good to see Olympia and Isis," Vesta murmurs, looking at Carina, who takes her hand and smiles.

"It would be good to see my daughters and all my off-spring," Mother says softly.

"Mother." Hera's voice is exasperated. "Do you realize what a trip to Earth would involve? The preparation? We would have to outfit that primitive Cruiser in orbit around us, we would have to discover a method of entering the solar system undetected, we would have to—"

Mother waves a hand. "Details. You know how details bore me." She calls back over her shoulder as she returns to her chaise to watch the games, "I know you girls can manage."

BODY GUARD by Claire McNab. 208 pp. A Carol Ashton Mystery.
6th in a series.   ISBN 1-56280-073-6 $9.95

CACTUS LOVE by Lee Lynch. 192 pp. Stories by the
beloved storyteller.   ISBN 1-56280-071-X   9.95

SECOND GUESS by Rose Beecham. 216 pp. An Amanda Valentine
Mystery. 2nd in a series.   ISBN 1-56280-069-8   9.95

THE SURE THING by Melissa Hartman. 208 pp. L.A. earthquake
romance.   ISBN 1-56280-078-7   9.95

A RAGE OF MAIDENS by Lauren Wright Douglas. 240 pp. A
Caitlin Reece Mystery. 6th in a series.   ISBN 1-56280-068-X   9.95

TRIPLE EXPOSURE by Jackie Calhoun. 224 pp. Romantic drama
involving many characters.   ISBN 1-56280-067-1   9.95

UP, UP AND AWAY by Catherine Ennis. 192 pp. Delightful
romance.   ISBN 1-56280-065-5   9.95

PERSONAL ADS by Robbi Sommers. 176 pp. Sizzling short
stories.   ISBN 1-56280-059-0   9.95

FLASHPOINT by Katherine V. Forrest. 256 pp. Lesbian
blockbuster!   ISBN 1-56280-043-4   22.95

CROSSWORDS by Penny Sumner. 256 pp. 2nd Victoria Cross
Mystery.   ISBN 1-56280-064-7   9.95

SWEET CHERRY WINE by Carol Schmidt. 224 pp. A novel of
suspense.   ISBN 1-56280-063-9   9.95

CERTAIN SMILES by Dorothy Tell. 160 pp. Erotic short stories.
                                                   ISBN 1-56280-066-3   9.95

EDITED OUT by Lisa Haddock. 224 pp. 1st Carmen Ramirez
Mystery.   ISBN 1-56280-077-9   9.95

WEDNESDAY NIGHTS by Camarin Grae. 288 pp. Sexy
adventure.   ISBN 1-56280-060-4   10.95

SMOKEY O by Celia Cohen. 176 pp. Relationships on the playing
field.   ISBN 1-56280-057-4   9.95

KATHLEEN O'DONALD by Penny Hayes. 256 pp. Rose and
Kathleen find each other and employment in 1909 NYC.
ISBN 1-56280-070-1   9.95

STAYING HOME by Elisabeth Nonas. 256 pp. Molly and Alix
want a baby . . . or do they?   ISBN 1-56280-076-0   10.95

TRUE LOVE by Jennifer Fulton. 240 pp. Six lesbians searching for
love in all the "right" places.   ISBN 1-56280-035-3   9.95

GARDENIAS WHERE THERE ARE NONE by Molleen Zanger.
176 pp. Why is Melanie inextricably drawn to the old house?
ISBN 1-56280-056-6   9.95

MICHAELA by Sarah Aldridge. 256 pp. A "Sarah Aldridge"
romance.   ISBN 1-56280-055-8   10.95

KEEPING SECRETS by Penny Mickelbury. 208 pp. A Gianna
Maglione Mystery. First in a series.   ISBN 1-56280-052-3   9.95

THE ROMANTIC NAIAD edited by Katherine V. Forrest &
Barbara Grier. 336 pp. Love stories by Naiad Press authors.
ISBN 1-56280-054-X   14.95

UNDER MY SKIN by Jaye Maiman. 336 pp. A Robin Miller
mystery. 3rd in a series.   ISBN 1-56280-049-3.   10.95

STAY TOONED by Rhonda Dicksion. 144 pp. Cartoons — 1st
collection since *Lesbian Survival Manual.*   ISBN 1-56280-045-0   9.95

CAR POOL by Karin Kallmaker. 272pp. Lesbians on wheels
and then some!   ISBN 1-56280-048-5   9.95

NOT TELLING MOTHER: STORIES FROM A LIFE by Diane
Salvatore. 176 pp. Her 3rd novel.   ISBN 1-56280-044-2   9.95

GOBLIN MARKET by Lauren Wright Douglas. 240pp. A Caitlin
Reece Mystery. 5th in a series.   ISBN 1-56280-047-7   9.95

LONG GOODBYES by Nikki Baker. 256 pp. A Virginia Kelly
mystery. 3rd in a series.   ISBN 1-56280-042-6   9.95

FRIENDS AND LOVERS by Jackie Calhoun. 224 pp. Mid-western
Lesbian lives and loves.   ISBN 1-56280-041-8   9.95

THE CAT CAME BACK by Hilary Mullins. 208 pp. Highly praised
Lesbian novel.   ISBN 1-56280-040-X   9.95

BEHIND CLOSED DOORS by Robbi Sommers. 192 pp. Hot, erotic
short stories.   ISBN 1-56280-039-6   9.95

CLAIRE OF THE MOON by Nicole Conn. 192 pp. See the movie —
read the book!   ISBN 1-56280-038-8   10.95

SILENT HEART by Claire McNab. 192 pp. Exotic Lesbian
romance.   ISBN 1-56280-036-1   9.95

HAPPY ENDINGS by Kate Brandt. 272 pp. Intimate conversations
with Lesbian authors.   ISBN 1-56280-050-7   10.95

THE SPY IN QUESTION by Amanda Kyle Williams. 256 pp. 4th
Madison McGuire. ISBN 1-56280-037-X 9.95

SAVING GRACE by Jennifer Fulton. 240 pp. Adventure and
romantic entanglement. ISBN 1-56280-051-5 9.95

THE YEAR SEVEN by Molleen Zanger. 208 pp. Women surviving
in a new world. ISBN 1-56280-034-5 9.95

CURIOUS WINE by Katherine V. Forrest. 176 pp. Tenth
Anniversary Edition. The most popular contemporary Lesbian
love story. ISBN 1-56280-053-1 10.95

CHAUTAUQUA by Catherine Ennis. 192 pp. Exciting, romantic
adventure. ISBN 1-56280-032-9 9.95

A PROPER BURIAL by Pat Welch. 192 pp. A Helen Black
mystery. 3rd in a series. ISBN 1-56280-033-7 9.95

SILVERLAKE HEAT: A Novel of Suspense by Carol Schmidt.
240 pp. Rhonda is as hot as Laney's dreams. ISBN 1-56280-031-0 9.95

LOVE, ZENA BETH by Diane Salvatore. 224 pp. The most talked
about lesbian novel of the nineties! ISBN 1-56280-030-2 9.95

A DOORYARD FULL OF FLOWERS by Isabel Miller. 160 pp.
Stories incl. 2 sequels to *Patience and Sarah.* ISBN 1-56280-029-9 9.95

MURDER BY TRADITION by Katherine V. Forrest. 288 pp. A
Kate Delafield Mystery. 4th in a series. ISBN 1-56280-002-7 9.95

THE EROTIC NAIAD edited by Katherine V. Forrest & Barbara Grier.
224 pp. Love stories by Naiad Press authors. ISBN 1-56280-026-4 12.95

DEAD CERTAIN by Claire McNab. 224 pp. A Carol Ashton
mystery. 5th in a series. ISBN 1-56280-027-2 9.95

CRAZY FOR LOVING by Jaye Maiman. 320 pp. A Robin Miller
mystery. 2nd in a series. ISBN 1-56280-025-6 9.95

STONEHURST by Barbara Johnson. 176 pp. Passionate regency
romance. ISBN 1-56280-024-8 9.95

INTRODUCING AMANDA VALENTINE by Rose Beecham.
256 pp. An Amanda Valentine Mystery. First in a series.
 ISBN 1-56280-021-3 9.95

UNCERTAIN COMPANIONS by Robbi Sommers. 204 pp.
Steamy, erotic novel. ISBN 1-56280-017-5 9.95

A TIGER'S HEART by Lauren W. Douglas. 240 pp. A Caitlin
Reece mystery. 4th in a series. ISBN 1-56280-018-3 9.95

PAPERBACK ROMANCE by Karin Kallmaker. 256 pp. A
delicious romance. ISBN 1-56280-019-1 9.95

MORTON RIVER VALLEY by Lee Lynch. 304 pp. Lee Lynch at
her best! ISBN 1-56280-016-7 9.95

THE LAVENDER HOUSE MURDER by Nikki Baker. 224 pp. A
Virginia Kelly Mystery. 2nd in a series. ISBN 1-56280-012-4 9.95

PASSION BAY by Jennifer Fulton. 224 pp. Passionate romance, virgin beaches, tropical skies. ISBN 1-56280-028-0   9.95

STICKS AND STONES by Jackie Calhoun. 208 pp. Contemporary lesbian lives and loves. ISBN 1-56280-020-5   9.95

DELIA IRONFOOT by Jeane Harris. 192 pp. Adventure for Delia and Beth in the Utah mountains. ISBN 1-56280-014-0   9.95

UNDER THE SOUTHERN CROSS by Claire McNab. 192 pp. Romantic nights Down Under. ISBN 1-56280-011-6   9.95

RIVERFINGER WOMEN by Elana Nachman/Dykewomon. 208 pp. Classic Lesbian/feminist novel. ISBN 1-56280-013-2   8.95

GRASSY FLATS by Penny Hayes. 256 pp. Lesbian romance in the '30s. ISBN 1-56280-010-8   9.95

A SINGULAR SPY by Amanda K. Williams. 192 pp. 3rd Madison McGuire. ISBN 1-56280-008-6   8.95

THE END OF APRIL by Penny Sumner. 240 pp. A Victoria Cross Mystery. First in a series. ISBN 1-56280-007-8   8.95

A FLIGHT OF ANGELS by Sarah Aldridge. 240 pp. Romance set at the National Gallery of Art ISBN 1-56280-001-9   9.95

HOUSTON TOWN by Deborah Powell. 208 pp. A Hollis Carpenter mystery. Second in a series. ISBN 1-56280-006-X   8.95

KISS AND TELL by Robbi Sommers. 192 pp. Scorching stories by the author of *Pleasures*. ISBN 1-56280-005-1   9.95

STILL WATERS by Pat Welch. 208 pp. A Helen Black mystery. 2nd in a series. ISBN 0-941483-97-5   9.95

TO LOVE AGAIN by Evelyn Kennedy. 208 pp. Wildly romantic love story. ISBN 0-941483-85-1   9.95

IN THE GAME by Nikki Baker. 192 pp. A Virginia Kelly mystery. First in a series. ISBN 1-56280-004-3   9.95

AVALON by Mary Jane Jones. 256 pp. A Lesbian Arthurian romance. ISBN 0-941483-96-7   9.95

STRANDED by Camarin Grae. 320 pp. Entertaining, riveting adventure. ISBN 0-941483-99-1   9.95

THE DAUGHTERS OF ARTEMIS by Lauren Wright Douglas. 240 pp. A Caitlin Reece mystery. 3rd in a series. ISBN 0-941483-95-9   9.95

These are just a few of the many Naiad Press titles — we are the oldest and largest lesbian/feminist publishing company in the world. Please request a complete catalog. We offer personal service; we encourage and welcome direct mail orders from individuals who have limited access to bookstores carrying our publications.